THE RED THREAD

Also by Roderick Townley

The Sylvie Cycle:
The Great Good Thing
Into the Labyrinth
The Constellation of Sylvie

Sky

THE RED THREAD

A Novel in Three Incarnations

Roderick Townley

A Richard Jackson Book
Atheneum Books for Young Readers
New York   London   Toronto   Sydney

Atheneum Books for Young Readers
An imprint of Simon & Schuster Children's Publishing Division
1230 Avenue of the Americas, New York, New York 10020
Book design by Debra Sfetsios and Tom Daly
The text for this book is set in Augustal.
Manufactured in the United States of America
First Edition
10 9 8 7 6 5 4 3 2 1
Library of Congress Cataloging-in-Publication Data
Townley, Rod.
The red thread: a novel in three incarnations/Roderick
Townley.—1st ed.
p.   cm.
"A Richard Jackson book."
Summary: Bothered by insomnia, nightmares, and
claustrophobia, sixteen-year-old Dana sees a therapist who
hypnotizes her into remembering past lives, involving her in
an age-old mystery and causing her to question what kind of
person she is.
ISBN-13: 978-1-4169-0894-4 (alk. paper)
ISBN-10: 1-4169-0894-3 (alk. paper)
[1. Reincarnation—Fiction. 2. Psychotherapy—Fiction. 3. Family
life—New Hampshire—Fiction. 4. Photography—Fiction. 5. New
Hampshire—Fiction. 6. Mystery and detective stories.] I. Title.
PZ7.T64965Red 2007
[Fic]—dc22   2006005212

For their generous help I would like to thank Joan Christy, librarian, Portsmouth High School; special education coordinator Donna Blessing and developmental disabilities specialist Jeanne Laghan, Portsmouth Middle School; and Steven Parkinson, director of public works, Portsmouth, New Hampshire.

For medical advice and good counsel, I thank Drs. Alan Forker and Damien Stevens, pulmonologists, as well as psychiatrist Dr. James Hasselle and psychotherapist Susan Hasselle.

My thanks, as well, to Venetia Gosling of Simon & Schuster UK, my agent Amy Berkower, and editor/mentor Richard Jackson.

I'm grateful to my daughter Grace for helpful suggestions, and to my son Jesse, a great encourager. Finally, deepest thanks to my wife, Wyatt, who holds the string that keeps my kite in the air.

For Elise Townley
with love and gratitude

Contents

IV The Hole

I
The Studio

Chapter One

Another Day in Paradise

THE SPACE WAS NARROW AND DIM AND SMELLED of dead rat. Grit from the floor bit his forehead. Sticky warmth worked down his cheek.

He had a moment of panic when he realized he couldn't open his right eye. It was his own blood that sealed it. He ran his sleeve across his face. No good. He pried the lid open with his fingers. Was it night? Why was everything so dark?

He found himself panting as if he'd been running up a staircase. Then he realized it wasn't lack of air but fear that winded him.

Slow down. Breathe.

Still panting, he glanced around. Hemming him in were walls of unfinished wood, not the gleaming paneling of the great rooms and hallways. But light, faint as it was, reached him from somewhere. Then he saw it, a wedgelike opening four feet above the ground, where wood abruptly changed to stone rising in the gloom. If he could reach it!

Holding to the wall, the boy fought to make his legs support him. He swayed uncertainly. Just ten years old, he was not tall for his age and had to stand on tiptoe to see. Through the throbbing in his brain he heard echoing shouts and the clump of booted feet down corridors. He squinted at vague shapes. Steadying himself, he realized he was in the chapel, behind the new marble altarpiece.

Behind it? Suddenly he couldn't breathe again. *How did I get here?*

Dizziness buckled his legs, but he held on till his vision cleared. A flicker of light. Someone was on the other side of the altar! The candlelight grew brighter. The boy waited, breathless. There were so many people to be scared of these days. Then came a scraping sound, quite loud, quite near, of stone on stone. To his horror, he saw the opening grow an inch narrower, then another inch.

"No!" he cried, pushing back against the marble. But he was too weak, and the altarpiece kept edging back toward him.

"No!" His voice was louder now. "Stop!"

The scraping ceased.

A face appeared at the opening.

"Oh!" The boy sighed with relief, recognizing the pointed beard, dented forehead, and intense gaze he knew so well. "It's you!" His eyes blurred with gratitude. This was the person he trusted above everyone.

The man did not smile or speak. He turned to listen to the thumping of running feet, then moved away from the opening.

"What's the matter?" the boy called out. "What are you doing?"

The altarpiece shuddered and moved slightly, then slightly farther.

"No! The other way!"

The stone moved again. Only a sliver of light remained.

"Don't!" the boy wailed. "Please don't!" His legs failed him and he collapsed in the darkness.

The stone shrugged another inch.

"Not you!" he moaned. The salt of tears mingled with the coppery taste of blood. "Not you, too!"

A final shove, and the massive stone was set in place, leaving the boy in an insanity of blackness.

With a gasp Dana Landgrave lurched up from the pillow, her eyes staring. Her mouth was dry, her heart beating hard. It took a few seconds to realize where she was. Yes, there were the glowing numbers on her clock radio, the milky gleam of the night-light reflected in the glass eyes of her bear. A gentle half light filtered through the window. The curtain stirred. Dawn.

She swung out of bed, planting her feet on the cool floor. She wouldn't risk going back to sleep and dreaming the dream again. It had haunted her a dozen times this spring, but this was the worst. It was as if she were there. But *where*?

Nowhere. She'd made it up. The doctor had told her it was natural for teenagers to have fears, about life, death, sex, you name it. What Dana had managed to do was turn those fears into a place—a place that she returned to, furnished, and made real.

So what was this altar business? What was that about?

Whatever it was, the dream kept coming back. And who was the boy? She shut her eyes, trying to think if she knew anyone like him. No one in her school, certainly. In other dreams, Dana had seen his face the way you'd see anyone, from the outside. This was much creepier. She'd *felt* him, as if she were thinking his thoughts.

The view from the window was obscured by mist, but Dana could hear the river. Its presence calmed her, vague, always flowing, always there, like a parent moving about a nursery. The dream had less of a hold on her when she looked outside. That was why she kept the window open at night—to hear the slap of waves in the back channel and smell the seaweed. And it helped with her claustrophobia, which was getting worse. It gave her a way out.

She switched on the bedside lamp. Slipping a sweatshirt over her head and pulling on her jeans, Dana wiggled bare feet into her sneakers and stepped from the room, pausing to grab the camera and keys.

The hallway was dim, filled with the sounds of nearby sleepers. There were the soft gasps of her brother on his ventilator, and from down the hall the loud, decisive snorts of her mother. Not very feminine, Dana thought with a half smile. Her father's breathing was inaudible, as if, even asleep, he were listening for the others.

Dana made a quick bathroom stop, throwing water on her face and running her fingers through her hopelessly curly hair. She shot herself a glance. Not bad looking, certainly, but not exactly pretty. Character. That's what people said: Her face had character. Another way to put it was that, at almost seventeen, her nose was too strong and her forehead too high. Was she going bald or something? Dana sighed, giving her curls a shake. How did she ever get a boyfriend?

She headed down the stairs and out the kitchen door, her sneakers crunching on the gravel. The gray minivan stood under the carport like a faithful animal in its stall. Veils of mist trailed through the empty streets. It was almost six, the hour when she took some of her best pictures.

The bell began tolling in the North Church across town. It could almost be another century, another country. She would have liked that. Fiddling with the camera, she turned a corner and stopped with a gasp. The boy from the dream! All the horror returned, his face staring out at her from a wedge of shadow between houses. She could even make out a line of blood threading his cheekbone! Instinctively she raised the camera and pressed the shutter, not even looking through the range finder, then shot again as she zoomed in close.

She glanced at the image she'd captured. *What?* she thought, and laughed. It was a white cardboard box tied with red string atop a trash can.

Was that her problem, an overactive imagination? Or was she hallucinating? Was she mentally ill?

Spotting an orange tabby crossing the cobblestones near Mechanic Street, Dana dropped to the ground, shooting as she went, and among many wasted shots captured one of the cat, at cat level, its paw raised, silhouetted against the glistening cobbles. Thank God for digital, Dana thought. If an image didn't work, you could just delete it, or edit it on the computer. A different world from her dad's clunky 35-millimeter, although she used that, too.

She ducked through an alley, peering up at the sharpening shadows of one building against the bricks of another, and the sky beyond, crossed now by two gulls. If it weren't for the photography elective, Dana didn't know how she'd get through eleventh grade. She still might not. Finals were two weeks away. She wouldn't have said it to anyone, but in a strange way she didn't *believe* in school—that world of grades and rules. It didn't seem real.

She made her way among the eighteenth-century houses near the quaintly spelled Strawbery Banke Museum and emerged on Court Street. A car honked and she jumped back to the curb. The town was getting itself in gear; she'd have to hurry if she wanted to change, eat, and get Ben ready. Returning to her house (nothing quaint about that old white saltbox off Marcy Street), Dana grabbed the newspaper and took the front steps two at a time, her camera swinging from her neck. Her parents were already in the breakfast room. They looked up as she breezed through, flopping the *Portsmouth Herald* on the table as she passed.

"Thanks, Button," said her dad, throwing her a smile. He was leaning back in his chair, holding his coffee mug against his chest.

"Dana?" her mother called.

"What, Ma?" She paused on the steps.

"Are you all right?" Her quick green eyes held an emphasis her daughter was meant to get.

"Sure!" Dana said in her flip way, but she knew what her mother meant: *Is that why you needed to go out this morning? Did you have those dreams again?*

"Well," said Mrs. Landgrave, "I'll fix you an egg."

"Okay."

"Tell Ben his oatmeal is ready. Oh, and don't forget," her mother called after her, "you see the doctor this afternoon."

Dana burst into Ben's room to find her brother already sitting up, looking at his collection of early English coins. On the wall behind him were pictures of coats of arms, printed out from the Internet. Ben was heavily into heraldry these days, as well as being a computer whiz.

He gave her a sour look. "Thanks for the help," he said in his whispery voice. He'd managed to disconnect the tracheotomy tube—the "trake" as he called it—and plug the stopper in the small plastic opening in his neck so he could talk. The machine was only for nighttime, to regulate his breathing when he wasn't conscious. Soon he'd be weaned off it altogether. He was one lucky eleven-year-old, as his father often and irritatingly told him. If the fracture had been two vertebrae higher, he wouldn't be able to breathe on his own. Not to mention his other bodily functions.

Dana helped him into the wheelchair.

"Any good pictures?"

She swept the camera off her neck and went over to him. "Take a look."

Ben could raise his arms if he had to, but they were weak, so his sister held the camera and went through the shots.

He grunted.

"You don't like them?"

"Didn't say that." His voice was breathy and soft—a sort of rush of bumpy air—and most people had trouble understanding him, but Dana was an expert.

"I don't much either," she said. "The cat's all right."

"Yeah," Ben said. "I like the cat."

"Say," Dana said brightly, "we've got to get you going."

"Let's not."

She gave him a light punch on the shoulder and pushed him across the hall to the bathroom. "He's ready!" she sang out.

"Coming," her father called. He trudged up the staircase to take over. While Dana made Ben's bed, Tom Landgrave took care of his son's bathroom needs, attaching the catheter that would help him through the day without having to use the facilities at school. With Mrs. Landgrave's recent successes at the law firm, the family had been doing better financially. But they'd gone into debt for Ben's ventilator, not to mention the specialized computer and the van with the wheelchair lift— and it would have been hard to add the cost of a nurse. Ben wouldn't have put up with one anyway.

Landgrave poked his head out of the bathroom. "He's ready for you, Button."

Dana came in with Ben's shirt as her father headed back down.

"This is going to be a good day," she said.

"Are you joking?" Ben watched himself in the mirror as she wet a comb and ran it through his hair.

"Aren't you going to see your friend Eric?"

"I guess."

"He's your research buddy."

"Not anymore."

Dana didn't know what to say. In the year since the accident, Ben had managed to keep a positive attitude, but some of his classmates began edging away. He couldn't afford to lose another friend. "Weren't you two working on a coat of arms or something?"

"He's gone out for softball."

That stopped her a minute. "Well, softball isn't forever. Maybe he could come over on weekends."

"Maybe."

Handsome little guy, she thought, giving him a last glance in the mirror before backing the wheelchair into the hall.

Fifteen minutes later, with a warm croissant in her pocket, Dana pushed Ben down Marcy to Pleasant Street to wait for the Cheese. That's what everybody called the Special Ed bus, which was half the size of the regular school bus and looked from a distance like, well, a brick of Muenster cheese.

She hummed tunelessly as they waited.

"You're in a good mood," said Ben.

"We get the yearbook today."

Ben grunted.

"Can't wait to see the pictures."

"Yeah."

"You don't know what I'm talking about, do you?" she said.

"Sure I do. All those clubs and things."

Dana was especially proud of her portrait of the Chess Club. Instead of lining the kids up in front of a curtain somewhere, she'd supplied them with crowns and bishops' miters. Then she'd brought them out in the parking lot, drawn a chessboard around them in chalk, and had them stand in squares representing a classic checkmate.

"Here we go," said Ben as the Cheese came around the corner and groaned to a stop. "Another day in paradise."

The wheelchair lift lowered and Dana helped him on. "Go get 'em."

He gave a little backward wave.

She watched the bus putter up the hill, then hitched her backpack higher on her shoulder and started along South Street, camera in hand.

Dana's good mood began to fade as soon as she reached the locker pod on the third floor and caught sight of Gianna Belkin, the yearbook's editor. Just the person, she reminded herself, approaching slowly, that she wanted to see. So why did Dana always flinch at the sight of her?

Gianna could be touchy at times, opinionated—but Dana wasn't such a piece of cake to be around either. Nor did Dana have anything against large people. Her regular lunch partner was a supersized girl named Trish Roth, who was a hoot to be with. But something about the way Gianna rooted around in her locker was unsettling. It made Dana think of a young bear pawing at its prey.

Her Irish ancestry did give Gianna one quite beautiful feature, of which she was very proud: the long, straight waterfall of red hair that flowed halfway down her back. And she could be charming, with a wide slangy smile that made people want to like her, teachers especially. Dana had tried to like her too, but it didn't work out.

"Hey, Gianna."

The girl turned her head before making the effort to turn her entire body. "Hey, Landgrave. We got books."

"I was hoping."

"Think you'll like them." She gave Dana a wink.

"When can I see a copy?"

"The cartons are in the storeroom," she said. "Grill has the key."

Dana nodded. Miss Grill, in the office, had the keys to everything.

Gianna smiled. It was one of her charming smiles, but Dana found it vaguely alarming. "There are a couple of amusing shots of you in there."

"Amusing?"

"You'll see." Gianna turned back to her locker. "We should have books to give out by lunchtime."

"Great." Dana knew when she was being dismissed. "Super."

There was no way she could concentrate during Precalc. What amusing pictures would there be of her in the yearbook? More to the point, what pictures would there be *by* her?

At the end of third period, when the yearbooks were finally handed out, Dana leafed quickly through and found out. The school club pictures she had labored so hard over were not there! The Chess Club, looking disconsolate, was grouped at a table, three boys seated, two girls and a boy standing behind them.

She stared at the photo while going through the lunch line. *Easy*, she told herself. *This isn't worth it.* She spotted Gianna's red hair across the cafeteria and her anger spiked. She parked her tray by her friend Tricia, who was leafing through her own copy.

"Hey," said Trish in her fluty voice, "this is pretty good! 'Ja see the ones of you?"

"Be right back." Dana headed across the room.

"Gianna," she said, standing over her. She held the book open to the Chess Club. "You thought this was *better* than the picture I gave you?"

The girl frowned up at her. "You're interrupting, Landgrave."

"Yeah, I know." Dana glanced around the table—class smarties all—then back at Gianna.

"Your picture was unusable," said Gianna, turning back to her creamed chicken.

"Unusable? How?"

She laid down her fork. This was not the charming Gianna. "You couldn't see the faces. This is a yearbook. People want to see kids' *faces*. I had to go and reshoot most of the pictures you took."

"*What?*" Dana leafed through. There was the Photography Club. Dana had made a high-spirited portrait, with everyone holding up cameras and snapping pictures of the unseen photographer.

"You sure like pictures of tables," Dana said drily.

"I didn't have a lot of time to get creative."

"Hey, what could be more creative than having the

Photography Club sitting around a table looking like a bunch of morticians?"

Gianna flashed a look so fierce that Dana dropped her eyes. The bearish impression was very strong. It had to do with Gianna's heavy nose and slightly open mouth, as if she'd just been chewing fresh meat. In fact, she was still chewing her creamed chicken.

"What is it with you, Landgrave? They were all holding their cameras in front of their faces. You couldn't see who they *were!*"

"At least they were alive." Dana counted two smirks from Gianna's table partners.

"Look. You didn't give us what we needed. End of story."

Dana caught herself. She was good at arguing, but sometimes she knew when to hold off. She turned away, her jaw clenched.

"Landgrave and her artsy-fartsy pictures," Gianna said, grinning at the others.

"What did you say?" Dana's heart was pumping.

The girl looked to the side. "You still here?"

"Still here."

"Then you don't have to ask."

Gianna wasn't prepared for the sudden shove Dana gave her, spilling Coke all over the table, onto Gianna's white pants and into the lap of the guy sitting next to her, who happened to be the captain of the debate team. He jumped up, cursing, as Dana strode off. She ignored her own lunch tray and the stunned look on Trish's face and continued out into the hall. Then out of the building.

She'd walked most of a block before she asked herself if she was skipping school. At the corner of Summit she stopped and opened the yearbook. The day had warmed into the seventies, and a breeze blew her curls.

There was one of the "amusing" pictures: Dana struggling to push Ben in his wheelchair up the incline of Daniel Street against an icy wind. Their expressions were not happy. Her brother didn't even go to this school. The picture would embarrass him even more than it embarrassed her.

Then came the biggest shock. She found two pictures of her own, out of the dozens she'd submitted. They were dramatic action shots of the Clipper soccer team on the field, and each had been given a quarter page. But they were different than she remembered. They'd been massaged by a computer so that a forest of cheering fans appeared in the background where no crowd had been. In small print under each picture was the photo credit: Gianna Belkin.

Dana found it hard to get her breath. She tore the pages out and slowly crumpled them. Mechanically she started walking. She turned left on Junkins and crossed the Mill Pond, a tidewater marsh favored by gulls and cormorants. Today a snowy egret stood on one leg, like a waiter trying to keep his uniform clean.

Dana watched it a long time. It watched her watching.

But even as she stood there surging with anger, a part of her remained detached, realizing that after all she was here at midday, free from school, with the simple sun overhead. She might dislike Gianna Belkin, but it wasn't real, not the way her dreams were real. In the world of high school there were no visions of a bloody child entombed in the dark.

Dana frisbeed the yearbook far out over the pond, scaring the bird into flight.

Chapter Two

The Friendly Toast

"I HEAR WE HAD A LITTLE TROUBLE IN SCHOOL today," said Dr. Sprague, scratching his cheekbone. He pushed back from his desk, tilting his leather chair against the wall behind him. "Want to tell me about it?"

Dana glanced at the door of his office, glad it was closed, although she could still hear Mrs. Robyns, the receptionist, clacking away outside. The only other sound was the humming of the aquarium across the room. "First of all," she said, "*we* didn't have trouble in school. *I* did."

"Figure of speech."

"It's condescending."

Sprague, a solidly built man in his disheveled fifties, swung forward onto his feet. He went to the window and looked out at the North Church, his dark-vested form blocking the light. "We can analyze me if you want, Miss Landgrave," he said, "or we can analyze you, whichever you think is a better use of your parents' money."

Dana was silent.

"Do you want to tell me what happened?"

"Nothing happened."

"I see." Morton Sprague paused by the bookshelves to contemplate the aquarium, an oversize tank containing a large and

16

very creepy-looking snapping turtle, either dead or asleep. Satisfied, he returned to the desk. He'd never been a handsome man, and his face had grown bucket-shaped with advancing middle age. His sad-looking dewlapped eyes settled over Dana, giving him a look rather like his turtle. He was waiting her out. She hated that.

"Gianna Belkin rejected my pictures for the yearbook," she said at last, twisting back and forth in the swivel chair.

He nodded. "She rejected your pictures."

"Except the ones she took credit for."

Sprague's eyes widened, then narrowed. He did that a lot, like he was letting in an idea, then closing the door to keep it from getting away. "And how did that make you feel?"

She grimaced. "Please."

"A simple question."

"How would it make *you* feel?"

"Your parents tell me they got a call from school."

Dana didn't respond.

"Apparently the young lady claims you attacked her."

Dana gave a short laugh.

"Is there a joke I'm missing?"

"If Gianna thinks that was an attack . . ."

"Is that why you walked out of school in the middle of the day?"

"Do you have spies or something?"

Dr. Sprague brought his hands together at the fingertips, like a cage, and leaned forward on his elbows.

"Do all of you do that?" said Dana suddenly.

"Do what?"

"That thing with your fingers. That's a shrink thing, right? They teach you that in shrink school."

Sprague set his hands down flat on his desk. "You caught me."
She gave a little smile.

"Now, Miss Landgrave," he said, "what do you say we try to find out something about *you*?"

"What about me?"

"Your anger, for instance."

Dana slumped down in her chair, her legs straight in front of her. "I thought we were trying to find out about the dreams."

"They could be connected."

"What makes you think that?"

"It's a shrink thing." He glanced at his watch. "We still have some time. I suggest we have another go at hypnosis."

She shrugged. "It didn't get rid of the dreams."

"No, it didn't. Failed experiment."

"Like those pills."

"Right. It seemed the place to start. If the antidepressants had worked we'd be home free."

She was barely listening.

"I'd like to try hypnosis again. Have you heard of age regression? I'd like to take you back to your childhood."

"Why not just ask me about my childhood?"

"We've been doing that, if you'll recall."

Dana sighed. Twice a week for the last two months she'd had to dredge up memories of her toddler days, her second-grade teacher, her feelings about having a baby brother, even about the accident. Waste of time, all of it.

"Whatever you say, Doc."

"Good. So if you'll switch over to the recliner . . ."

With a sigh she uncoiled herself and plunked down on the La-Z-Boy. Sprague came and sat in a straight chair beside her.

"Now," he said, "let's clear your mind and see what we can do. Are you ready?"

Dana relaxed into the recliner and lightly closed her eyes, as she'd done in the previous session. The doctor asked her to concentrate on her breathing, counting down slowly from fifty, one breath at a time. He then switched to the image of stairs. She liked this part, imagining herself walking down a long curving staircase, her bare feet sinking into plush carpet, her hand gliding along the banister. With each step she became more relaxed, her eyes heavier. Long before she reached bottom she'd lost track of where she was.

Dana was an easy subject. In a way, she was already self-hypnotized much of the time. Kids in school would tease her about the "Dana stare." She was smart, certainly, but her grades didn't always show it because she'd forget her assignments or be caught gazing out the window when the teacher called on her. At home she regularly burned the toast and more than once filled her milk glass over the top. Her mind was who knows where, on her photography, or on mental images of people she'd never met. The boy in the dream was only one of them.

"I'm thinking," Sprague said quietly, "we might go back to when you were ten. Can you think of a scene from that year that was comfortable for you? That felt safe?"

She nodded slowly.

"What are you thinking of?"

"The swing set. Backyard."

"Were you happy there?"

"Secret place."

"How does it make you feel, being there?"

She smiled. "Safe."

"Good. And you can go back to that safe place whenever you want. Whenever you need to. I'm wondering, though, is there another time back then that wasn't quite so comfortable?"

"Not comfortable?"

"Maybe not as safe?"

She was silent a few seconds. "Yap," she said.

"Excuse me?"

"Miss Yapko."

"Who is she?"

"Fourth grade."

"Your teacher?"

Dana's mind had already raced ahead to her fourth-grade spring art project. She was not remembering the scene; she was *in* it.

Miss Yapko stood before the class. Beside her was a table covered with a dozen dioramas. "Who helped you with your project?" she said sharply.

Dana was so surprised she didn't answer at once. "Nobody helped me."

"Stand up when you answer me."

Mortified, Dana got to her feet and stood in front of Dr. Sprague's divan. She felt a surge of heat rise into her neck, her ears, her scalp. She could feel the eyes of her classmates on her.

"You thought of this all by yourself?" The teacher squinted at the girl's diorama, a complex depiction of Bambi's mother about to be shot by a realistic cardboard rifle suspended by wires in the air. Especially interesting was the depiction of the rifle's stock, which was disproportionately larger than the barrel. It was meant to appear closer to the viewer's eye, as if the viewer were the shooter. At age ten little Dana Landgrave had already grasped the concept of perspective.

"Well?" snapped Yapko. She saw the girl's hesitation and sensed triumph.

"Ben helped some."

"Ben? Who's Ben?"

"My brother."

"Come up and show me what parts he did."

Dana's legs felt like cement.

"Did you hear me?"

She imagined herself making her way to the table. Her body shuffled up to Sprague's desk.

Yap (as she was universally called behind her back) folded her arms. "So your older brother helped you."

"Younger."

"What?"

"He's five years younger. He did some of the gluing."

Yap was momentarily without a reply.

"Especially the bugs on the background. See there, and there? He caught 'em and glued 'em."

"That's not the sort of help I meant," Miss Yapko said. "I meant the whole design, the concept, the construction."

Dana looked confused.

"This," said Yapko, "is way beyond fourth-grade work."

The girl looked up into her teacher's face, her heart beating hard. "You think"—she could hardly say the words—"I *copied* off somebody?"

"Didn't you?"

"No!"

"Using that tone is not going to help you."

"I didn't copy off anybody!"

"I want you to lower your voice, young lady."

Quietly, as if not to interrupt, Dr. Sprague's voice came in. "What are you feeling now, Miss Landgrave?"

Dana's eyes sprang open and she stared straight ahead. She was breathing hard.

"Tell me," he soothed.

She whispered. "Scared."

"Tell me more," he murmured. His reassuring baritone was little more than a background hum. "What are you scared of?"

"I want to hit her."

"I see."

"I want to kill her!"

Dana's eyes closed. She saw herself give the diorama a tremendous push that propelled it off the table, knocking against the blackboard and splintering on the floor.

Her body, still standing, squirmed around as if in physical pain. She wanted to be free of the trance. Slowly the doctor took her forward in time to her present age, instructed her to remember everything, and allowed her wake up.

She stared at him and then at the pipe stand, paperweight, and humidor that lay scattered on the carpet. "I don't like you," she said evenly.

"That's all right," said the doctor, bending to pick up the things she'd knocked off the desk. "I might as well join the list."

"What's that supposed to mean?" She sat down in the swivel chair and folded her arms.

"You're angry with your teacher, so you throw your diorama on the floor. You're angry at Gianna, so you throw the yearbook in the pond."

Dana was silent.

"You feel unjustly treated."

"I *was* unjustly treated."

"Maybe. What's interesting is that both times your reaction was violent. And both times it was your own work you destroyed."

She glared at him.

"So who are you really angry at?" he pursued.

"Right now," she said slowly, "you."

"I can see that."

"Can I go now?"

He glanced at the wall clock. "Of course."

Chase Newcomer was waiting for her downstairs when she came out. A tall, athletic kid with a good-humored, clean-cut face, he wore his varsity sweatshirt like a cape, the arms tied loosely around his neck. With his sunglasses perched high on his head, he looked as though he'd just stepped off a yacht. There was no yacht, of course. His parents were not in that tax bracket. His dad was the news producer at a local TV station.

She frowned. "What are you doing here?"

"Missed you in English class." He pushed back a careless flop of blond hair.

"Yeah, well."

Chase nodded toward the upstairs window. "How'd it go?"

"Sprague's a jerk. Your dad should do an exposé."

"Sounds like progress."

"Don't you start."

"Want to grab a bite?"

"Sure."

He slipped an arm around her waist as they headed down Islington to the Friendly Toast. They tried for privacy in a booth toward the back, but Chase was easy to look at and hard to miss.

"Hey, Chase. Sign my yearbook?"

Newcomer looked up into the lively blue eyes of Mary Bing. Even amid the smells of bacon and hamburger you could catch the perfume. She was the kind of girl cashmere was made for.

"Sure."

She pulled out a gold pen for him. Finally she noticed he was not alone. "Hey, Dana."

"Hey, Bingo."

Chase signed with an actorish flourish, but Mary hung around, asking what schedule Chase had picked for the fall and how the team was doing. "Great picture of you in the yearbook."

She was talking about an action shot of the soccer team. Chase was booting the ball through a spray of mud.

"Thanks. Dana took it."

"Really?"

The girl held the book in front of her hips and swung back and forth as she talked. A perpetual motion machine, that girl. Finally she left, and Dana picked at her fries.

"What?" said Chase.

"She likes you."

"Think so?"

"They all do." She gave a nod at the table of gigglers Bing had returned to.

"Isn't it pretty to think so."

Dana looked at him. "You're weird." She went back to not eating her fries. She stared at a truly ugly, mustard-colored ceramic lamp on the table. "Why do you like me?"

"I don't, really."

"Then how come you hang around?"

"Maybe I should ask your shrink."

"Want some of my fries?"

24

"Thanks."

She set the plate between them for easy access. "I had the dream again."

He held a fry in his hand, forgetting to eat it. "How bad?"

She shook her head.

"Same kid?"

"Yeah, except this time I could hear his thoughts."

"Freaky." He beheaded the fry. "How come I never dream about anything interesting like that?"

"You're lucky."

"Maybe I'm just shallow."

She smiled. "Don't change. I need you shallow."

"Oh, I ran into Belkin."

Dana shot him a look. "Yeah?"

"What did you do to that girl?"

"What did she do to *me*?"

"I asked first."

Dana shrugged. "I gave her a little shove."

"That's it?"

"I might have spilled her Coke."

He leaned against the back of the booth. "Here I thought you'd killed her grandmother."

"She wouldn't care if I killed her grandmother. It was her white pants."

"Well," he said quietly, leaning forward, "she's not wearing them now."

Dana looked around to see Gianna Belkin, large as life. Larger.

"Oh, jeez," Dana murmured.

Gianna's eyes were unnaturally bright. "What do you know?" she said. "The absentee."

"What do you want, Gianna?"

"What do I want?" Her mouth remained open between sentences. It was one of her more disconcerting habits. "I suppose seeing you suspended would be high on the list."

Dana traded a glance with Chase. "Why would I be suspended?"

"Attacking another student?" Gianna suggested.

"I never attacked you."

"There were about a thousand witnesses."

"Then they know what happened."

"They do. Two of them have already talked to Grill."

"About what?"

"You'll find out Monday."

Dana had forgotten about Monday. The school secretary had called her parents about it. "Oh, yeah."

"We'll all get to tell our story to the principal."

The thought of it made Dana angry all over again. "What story? I barely touched you."

"Not touched. Punched. My shoulder's still bruised."

"Why are you saying this?"

She pulled the wide neck of the sweatshirt to one side. "Take a look."

It did, actually, look a lot like a bruise.

"I didn't do that."

"Good, Landgrave. Stick to your story. Maybe you'll get somebody to believe it. Hi, Chase." She gave him a tiny wave as she turned and tugboated out the door.

Dana leaned across the table. "*I didn't do that*, Chase."

He swirled cold coffee around the plastic cup. "Of course you didn't."

"Do you believe me?"

"Of course I do." He paused one beat. "Just don't do it again."

"Chase . . ."

He leaned back. "Whatever. I'm sure she had it coming."

"Chase, you are the most infuriating—"

"Hey," he said, holding his arms up in front of him and laughing, "just don't hit me!"

She had to smile in spite of herself. "Let's get out of here."

"Deal."

Chapter Three

The Dana Stare

TOM LANDGRAVE LOOKED UP FROM THE HOLE IN the ground he'd been peering into. "Hey, kids! Catching some air?"

Dana smiled. It was good to see her dad at the work site. She'd never had the chance when she was younger and he was working on fishing boats. But he'd come in to land a few years ago and taken a job with the city working on drainage projects. His tanned, comfortably wrinkled face and calloused hands gave a touch of sanity to Dana's life, and she took Ben there on walks whenever she could. Today was a warm, windy Saturday with Monday nowhere in sight.

"Come on down," Landgrave called, squinting through the chain-link fence. "I have something to show you."

"Okay with you?" Dana said.

Ben shrugged.

Tipping the chair back onto the rear wheels, she let it bump off the sidewalk. She had to hold on tight as they started down the dirt ramp. Three other men were working there. She recognized the one named Chick, a leathery guy in his fifties. Tom Landgrave was their boss, but you wouldn't know it.

"Ever seen anything like this?" Landgrave said.

Dana parked Ben beside an ancient-looking stone opening

that led straight into darkness. From somewhere below came the sound of rushing water. "What are we looking at?" she said.

Ben grimaced. "We're looking at a sewer pipe."

"Actually," said Landgrave, "this is what they call the box. The pipe itself is down there. We're replacing both." He took a bandanna from his back pocket and wiped his hands on it. "It's from the seventeen hundreds."

"We risked our necks," Ben said in his rasping voice, "to look at a sewer pipe."

Landgrave tousled his son's hair. "But look at the stonework. There's another one over here. Nineteenth century." He trudged a hundred feet to the east, and of course Dana had to follow with her cranky brother.

"This was built by the ale maker Frank Jones to carry waste water to the river from his brewery."

Dana and Ben dutifully peered into the darkness.

"Yep," said Ben. "Another sewer, all right."

The guy named Chick was poking at a mound of earth with a shovel. "Your dad's a special guy."

"No kidding," Ben said.

Chick's thin mouth cracked in a smile. "I keep telling him he should work for the historical society."

It made Dana happy to hear her father talked about. "I know," she said.

"He can tell you the story of every pipe in the city," said Chick.

"Well, it's *interesting*," said Landgrave.

"Interesting," drawled Ben.

"It's our past. You can't set your compass by the present. You want to know where you're going, you got to know where you been."

"See what I mean?" Chick poked at the dirt with his shovel.

Dana went up to her father and kissed him on the cheek.

He gave her a bewildered smile.

"You can tell me about sewer pipes any time you want," she said.

Monday came too soon. It started with a Precalc pre-final (a sort of dress rehearsal for next week's real thing), followed by an appointment with the principal to discuss recent lunchroom events.

At the last moment Dana pressured Trish Roth, her friend and cafeteria mate, to come with her to make her feel less outnumbered. Gianna Belkin could outnumber you all by herself, and she'd increased her advantage by bringing along two witnesses, both honor students. One of them was the debate captain who'd been splashed by the spilled Coke, the other a quiet girl named Bev, who was Gianna's yearbook assistant. To make things worse, Miss Grill was present, yellow pad on knee, ready to take notes. She looked up as Dana and Trish found seats.

"Don't worry," Trish whispered, her round face apprehensive.

"How can you say don't worry?" Dana's stomach was making strange noises from the apricot Danish she'd eaten an hour ago.

Trish looked around the room. The room looked back. "You're right," she said. "Go ahead and worry."

"Thanks for coming, everyone." The crisp voice belonged to the principal, Martin Sharpe, a man as narrow as his name. He settled himself behind his desk. "Let's get right to it. Miss Landgrave? You've been accused of starting a fight with Miss Belkin. True?"

The Danish lurched in Dana's stomach. "No, sir."

Sharpe narrowed his eyes to a point. "Miss Belkin is sporting quite a bruise on her shoulder. How do you explain that?"

"I can't."

"You can't?"

Dana swallowed. "No, sir. I didn't cause it, so I can't explain it."

Sharpe's eyes slashed over to Gianna. "Miss Belkin, tell us again what you told me."

"She punched me." Gianna cast a disgusted look at Dana. "I had to reject some of her pictures—most of them, actually—and I suppose she was upset."

"As you just heard, she denies it."

Gianna smiled. "I thought she would, which is why I brought two witnesses who were with me when the attack occurred."

"Nice to see you're prepared. Go ahead."

Gianna launched into an account of Dana's "unprovoked attack," while her supporters nodded in agreement at appropriate intervals. Dana was amazed at the distortions coming out of the girl's mouth. Gianna had a lot to say, and after a minute or so Dana's mind started to wander. There was something about the girl she hadn't noticed before. A resemblance, but to whom? Gianna definitely reminded her of someone.

"Then when I turned back to my friends," said Gianna, winding up, her voice confidently loud, with a touch of spittle in the corner of her mouth, "*she* came up behind me and punched me really, really *hard*." Reflexively she rubbed the injured shoulder.

"You say she punched you on the shoulder."

"Yes. Really hard. And she spilled my drink all over my pants. The stain won't come out."

Sharpe turned to Dana. "Miss Landgrave, what do you have to say?"

Dana didn't hear him. She had fallen into the "Dana stare" that her classmates often razzed her about. It could happen at any time and didn't seem related to where she was. The first thing she noticed was that the light was growing dimmer and the principal's gestures slower. Most alarming, something was happening to Gianna! Dana shook her head, certain she was seeing double—two Giannas, or Gianna and someone else. A moment later, the bearish girl with the flaming hair had begun looking like a man in his forties, dressed outlandishly as though for a costume party.

Dana's heart beat hard. *Is this a joke?*

The man was wearing one of those wig things like George Washington, but he was definitely not George Washington. Dana glanced around to see if anyone else had noticed, but no one was looking at him. Didn't they *see*? He had the same bright, attacking eyes as Gianna, the same carnivore mouth, slightly open—but a different person entirely! Dana couldn't stop looking at him. Handsome in a middle-aged way, he wore a blue waistcoat over a ruffled white shirt with a flare of lace at the cuffs. His outfit was not just a few years, but a few centuries out of style.

"Miss Landgrave?" The principal's voice was impatient.

Trish nudged her.

Dana's stomach made an audible complaint.

"Miss Landgrave? Are you with us?"

"Why don't you *answer* him?" Trish hissed.

Dana mumbled back, "What did he say?"

"Excuse me," said Sharpe, "what are you two whispering about?"

Trish gave her friend an alarmed look, then she cleared her throat and raised an arm. "Um, may I say something?"

The principal nodded.

"I was not at Gianna's table," she said, her voice quavering, "but I can tell you what I saw."

"Briefly, please."

Trish clasped her hands before her and gazed down at them as if in prayer. It was possible that she actually did say a quick one before she looked up.

"I could tell Dana was angry," she began. "She was holding the yearbook open while she talked to Gianna. I couldn't hear what they said, but I think Gianna must have made some remark, because Dana turned and went back. They both said something more, and then Dana gave her a shove on the shoulder."

"A shove?" said Sharpe. "Not a punch?"

Dana shook her head to clear her thoughts. She watched Miss Grill madly shorthanding on her legal pad.

"A shove," said Trish. "It was not that hard. Hard enough to spill the drink, but that's it."

"Not true!" crowed Gianna.

Dana was looking from one to the other. She knew all this talk concerned her, but she was still in two worlds. Gianna was recognizably Gianna, but she was also that other person, now rapidly fading.

Am I going crazy?

"What is not true, Miss Belkin?" said Sharpe.

"It was a *punch*. Here, look." She pulled the neck of her blouse to the side, revealing a yellowing bruise.

"That's enough, Miss Belkin. We concede the bruise."

Suddenly Dana understood something, and without thinking she stood up. In a room full of sitters it was a dramatic move. "Except for the bruise, Gianna," she said, now fully herself again, "you agree with what Tricia said?"

"I suppose."

"You made some remark, right? And I came back. . . ."

"What's your point?"

"And I came up behind you?"

"Like a coward, yes."

Everyone, including Trish, was looking at Dana as if her mind had jumped the tracks.

"Your *point*?" Gianna's eyes flamed.

"Could we see that bruise again?" said Dana.

Sharpe held up his hand. "We all saw the bruise, Miss Landgrave."

"Where was it?"

He sighed. "It was on the front of . . ." He stopped. Everyone looked at Gianna.

"Yes," said Dana. "Exactly. On the front of."

The room fell silent. Even Miss Grill paused in her shorthand.

"Looks like you dodged a bullet." Dr. Sprague was leaning back in his squeaky leather chair and chewing on the stem of an unlit pipe.

"Yeah," said Dana. "Now *she's* in trouble. For lying."

"Are you happy about that?"

"Ecstatic."

"I see. So you're out of the woods, then?"

Dana sighed. "I have to see the school counselor and pay to have Gianna's pants cleaned."

"Beats getting suspended. What's the counselor for?"

"Anger management."

"Lovely. Did you ever find out where your friend got that bruise?"

Dana snorted. "She was lugging boxes of yearbooks. Didn't watch where she was going."

"Narrow doorway?"

"All doorways are narrow for Gianna."

Silence filled the office. Dr. Sprague seemed in no hurry. Dana could hear his teeth on the pipe stem. "I'm interested," he said, "in something you said before. You said you were looking at this young lady and thought she was someone else."

Dana nodded.

"Can you be more specific?"

"It's not that I *thought* she was someone else. I *saw* someone else."

Sprague took this in for a few seconds, widening and then narrowing his eyes. He got up and went to the aquarium to contemplate his snapping turtle. It seemed to help him think. "I'm wondering," he said, returning to his chair, "if you'd be game to try something a little unorthodox."

"Like what?"

"Have you ever heard of past life regression?"

She shook her head.

"It's just what it sounds like. We get you into a hypnotic state, as we've done several times already. Then I take you back, or try to, to a former lifetime."

Dana frowned. "What makes you think I've had a former lifetime?"

"Maybe you haven't. Then we'll have another failed experiment to add to the list."

"This is too weird." Dana was beginning to wonder, in fact, and not for the first time, if her doctor was entirely sane. For one thing, that turtle. Who'd have a snapping turtle for a pet?

"Have you ever tried this before, or am I the guinea pig?"

Sprague's face grew solemn. "I had it done to me."

"You *did*? *When*?" Dana's pipe-chewing shrink with the mustard stain on his sleeve hardly seemed the type to push the frontiers of science.

"As part of my studies, years ago. A new analyst used to have to go through psychoanalysis before they set him loose on the public. I asked my professor to take it a step further."

"What happened?"

Sprague held up his hands. "Hard to explain. Something did happen, that's for sure."

"Were you somebody famous?"

"Why is that the first thing people want to know?"

Dana shrugged.

"Anyway, I can't answer you. I saw only pieces of the puzzle. Disconnected scenes. They didn't last long enough to make sense. I didn't even learn who I was."

She nodded.

"I've tried to find out since, but I never was able to get back. The door opened, just slightly, then it closed. I suppose I was lucky it opened at all." He laid his pipe on the shiny desk. "Miss Landgrave," he said, "I wouldn't suggest this except that you keep seeing faces of people you don't know."

"Maybe I knew them in the past?"

He raised a heavy eyebrow.

"Do you think," she said, "I'm seeing ghosts?"

"I don't know what a ghost is. I know what memories are. I'd rather think these are memories."

"Memories from a past life." Dana was silent, but in the silence she felt growing excitement. "When do you want to start?"

"How about now?"

"Now? You mean *now*?"

He watched her.

"What if I don't get back?"

"Meaning?"

"What if I get into another lifetime and can't get back to this one?"

"I don't think it works like that. You're not *going* there. You're *remembering* it."

"You don't *think* it works like that? You don't know?"

He stroked his cheek thoughtfully with the side of his finger. "No, I don't."

"Not very reassuring."

"Want to skip it?"

Dana thought of the man in the periwig and blue waistcoat she'd seen in the principal's office. She thought of the boy from her dreams. His wounds, his pleading eyes. She *had* to find out who he was—who she herself was.

Her mouth set in a determined line. "Let's do it."

Chapter Four

Bump

THEY TRIED TWICE THAT AFTERNOON AND
failed both times. The first time, as Sprague led her backward,
her mind became tangled in images of the bus accident that
had crippled her brother. As soon as Dana's mind locked
onto the wet curve of Route 1 heading south of town, there
was no use trying to continue the regression. There was only
the squeal of tires as the bus swerved to avoid a merging
sedan, the loud bang as the side mirror clipped a pole, the
terrifying loss of balance as they went over, everyone hurled
screaming from their seats. . . .

Dana, who'd been sitting with her friends and her brother
near the front, felt a burning pain in her shoulder as she
searched madly for Ben. She found him under a seat, his head
at an unnatural angle. The image of his half-shut eyes, one of
them fluttering slightly, would stay with her always.

She was the first to crawl from the wreck. Seeing the lights
of the Bowl-O-Rama, she limped inside and managed to call
9-1-1. Even under hypnosis she couldn't remember how she
got back to the bus, where she helped bleeding people,
including her friend Trish, who had a dangerous-looking cut
over her eye. Something told her not to move Ben, and she
stood guard over him until the ambulance arrived.

When Sprague gently brought her out of the trance, her forehead was damp.

"Maybe we should try this another time," he said gently.

Dana pressed the heels of her hands against her eyes. "No. Let's do it now."

"I think we should wait."

"No!"

He nodded. "Well, if you feel ready."

"I'll never be ready."

This time they started with her earliest clear memories and worked back from there: little five-year-old Dana kneeling on the window seat on the second floor of the Marcy Street house. She watched as a car drove up and people got out. "Mommy!" she called. Her mother, not hearing her through the pane, emerged with a blanket-wrapped bundle. It was the baby brother Dana had been hearing about. She jumped down and raced for the stairs.

"Very good," came the doctor's voice, interrupting her. "Now let's go back to a memory before that."

"Before Bennie?"

"You're very safe. It's all right. You can remember."

Dana frowned. "Peas."

"Excuse me?"

"Rolling peas."

"Rolling peas? Where do you see this?"

"On the tray. They are rolling." Dana's voice sounded babyish.

"Where is the tray, Dana?"

"On the high chair."

"What is happening around you? Can you tell?"

Dana's head tilted to the side, then to the other side, clearly uncomfortable. "Yelling."

"Who is yelling?"

"Mommy and Daddy."

"Can you see where they are?"

Dana's eyes remained closed. "Kitchen," she said in a little voice.

Sprague's voice was soothing. "What are they arguing about?"

She shook her head.

"All right. It's not important."

"The peas are rolling."

"It's all right, Dana. Let's go back further now, to a time before this. A moment that was important to you."

The girl flinched and squeezed her eyes shut.

"What is it?"

"Ah!"

"What is it?"

"Eyes!"

"What about your eyes?"

She tightened her eyes still further. Her whole body began trembling. "Light!"

"Is it hurting your eyes?"

She half-raised her arms before her. A tear escaped her.

"You seem to be shivering."

"Cold! Freezing!"

"Is there pain anywhere else?"

"Shoulder!"

"That's all right. The pain is over now. You are safe. Let's go back to a time before the pain. Before the terrible light."

After a few seconds Dana's expression cleared. Her eyes remained closed as the suggestion of a smile tugged gently at her lips.

"Where are you, now, Dana?"

No response.

"Can you tell me what you see?"

"Nothing."

"What sort of place is this?"

"Warm."

"Warm. Can you hear anything?"

"Yes."

"What do you hear?"

"Far away."

"Voices?"

"No."

"Can you imitate the sound?"

Dana hesitated only a moment. "Bump, bump, but far away."

The doctor was silent, as if listening for the sound himself. "All right," he said. "Let's go even further back. You can do it. Go back to something that happened before this."

Dana was silent. Then she whispered, "Ba-bump. Like that."

"Can you go back to an earlier memory?"

"Bump," she whispered.

"That's all right. That's enough for now. Let's come back."

Sprague slowly progressed her through babyhood and early childhood until she reached her teen years. He allowed her to float back to the present, instructing her to remember everything.

Her eyes opened. She felt tired, but calm. "We didn't make it, did we?"

"Make it?" He shook his head slowly. "But you should be pleased. We got further than we've ever gotten before. That thudding sound may have been your mother's heartbeat."

"You mean, before I was . . . ?"

"Before you were born, yes."

She thought about it. "Maybe that's all there is. Maybe there's no past life."

"You could be right."

"But you don't think so," she said.

He gazed down at his nested hands, then looked up to meet her gaze. "No, I don't."

That evening Dana was mostly silent as she cut up the salad. She was helping her dad get dinner—his special breaded chicken and whipped sweet potatoes, the kind with a roof of marshmallows on top. Her mother wasn't back yet from her day trip to Boston, but she'd called on her cell to say she was turning off 95 and would be there soon. Mrs. Landgrave went to Boston a lot, and sometimes New York and Chicago. This time it was to meet with product liability experts and depose witnesses for an upcoming trial. Dana understood that she was one of the best litigators in the state.

And maybe the worst cook. Dana preferred her dad's comfort food to her mother's twigs and nuts. Tofu burgers were a particular trial. Still, for someone so often absent, Becca Landgrave was conscientious. She ran the household like a business, or tried to, and everyone had his chores. Ben's didn't involve much lifting, of course—his main job was setting out the knives and forks—but it was the principle of the thing. There were a lot of principles in the Landgrave household.

The grumble of a car engine reached them, and the crunch of tires on gravel. "She's home!" Landgrave sang out. He opened the oven a crack to check on the chicken and was met with a wave of fragrant heat. He popped the sweet potatoes in to brown the marshmallows.

"Yum," said Ben.

The front door squealed, and Becca Landgrave's head popped in, her green eyes vivid under arched brows, her tightly curled hair almost a form of weaponry. Then the rest of her slid in, too slim a stalk for that remarkable head. She was a very pretty woman. You could see her children in her. Ben got her short stature, regular features, and quick tongue. Dana got the curly hair. It was not a gift she was happy with.

"Looks like the gang's all here." Becca surveyed the kitchen.

"You bet." Tom Landgrave kissed his wife's cheek and took the bottle of Chablis from under her arm. "What's this?"

"Celebration. Looks like they're going to settle."

"Good going!"

"Yeah, pretty nice."

It was a good thing when Becca didn't have to go to trial, and this was a big case, lots of preparation with no guarantee how it might have turned out.

"How much?" he said.

Becca shot him a frown.

"*That* much?" he exclaimed.

"How much, Mom?" said Ben.

"See what you've started?" Becca gave her husband a shove. "Hi, kids." She gave each a smooch on the forehead and sat down. "*Quel* day!"

"Hope you like chicken," said Tom. "Dana, could you set out the plates and get your mother's jacket?"

"Not too much dinner for me," said Becca. "We stopped on the way."

"We?"

"Bernie and Pauline and I. We had to celebrate when the word came."

43

Dana already knew her mother had stopped to celebrate. The unnatural brightness of her eyes had told her that the moment she walked in.

"Try a little. Dana made an incredible salad."

"Maybe a little." Becca slipped off her maroon suit jacket. Beneath was a cream-colored silk blouse that came together in front with a floppy bow.

Tom Landgrave served up steaming helpings, including a special plate for Ben—everything cut up extra fine. It was a break from his usual mush.

"Mm," said Becca, forking a mouthful. "But do you always have to use so much butter?"

"Trying to fatten you up."

She let that pass. Usually she wouldn't. Family nutrition was taken seriously.

Tom uncorked the wine, pouring a glass for her and half a glass for himself. "Tell us what happened."

"How much do you want to know about asphalt grinding equipment?"

The others looked at one another.

"What I thought. Anyway, long story short, the equipment was faulty, and they knew it before they sold it to the D.O.T."

"The D.O.T.?" said Ben.

"The Department of Transportation. We had the goods on them, internal memos, everything. By the way," she said, "the office gave me the okay for London."

Tom's fork, laden, paused in midair. "London?"

"The law convention end of next month. We talked about it. Don't you remember?"

Dana and Ben glanced from their mother to their father and back.

"Well," Tom said. He seemed to lose his train of thought. "That's great."

Becca took another sip of Chablis. "I'd be making all kinds of contacts."

"Maybe we could all go."

"Yeah!" Ben rasped.

Becca laid down her fork. "I don't think the settlement's *that* good."

For a minute no one ate anything.

"Tom." She drained her glass and refilled it. "Why do you always bring things up in front of the kids before we've talked?"

"I just thought of it."

"Well, then *think*. It's not practical. Getting Ben around, for one thing."

"I can do it, Mom," Ben piped, his face shiny with hope. "The trake's coming out in a few weeks."

"And it's not affordable."

The room sank into silence.

Becca took a forkful of chicken. "You get everyone all stirred up."

"You're right," he said. "Say, anybody in the mood for pie?" His face, comfortable as an old sofa, beamed at his son.

"I'd *like* to take everybody," Becca said. "I would. I just don't see how it would work."

"I'd help," said Dana. "You know, with Ben."

Becca's impatience was starting to show. "Can we *not* talk about this right now?"

"Right," Tom said.

They were well into dessert before anyone spoke. It was Becca, asking Ben about school. She got a shrug for an answer.

That was about all she ever got on that subject; and anyway, Ben was still upset about London.

"So how about you?" Mrs. Landgrave turned to Dana.

"The usual."

"How's homework? Got a lot?"

"Not really."

"Meaning?"

"It's the end of the year. We don't have homework."

"You have finals."

"Mmn."

"So?" Mrs. Landgrave's eyes were getting brighter, which was generally a warning sign. "What's your first final?"

Dana sighed. "Precalc."

"Don't you need to study for it?"

"It's a bore."

"Math is a bore?" Mrs. Landgrave looked at the ceiling, as if seeking divine help. "Math is a *bore*? I *think* in math. It sharpens the mind."

Dana examined her half-eaten pie and melting ice cream.

"It's okay, Bec," Tom soothed. "Everybody's just had a long day."

Becca sloshed the last of the wine into her glass, spilling some. "Maybe if you studied a little more math, you wouldn't be so vague all the time."

Ben smirked.

"Mom," said Dana quietly, "I know you're good at math. People's minds are different, that's all."

"Mind is mind."

Dana knew better than to continue, but she had figured it out that afternoon, and she felt strongly. "Not really," she said. "You think in numbers. I think in pictures."

"You don't *think!*"

A horrible sound came from Ben, a loud wheezing, like an old car that was trying to start and couldn't.

"He's choking!" Becca cried.

Her husband was already there, thumping on the boy's back. "It's okay. Come on, buddy!"

Ben's face reddened and his eyes grew teary from the effort to cough up whatever it was that had gone the wrong way. It was always a danger that some bit of food meant for his stomach might go down his windpipe.

"Come on, that's it!"

Gradually Ben came out of it, but he was exhausted. He held on to the edge of the table to steady himself.

"I'll be glad when that trake is out of there," said Tom grimly.

"It's my fault," said Becca. "Too much excitement."

There was always excitement with Becca Landgrave. Dana looked at her across the table, the dynamic little litigator with the tight, copper-colored curls. *Mama, I was living inside you this afternoon. I listened to your heartbeat.*

She felt a pang of despair, remembering. *I listened to your heartbeat, Mama. It was the same as mine. I never felt so warm.*

If only she could say that to her. That simply.

Almost midnight, and everything was arranged. The castle-shaped night-light cast its milky glow. The bear she was much too old for sat propped by the pillow. The door and the window stood partly open, allowing routes of escape in case of emergency. A three-quarter moon, in an upper pane, glazed the dresser with silver, like an illustration from a children's book. So why was Dana staring at the ceiling, certain that sleep would not come?

The dreams. Terror of the narrow space. Blackness with no way out.

Her mouth was dry, and a familiar dizziness set the room in motion around her. She thought it was because of her shallow breathing, and she tried the technique the doctor had taught her, breathing slowly and deeply, slowly and deeply.

Her hand fumbled with the cell phone on the night table. Without taking her eyes from the shadowy corner of the room, she dialed Chase Newcomer's number. She knew it by feel.

"Hey," he said softly.

"Hey."

"Bad night?"

She didn't answer.

"Guess that would be a yes."

She started her breathing exercises again.

"Are you still there?" he said.

"Keep talking," she murmured. "It's helping me."

"You want to go to Hampton Beach this weekend?"

"Okay."

"They've got new games in the arcade."

"Good. Okay."

"Or we could be smart and study for finals."

"Fine," she said between deep breaths.

"You'll agree with anything I say, won't you?"

"Long as you keep talking."

"Want to run away with me to South America?"

"Okay."

"I like this. You want to do my laundry?"

"As long as you keep talking."

"I can talk all night."

"I noticed."

They fell into a comfortable silence. Dana was starting to feel better. "You really don't mind," she said, "me calling you like this?"

"No problem."

"I mean really."

"I just keep the phone on vibrate, like we said. Doesn't bother anybody."

"It bothers you."

"I was just wasting time sleeping."

She smiled. "You're okay."

"I know."

"You can go back to wasting time again."

"You sure?"

"Yeah. Go to sleep."

He yawned. "Maybe I will."

"Me too." She snapped the phone closed and laid it on the night table. Her smile faded. Between the night-light and the moon, her room was awash in silver gray, like a TV left on with the sound off. Something was not right. Dana was sure there was somebody outside the door. Her heart bounded in her chest and she jumped up, closed the door, and locked it.

She locked the window.

That helped until she realized she had locked herself in. She went to the window and flung it wide.

An eon later dawn came. She was still rigid on the bed, staring at the ceiling.

Chapter Five

Hannah

"AT LEAST," SAID SPRAGUE, LEANING BACK AND
lacing his fingers behind his head, "you didn't have nightmares."

"For that you have to actually sleep."

"True." His eyes, almost closed, blanketed her like fog over
an airport.

"What are you looking at?" she said.

"I'm thinking."

"You look creepy when you think."

"So I'm told."

"You look like that snapping turtle."

He didn't answer.

It made her feel squirmy sitting there. It reminded her of the
time she was in the park and an old guy in his forties sat across
from her and undressed her with his eyes. Sprague was undress-
ing her soul.

"I still think your problems may come from a past life."

"What makes you think that?"

"Call it a hunch."

"Aren't you supposed to *know* things?"

"Sorry, not part of the job description."

"Then why am I talking to you?"

"Good question." He contemplated her silently. "Do you want to quit?"

"Not yet."

"You want to see if I'm right about the past lives?"

"Yeah."

"So do I." He indulged in a rare smile. "Shall we steam ahead?"

She shrugged.

"Miss Landgrave, I need more than a shrug."

She nodded. "Let's do it."

"All right. Assuming you've had past lifetimes, the problem is how to get to them. Going step-by-step hasn't worked. We'll have to jump."

She narrowed her eyes. "What's that mean?"

"First let's get you hypnotized."

Dana moved over to the couch while Sprague lowered the blinds. At his direction she closed her eyes and started counting backward slowly from fifty. Then they started down the imaginary staircase with its curving banister and thick carpet. She was gone before she'd taken a dozen steps.

"I want you to remember the meeting in the principal's office," Sprague intoned.

She nodded.

"Are you there now?"

"Yes."

"What do you see?"

"I see Mr. Sharpe behind the desk. And Miss Grill."

"Who else?"

"Trish is next to me. She's trying not to show how scared she is."

"Turn and look at Miss Belkin."

"I see her."

"Good. What happens next?"

Dana was silent a moment. "It's like everything's slowing down. I can almost see . . ." Her voice drifted away.

"What do you see?"

"It's a man. He's sitting where Gianna was. Or they're both sitting in the same place."

"Tell me about the man."

"He's dressed up in some kind of weird costume. He's got on one of those wigs they used to wear a long time ago."

"What else?"

"There's a lacy thing around his neck, and he's wearing a blue jacket."

"Concentrate on his face, Dana. Do you recognize him?"

She fell silent.

"Well?"

"Of *course* I recognize him."

"Keep concentrating on his face. See him clearly."

She nodded.

"Now go back to another time when you saw him."

"Another time?"

"Yes, a time before this."

Dana's eyes remained closed.

"Are you there now?"

She was silent.

"Miss Landgrave? Are you there?"

Her lips barely moved. "Yes."

The eyes were blue and very keen, the brow nobly high, mouth friendly, nose assertive, lips parted as if in the act of calling out,

"I say there, my good man." A fine piece of work, really, Dana realized, stepping back from the painting to take in the ornate frame and the wall, a rich Pompeian red, behind it.

Gazing at the portrait, she could almost smell the man's hair powder, made from the ground-up roots of irises. A most pleasant scent, people said, but it made her gag. Everything about him, from his shirt frill to his knee breeches and stockings, followed the latest fashion. Everything offended her.

She'd often seen Gavin Traxler, the portrait's subject, with just this expression—and in the same velvet waistcoat—regaling dinner guests with observations and sly asides. Such parties he gave, the booming laughter of Dr. Johnson or the high-pitched titter of Mr. Boswell reaching all the way up to the studio on the top floor, where Dana worked till late at night finishing the background trees or foreground draperies of one of Traxler's celebrated paintings.

Dana would seldom be invited to the dinner parties, but sometimes, as Traxler's unmarriageable niece, she was allowed to be seen and not heard near the end of the table. She was not expected to join the conversation. That was not quite true. Sometimes Dr. Johnson would try to draw her out on some subject he conceived would interest her; but her dull answers discouraged him. She was not witty in that way. She was witty with her brush, not with her tongue.

"*Hannah!*" A woman's carrying voice reached her from upstairs.

"Yes, mother?" Dana's answer was automatic, as was the tangle of feelings that went with it.

"Come *up*! Your uncle needs you!"

Dana placed a hand over her breast. Suddenly the full sense of where she was overwhelmed her. "Coming!"

This was her home. Her name was Hannah. She shot a glance at the round nautical mirror by the staircase. In its convex surface a plain-faced woman of thirty gazed frankly back at her, her jaw square, almost mannish, her mouth thin. Dana caught her breath, not at the strangeness of the sight, but at its depressing familiarity.

Just then—her heart skipping with sudden fear—she noticed another face in the mirror, someone behind her. She whirled around. It was Pickerel the footman, standing under the archway to the hall.

"How long have you been there?" she demanded breathlessly.

"Didn't mean to startle you, miss." His long, rather solemn-looking face slid into a quiet smile, causing her to remember that he wasn't a solemn man at all. "The master sent me down to fetch you. But I see you've already heard."

Dana blushed. She wasn't supposed to be in the great room by herself this time of day. During work hours her place was upstairs in the studio, making herself useful.

"It's hard *not* to hear my mother," she said.

Pickerel gave her a consoling smile.

Dana felt suddenly numb, overcome by an amazed rush of sensations. She knew this James Pickerel. They *liked* each other. They liked each other very much. How could she have forgotten something as important as that?

His long-boned face was not what you'd call handsome—homely-handsome, perhaps. In his worn black suit he looked like a mortician's apprentice. All those poor efforts at respectability, how pitiable they seemed to her: the black breeches, the only ones he had, shiny from use; the limp neckerchief, the frayed cuffs. Tomorrow, she remembered, was his day off, when he would take a proper bath and go out with friends as poor as himself and spend a few coppers at the Nell Gwynne for a pint of ale.

It struck her as remarkable that, given his difficulties, James managed to keep his spirits up. He even kept hers up. His favorite expression, tossed off with a shrug and a smile, was simply, "There's always a way."

Of course, there *wasn't* a way for them. Not always, not ever. Her uncle had made that clear months ago when he'd caught them in conversation in the back hall. A Traxler, no matter how plain or how old, could never marry a footman.

She remembered now that she had something for him. She felt in her apron. "Here," she said, "put this in your pocket."

He frowned.

"Come on, James. It's an extra scone from breakfast. Take it. You'll be wanting it later. They feed you little enough."

"Am I stealing crumbs from the table now?"

"Hardly stealing, when they'd just be feeding it to the parrot."

"Worse and worse."

"James," she said, wrapping the scone in a handkerchief. She tucked it into his pocket and gave it a pat. "Try not to be an idiot."

He gave her a rueful smile. "And how do I manage that?"

"Listen to me, that's how." She stood on her toes and gave him a kiss on the cheek. She noticed how natural it felt doing that.

He nodded. "Thank you, Hannah."

Yes, she remembered, as she headed to the staircase, he had recently taken to calling her by her first name when no one was around. At the first sign of others, it was "Miss Traxler" again.

How she hated "Miss Traxler."

• • •

Dana frowned, her eyes still closed. Her head moved back and forth.

"Are you in pain?" Dr. Sprague asked quietly.

Her eyes closed more tightly. "Don't want . . ."

"What is it?"

"Do I have to go up?"

"It's all right. You're safe. You can go up. No one will hurt you."

"I know."

"Go on, Dana. Trust me."

She didn't answer.

"Do you trust me?"

Slowly she nodded.

"Damn well about time!" The man's back was turned as he worked with the panels of a machine set up on a worktable. "Help me with this. Mrs. Thrale will be arriving any moment."

"Yes, Uncle." Hannah knew all about the apparatus. They used it for most first sittings, to get the face right. A clumsy business it was, a wooden box the size of a child's coffin with a lens of convex glass at one end and a hinged door at the back. And this was the *portable* kind.

"Dust off the glass, will you? How am I supposed to see?"

Silently, she took a soft cloth from the cupboard and dampened it with alcohol.

Quick steps on the stairs made them both turn. It was James. "The lady has arrived, sir, with Mr. Thrale and another gentleman. I've seen them into the parlor."

"Brought them tea, have you?"

"Mary is bringing it, sir."

"Good." Traxler smoothed back his hair and gave a tug to

his waistcoat, then turned to give his niece a warning glance. "When Mrs. Thrale comes in, I want you to try to be pleasant. Answer when she speaks. Show some life!" With that, Traxler started down the stairs, arranging his mouth in a smile.

A grating voice screamed from the corner. Hannah jumped. It was only the parrot, shifting from one foot to the other in its shiny brass cage.

"Don't you start ordering me around too!" she said aloud. She took a soda cracker from a saucer and held it out. The parrot snapped off half of it, made a mess of it, and cocked its head. It came back for the other half, but instead bit Hannah's thumb.

"Ow! You horrible creature!" She turned away, sucking her wound and then looking at it.

Her thumb in her mouth, she inspected the apparatus on the worktable. Cheating, was how she thought of it. Her uncle was a fair draftsman, but weak when it came to faces. The *camera obscura* allowed him accuracy without the troublesome need for talent. Light came through the lens at the front of the box and was redirected by a mirror to a smooth surface where the image could be traced. Later it would be transferred to the canvas. Often it was Hannah who did the transferring, after which her uncle would add expression, a touch of melancholy, perhaps, the hint of a smile, or a playfully lifted eyebrow. He was really quite good at expression. Famous for it.

The picture on the easel now was a good example, a portrait of the large-nosed Scottish economist Adam Smith. He was not smiling, but Traxler had managed to capture a twinkle of amusement in the great man's eye. Hannah was working on the background, as she always did. In an attempt to soften the subject's heavy features, she'd hit on the idea of painting a tapestry behind him, its reds muted by shadow and partly obscured by the swag of a curtain. She didn't know where the idea had come from—it had just bolted into her mind—but it was the perfect touch. Even her uncle approved.

A rumble on the staircase, a swishing of silk, and a high-pitched laugh announced the approach of the Thrale party. Hannah quickly put away the Smith portrait and placed a blank canvas on the easel, just as Traxler's head appeared at the top of the steps. A lively lady, plump as a robin, followed close behind, her cheeks flushed pink and her upswept hair held in place by diamond-crusted combs. Behind her came her husband, the wealthy brewer, and one of his men. James Pickerel followed in the rear.

"Pickerel," Traxler drawled, "don't stand there like a post! Build up the fire. And Hannah, find a seat for Mr. Thrale. No, the *bigger* one! Let's make the man comfortable."

Hannah pulled a thronelike chair to the center of the room and held it as the brewer gave her a good-natured nod and sat down. The studio was really quite impressive—and intended to impress. Octagonal in shape, it was as much a showroom as a working studio, with Oriental carpets on the floor and several of Traxler's more dramatic portraits on the dark-paneled walls.

Offering his hand, the artist led Mrs. Thrale to a seat on a raised platform. Folds of velvet curtain hung behind her, although they probably wouldn't figure in the finished painting. Hannah would add the background later from her imagination. No tapestry this time, she decided. A vine-covered column, perhaps, with a vista of distant mountains and an approaching storm. Storms were much in favor this year.

"Hannah, haven't you prepared my palette?" He waved the empty board in front of him like a fan.

"I was—"

"Come on!" He turned a lively eye on Mrs. Thrale. "Do you have as much trouble with your servants, madam, as I have with my niece?"

"Infinitely more, I'm sure."

"Not possible. I must repeat everything twelve times."

The lady turned a mischievous eye on the blushing Hannah. "I cannot believe this is true, Miss Traxler."

Hannah said nothing. *Show some life!* she scolded herself in her racing brain. *Say something!* "Perhaps not twelve times," she brought out at last, with a curtsy.

Mrs. Thrale turned to Gavin Traxler. "Not twelve times," she trilled. "Delightful!"

"You see what I'm up against, madam," he replied, smiling.

"Not at all! She's superb!"

Hannah went to the paint cabinet, her ears burning.

"I expect as much wit from my niece," said Traxler, tilting his head back, "as I do from General Braddock there."

"You mean the parrot?" said Mrs. Thrale.

As if on cue, the bird let out a screech.

"Oh! What an awful sound!" Mrs. Thrale laughed. "Why do you keep the creature?"

"Which creature do you mean? General Braddock or Hannah?"

"Gavin, you are so wicked!"

"Hannah is one of my charitable works. I'm teaching her to paint."

"Really!" Mrs. Thrale looked from him to Hannah with mock amazement. "Well, I hope you won't have her daubing at *my* portrait. I'm paying for pure Traxler. Traxler the Elder."

"I assure you my niece merely helps with the apparatus, gets the materials ready, that sort of thing."

Merely! thought Hannah, blushing furiously. *I merely save your career, you talentless fop!*

In the hour that followed, no one spoke to Hannah except her uncle, and that was to order her to fetch more cadmium for his palette, align the *camera obscura*, adjust Mrs. Thrale's hair, and ring for tea.

Dr. Sprague had been listening intently to all this and scribbling on his pad. Unable to contain himself, he interrupted Dana and instructed her to take a mental jump forward. "I'm going to count slowly from one to five," he murmured. "As I count, time will move forward. When I reach five, you will be here in Portsmouth, in the high school principal's office. Do you understand?"

Dana nodded.

"You will be at the meeting in the principal's office, and you will see the image of this Traxler person sitting in Gianna's chair. Are you ready? One . . ."

When Dr. Sprague reached five, Dana watched Traxler's aquiline nose thicken into Gianna's and his blue eyes turn brown.

"Where are you, Miss Landgrave?"

"I'm there."

"In the principal's office?"

On one side, she saw her friend Trish Roth. And there was Mr. Sharpe tapping his pencil on the desk blotter.

"Now I will count forward again from one to five, and you will gradually come all the way back to the present moment. Do you understand?"

She nodded.

"By the time I say four, you will open your eyes. And when I reach the count of five, you will be wide awake."

He began counting. At three he told her, "You are becoming more aware of your body. You are aware of the light outside your closed lids."

He paused. "Four. You are slowly opening your eyes."

Her eyes remained closed. She was frowning.

"Are you back?"

Instead of answering, she opened her eyes.

"Five. You are awake. Completely alert."

She did not look alert.

"We did it!" Sprague cried.

She looked at him oddly. Then she remembered something, and her face darkened. "Horrible man!" she scowled.

"Dana."

"Can you believe it? He treats me like his servant!"

"Dana, you're back!"

"I'm a *much* better painter than he is!"

"Snap out of it!"

"What?" She closed her eyes and then opened them and looked around, as if she'd never seen the room before. "Oh," she said, touching her forehead. "Hi, Doc."

"Dana, listen." He leaned forward in the chair. "We did it. We went and came back!"

"We did?" A smile spread slowly across her amazed face. "We did." Her smile widened. "We really did, didn't we?"

II

The Locket

Chapter Six

Rooms on Russell Square

"*WHAT IN GOD'S NAME ARE YOU DOING TO MY daughter?*" Becca Landgrave was practically shouting into the phone. She listened briefly, then broke out again. "I know, but I didn't give you *permission* to conduct experiments on her. What are you, some kind of mad scientist?"

Dana was at the kitchen table listening. She wanted to disappear.

"Yes, I know," Becca continued. She bit her underlip and held the phone away from her like a club. "I'm happy you had some sort of success," she said, resuming. "Not that I believe in any of that. But the point is, we didn't give you *permission!*"

She listened again. "Yes . . . yes. Yes, I know. . . ."

In the end she agreed to come in with her husband and meet with Dr. Sprague. She hung up and turned a dark look on her daughter. "We have to get you a new doctor."

"No, Mom."

"I didn't know he was a nutcake."

"He's not, Mom. It really happened."

"You really *thought* it happened."

Dana didn't answer. Where did her mother come off telling her what happened and what didn't?

"Anyway," said Becca, "your father and I are going to have a talk with him."

Dana nodded.

Becca folded her arms. "Do you really like this character?"

"Like him?" Dana thought of the click of Sprague's teeth on his pipestem. She thought of his heavy brows, his unsettling silences, and his creepy taste in pets. "Not very much. But I need him."

"Need him? How?"

"I think we're getting somewhere."

"I think he's loony tunes."

"I still think we're getting somewhere."

"Well," said Becca, easing up a little. She slopped black coffee into a mug on the counter. "We'll talk."

Dana wasn't there for the conference with Sprague, but it must have gone well, because she continued to see him. *Did he hypnotize Mom or something?* Dana wondered.

Then there was the matter of the trip. Although Dana continued to hold out hope, it seemed unlikely that she'd be allowed to go. Its only purpose was Mrs. Landgrave's law conference, and she couldn't be spending time shepherding the family around London. As she'd told them, making it sound as dull as she could, she'd be stuck inside conference rooms reading name tags and listening to PowerPoint presentations.

But as Dana eventually learned, Dr. Sprague had spoken up forcefully about it. His patient, he said, needed to get away from Portsmouth this summer. For one thing, he was going to be out of town himself and wouldn't be able to see her. He'd be reachable by e-mail, he said, if there was a need to communicate.

The truth, Dana suspected, was that their recent sessions

had been disappointing. There'd been that stunning success regressing her to her former life, but in the sessions that followed they hadn't been able to repeat the trick. The panics and nightmares continued and even grew worse. A change of scene, Sprague said, might be therapeutic.

Tom Landgrave thought it a fine idea, but Becca resisted. She didn't have a problem, really, with Dana, but was firmly against taking Ben. That would make every day a "logistical nightmare."

Dana was in the living room reading about the Boxer Rebellion when she heard her parents in the kitchen, talking.

"I'd be along to take care of him," Tom said in a low voice.

"I don't know. I guess I'm scared." It wasn't often that Becca admitted to weakness, and Dana began paying attention.

"I know you are."

"What if something happened?"

"I know."

They'd almost lost their son a year before, and the accident had changed them. Since then they'd never taken Ben traveling or tried anything risky. Now he was being weaned off the trake—a hugely encouraging step in his recovery. But there was no sign of response in his lower body. The catheter was still needed, and with it came the constant danger of infection.

"Well," Becca said.

"I think it might be good for him," Tom murmured. "For everyone."

"Ow! My ears!" Ben complained as the plane banked and began its descent through the darkness. Tom Landgrave unbuckled and stood, and his wife twisted around in her seat. When they saw Dana already at the boy's side, their shoulders relaxed.

She crouched. "Easy, Ben. You okay?"

Ben nodded tightly.

"I know. All our ears are popping."

"Hey, kid." It was Chase. He was grinning as if all this were lots of fun. "Try opening your mouth real wide, like this." He made a face so grotesque that Ben had to smile.

"Go ahead," Chase urged. "Try to yawn."

Yawning wasn't a thing that Ben was good at. Two weeks ago the trake had been taken out, and his throat was still tender. A bandage covered the opening till it healed over.

Dana returned to her window seat. She didn't want to miss the first glimpse of England. Blackness was giving way to the first gray of dawn, and she could make out tiny points of light in the farmhouses.

"Hello, little English people," she murmured against the window. A wheezy laugh from Ben made her turn around. *Thank God for Chase,* she thought; then she added another "thank God" that her parents had let him come. It was no financial burden, because he was paying his own way. Still, it surprised her that they'd let him be part of the trip, the Landgraves' first outside the United States.

It was Sprague who'd promoted the idea of having Chase Newcomer go along. He was an easygoing, good-natured kid who'd be a companion for Dana and another pair of hands in case problems came up with Ben. He'd even been to London a few years before and was familiar with the place. It was hard for Becca to say no.

Thank you, Dr. Weird, thought Dana as she watched the sky lighten. *You did good.* This sure beat a summer kicking around Portsmouth, fighting crowds and seaweed to get into the water, and then staying up all night to avoid the dreams. Now, with

England coming into focus, green and gray and marvelous, she dared to hope that the nightmares were behind her.

"Pretty nice," Chase murmured in her ear.

"How's Ben?"

"Better. You going to finish those?"

She pushed the bag of peanuts toward him. "How'd you get him to calm down?"

"Oh," he said, "there's always a way."

She gave him a look. When had he said that before?

"We got to talking about the family crest he's designing."

Dana smiled. "Another one?"

"He wants to put a seagull on it instead of a falcon."

"Makes sense." She was looking out the window. "Can you believe this is happening?"

He shook his head, in the process nuzzling her neck with his nose.

Dana glanced at the back of her parents' heads, three rows ahead. She pushed him gently away. "Look." She pointed. "Is that a city?"

A field of lights loomed up ahead as the plane lowered.

"And a river," he said.

"Oh!"

"Welcome to London."

Everything was more complicated with Ben, a kid with tricky needs and many complaints; but with Chase helping and a rented town car purring at the curb, the Landgraves got through customs without a crisis. The worst moment came as the car pulled into traffic and jetted ahead, clearly on the wrong side of the road. Ben flung up his arms to protect himself.

"Ben!" cried his mother. "What is it?"

Tom stroked the boy's head, which was hidden in his hands. "It's okay, Ben. The English drive on the left side. You'll get used to it."

Ben closed his eyes as the car swerved.

Chase gave Dana a quizzical look.

"It's the accident," she explained. "That's it, isn't it, Benny?"

He nodded, keeping his head bowed. So much for taking in the first sights of England. An eternity later the car pulled up to an ancient-looking hotel on Russell Square.

The lobby was high-ceilinged and hung with stalactite-like chandeliers; but the figured carpeting was faded and frayed, and the woman at the check-in desk was a gum-chewer who couldn't seem to work up an interest in the new arrivals. Becca had to use her tone—the clean-up-your-room-this-instant tone that sometimes worked with Dana—before she could get the woman's proper attention. By the time they'd wrestled Ben's wheelchair and a tippy luggage cart onto the elevator and made their way down several airless corridors to their rooms, the family was worn out. Their bodies were under the impression that it was three a.m., but all London thought it was mid-morning, time to be up and about. Dana collapsed on the creaky bed she would share with her mother. Tom would bunk with Ben next door, and Chase had his own, smaller room at the end of the hall.

Mrs. Landgrave, as the person in charge, suggested that everyone unpack and freshen up. For Dana that meant taking a shower, then fixing her makeup and squeezing into a nicely faded pair of jeans. Over it she threw a white acrylic sweater with a floppy collar. She scrutinized herself in the mirror and had to admit she didn't look bad.

The family convened in the lobby. Everyone had changed.

Ben was in a bright sportshirt, and his mother in a conservative suit, for her conference. Chase looked great—when did he not?—in a blue shirt and white jeans, his ever-present shades perched high on his blond head. Dana's dad looked the same as always; but even he had made an effort, changing from one pair of shapeless tan khakis into another and running a wet comb through his graying hair. He came downstairs whistling "Wouldn't It Be Loverly" until Dana stared him to silence.

"What's the next move, gang?" he said genially. "Something to eat?"

"Money, I think," said Becca.

Chase, pushing the wheelchair, led the way to an ATM he'd spotted by the post office, catty-corner from the hotel. Becca gave him the nod and watched as he expertly extracted fifty British pounds. Following his lead, she inserted her card and tapped in her code. The machine gave a little groan and spit out enough money to see everyone through the next two days. Even Ben was allowed a ten-pound note, which he held up to examine the watermark.

"Well," said Tom Landgrave, looking around with satisfaction, "here we are."

Here they were indeed, standing around on a sidewalk in London, of all places, home of the Queen and Peter Pan, with a warm breeze tossing their hair and banknotes lining their pockets. Their spirits were high, as if they'd simultaneously realized something wonderful. Even Ben, softly gasping in his wheelchair, was going on a full tank of nervous energy.

"Let's walk around the park, what do you think?" Dana said. She had her camera out and was looking across to Russell Square.

No one objected. It was a way of being outside without getting run over by taxis careening insanely around corners on the wrong side of the street. The horseshoe-shaped walkway led under a leafy arbor and great old sycamore trees. Dana fell behind, taking angled pictures of the arbor, while Chase trotted ahead, pushing the wheelchair. Ben giggled wildly until Becca called out to them to slow down. "No accidents on the first day, please."

Chase came to a stop by a glass-enclosed restaurant with little white tables set outside on the patio. Café in the Garden, it was called. "Anybody hungry?"

"Perfect," pronounced Becca.

It was actually quite ordinary, but anything would seem perfect this first bright morning in a foreign yet strangely familiar country, where everyone spoke a familiar, yet strangely foreign language.

"What's this?" Ben pointed to "bangers and mash" on the menu.

"Oh that," said Tom, leaning over. He explained that it had to do with mashed potatoes and sausage of some sort. "You want to stay clear of the sausage, I think."

Ben settled for watery scrambled eggs sitting on triangles of unbuttered toast. Until his throat healed, he would need to be a little careful. But the doctor said he'd soon be eating like everyone else. The wonderful part was that his speech was nearly back to normal.

During lunch, plans were laid for the afternoon. Tom asked if Chase and Dana would be willing to take Ben with them as they explored. Dana had been hoping for a different sort of day, but Chase piped up, "Sounds great!"

"Thanks," said Tom. "I thought I'd browse some old bookstores near the British Museum."

Becca thought it was reckless to let the kids wander around

by themselves on their first day in a foreign city. She made sure Dana was supplied with maps, phone numbers, and instructions. They were all to meet back at the hotel at six.

"Mom, we'll be fine."

"I know. I'm glad you're along, Chase. You're the sensible one."

"Don't worry, Mrs. L., I'll get them back safe."

"Six o'clock or I call the National Guard."

"Mom, we're in England," Dana said.

"The Queen's Guard."

"Dana," said Ben when their parents had gone, "we gotta see London Bridge."

"We could take one of those sightseeing boats," Chase said. "It goes right underneath it."

Chase, as the one who'd been there before, led the way down Kingsway toward the Victoria Embankment, where he had a vague idea they would find boats. Of course, he'd been Ben's age on his last visit and had forgotten almost everything. The trek was longer than he'd remembered, and around Great Queen Street they decided to take a rest. Chase bought them all ice cream and led them to a drinking fountain by Lincoln's Inn Fields. Dana brightened to see the place. She hurried through the entranceway and slid onto a bench, looking around with interest. Chase sat beside her, and she took a picture of him licking his melting ice cream.

Ben was being Ben, picky and particular. He wanted to know why they called the place Lincoln's Inn Fields. It obviously didn't have to do with Abe Lincoln, and it wasn't what you'd think of as a field.

"Used to be," said Dana, stretching. She watched a young mother in an alarmingly short dress come by pushing a pink pram. Two benches away a homeless man sat hunched over his bundles. The sun felt good. "And there was a theater," she waved her hand.

Chase looked at her curiously.

"You got a good view of it from the top window," she went on.

"From *what* top window?" he said.

"Oh, from . . ." Dana turned around and gestured vaguely at the row of houses across the street.

Chase and Ben were both looking at her now. Ben, in fact, seemed alarmed. She suddenly realized what she was saying, and turned and looked carefully at each house. "I don't see it."

"Don't see what?" said Chase.

"The house. It was right . . ." She shook her head.

Chase put his arm around her shoulder. "You're an interesting person," he said.

"No, really, I used to . . ." She lowered her head. "Never mind."

"You used to what? *Live there?*"

She looked at Chase, trying to see if he was mocking her. She saw only concern. "For a minute I thought so," she said.

"Wow," said Ben, impressed. "I never knew you were actually crazy."

"I'm not!" She got up and went to the edge of the park, examining the houses along that side. "I don't think."

Chase came up beside her. "Where did you remember the house?"

"Around the middle of the block. It was a big brick thing a few doors down from Mr. Soane's place. It had an iron gate and . . ." She closed her eyes to think. "And, yes, two angels on either side of the roof."

He scanned the street. "I don't see anything like that."

"I remember because I used to look at them whenever I went in. I would think, 'Well, there are no angels *inside* the house.'"

"She's making this up," Ben said, clearing his throat.

Chase ignored the remark. He looked at Dana. "Do you remember when this was?"

"I don't know. It was when they had a theater in the park."

"There isn't any theater." Ben was frowning.

Chase went quiet. He looked down, examining his shoes.

"I know it sounds nuts," Dana said. "It sounds nuts to me, too."

Chase walked off a few feet by himself.

She watched him. "I can't ask you to believe me."

He turned to her and shook his head. "I have to believe you, because you're obviously not making it up. Sorry, Ben, but she's not. She doesn't do that."

"I'm not smart enough to do that," said Dana.

"Well, I don't know about that. You going to write the doctor about this?"

"I guess I do have his e-mail."

"He'll say you're crazy," Ben said.

"Ben, cut it out!"

"Probably," said Chase, giving his hair a flip, "he'll be excited."

"I'm a little excited myself." She turned in a slow circle, her arms out, taking everything in. "This could be where I lived my last life."

"No such thing," said Ben.

"How do you know?" she demanded hotly.

He didn't answer.

"You don't believe in past lives because you don't remember yours!" Her words came out a little harsh, but he was being

75

bratty about it. "I mean, I'm starting to remember places I've never been before. People I've never seen before. Once you start doing that . . ."

Ben made a face. "I don't want to!"

"You don't want to remember?"

He looked angry enough to cry. Suddenly he burst out, "I don't want to live another life! God! Isn't *this* one horrible enough?"

Chapter Seven

The Man in the Dark Coat

THE AFTERNOON WAS OVERCAST AND DARKENING, rain imminent, but the outdoor market still teemed with people. Between the hawkers and the hagglers you could hardly think.

Dana glanced into one stall, then hurried to the next, searching intently but keeping on the move. As she went she tried to keep her head low and stay close to doorways. She'd seen him twice and managed to shake him both times, the man in the dark coat. She knew she couldn't escape his eyes for long. But first she had to find . . .

Had to find what? All she knew was that she had to have it—whatever it was—and she'd know when she saw it. Not this, not this. Not the silver necklace. Not the flatware or tortoise-shell combs.

She hastened on, aware that the colors were ebbing all around her. The dimming light drained the orange from the banners, the blues from shawls and dresses, the flush from cheeks. As the weather threatened, the scene seemed to turn into a mass of ghosts squabbling over the dull possessions of the dead.

Suddenly, before her, at a turn in the street, stood a chalk white woman. It was a statue, Dana realized. The woman's hair hung to her waist in curling white strings, and her eyes were closed, her arms raised partway before her, as if she were blind—or dead and fumbling her way back to life.

Something about her looked familiar. Was it Dana herself? A blind, dead statue of herself? What did it mean? Dana dropped her eyes and hurried on.

The man in the overcoat was closer now. She could feel him. She ducked behind a pillar and looked back over the crowd.

Ahead, the rows of stalls curved as the street bent downward. A fruit seller juggled apples in front of his cart. Then came lace makers, tinsmiths, knife sharpeners. No time, go on.

She felt the hair rise along the back of her neck, as if her pursuer were just behind her; but when she wheeled around, there was only a large, florid-faced man holding up a ham the size of his head.

The first drop of rain landed on her wrist. Another landed on her shoulder.

Meanwhile the offerings in the stalls were becoming more and more bizarre. An elderly man with one drooping eyelid held up a platter on which, nicely arranged, lay the heads of several small monkeys, their eyes sewn closed with white thread. Dana turned away with a shudder. In the next stall a humped woman grinned up at her, offering ginger cookies crawling with ants.

Dana backed away. A crowd was clustering around a jewelry stall. She tried to force her way through.

She grunted as a big woman bumped her. "Let me by!" Dana pushed the woman aside, ignoring her curses. On the edge of her vision she caught a glimpse of something dark. The coat! The man had seen her! Dana struggled to the display table and scanned the glittering pendants, earrings, and pins spread out on a linen cloth.

Excitement jolted through her. It was here, what she was after, she was sure of it. But as she watched, several of the pendants seemed to move! She stared, disbelieving, but there was no doubt. Tiny legs poked out from under brilliantly colored backs.

Insects!

Not all insects, she realized a moment later. There were real gold, malachite, jasper, and onyx among the bright carapaces of creeping vermin. This was a test, one she had to pass quickly if she were to find what she had to find.

Just then she noticed, in the upper corner of the table, a fold of linen concealing most of a small silver object. Immediately Dana reached out, her heart pumping, just as a black-gloved hand thrust past her and roughly grabbed it, scattering everything else, insects and jewelry alike.

Dana was so shocked she could only stare at the man's face, a narrow bone of intensity with burning eyes and a thin crease for a mouth. Beneath it, like a scraggly comma, hung the dark wisp of a beard. She knew this man—that was another shock— yet in the twist of the moment she couldn't remember where she'd seen him before.

"You!" she breathed.

The man had already turned and was running ahead, shoving aside anyone in his path.

"Hey!" the stall keeper shouted. "Stop!" Others picked up the cry.

Dana started after him. "Come back!" she shouted. "That's mine!" Raindrops struck her forehead. "Stop him!"

The man in the dark coat was getting farther ahead. A candle maker, several stalls up, saw what had happened and tried to block the way, but a gloved fist bloodied his face and left him staggering. The thief surged on, with Dana and others in pursuit.

That was when the sky let loose with a guttural roar. The rain pelted down, scattering the crowd. Many headed for awnings; others held newspapers over their heads. In seconds the man in the dark coat had a nearly empty street before him, and he sprinted on. Dana raced to keep up, though her eyes were stinging and her hair was plastered to her head.

It was just Dana and the man now, the world reduced to two. The street grew steeper and the cobbles were slick. Suddenly she slipped and landed hard on her hip. . . .

"Ow!"

"What is it?" It was her mother's voice in the darkness.

Dana opened her eyes. She was dry, no rain, in the pitch dark. "Ow, my hip."

"Dana, where are you?"

"I'm on the floor."

The light clicked on, and her mother's face, seamed with concern, peered over the edge of the comforter. "What are you doing down there?"

"I guess I fell out of bed."

"Are you all right?"

Dana didn't reply.

"We'll ask tomorrow about getting a bigger bed," Becca said.

"Good idea." Dana climbed back under the covers. She was still breathing hard, as though she'd been running and had miles to go.

"You know," said Chase, leaning back in the teetering metal chair and sipping his coffee, "it almost sounds like Portobello Road."

"What does?"

"Your dream. Sounds like the outdoor market they have every week in Portobello Road. The crowds, all the little stalls. We ought to go."

"Okay." Dana zipped her windbreaker against the morning chill and bit into a wedge of toast. She and Chase were by themselves for a change in the outdoor café, having left the dawdlers to find their own breakfast in the hotel dining room.

Chase opened his laptop on the table.

"You think he's answered yet?" Dana said.

"Let's find out."

Last night she'd sent an e-mail to Morton Sprague telling him about the strange events in Lincoln's Inn Fields. She'd described the house that wasn't there and how odd it made her feel not to see it.

"I don't even know where the guy is," she said. "I just know he's on vacation. He could be somewhere they don't have e-mail."

"Mars?"

"Don't be funny."

"We're receiving," said Chase, setting down his cup. "You've got something." He turned the machine so they both could read it.

"Bravo!" the message began. "I admit I was hoping for something like this when I asked your mother to let you go. But I didn't allow myself to believe it would happen. Stay open to further guidance. You *are* being guided, you know. You must tell me everything."

It was signed simply "Sprague."

There was a P.S. "I checked the Internet. There *was* a theater in the park. Built 1705, torn down 1848. There's your time frame."

And a P.P.S.: "Couldn't find much on your Gavin Traxler. There was a painter by that name. Apparently not a very important one."

They looked at each other.

"Guided?" said Chase.

"I told you the guy is weird." Dana gazed out over the square. A Pakistani man in dirt-colored clothes and an oilcloth turban was raking under the sycamores. "Interesting about the theater, though."

"I'll say."

The Landgraves were finishing breakfast when Dana and Chase came in. Mrs. Landgrave was there too, since the first seminar that day didn't start till two. She suggested they head to the British Museum, which was a few walkable blocks away.

"Why don't you just park me somewhere?" said Ben. "I'll listen to my CDs till you come out."

Dana gave him a punch on the arm.

"By the way," said Becca, producing a postcard, "you got some mail."

"Me?" Dana squinted at the card.

"Nothing for me?" said Ben.

"Were you expecting something?" his mother said.

"I don't know. Maybe Eric."

"Well, why don't you write to him?" said Becca. "He'd love to hear from you."

Ben wasn't much of a letter writer, and Eric, his fellow heraldry expert, was even worse.

Dana's card was from Trish Roth. The message was simple:

I am insanely jealous, so you better bring me
back something really good. One of those palace
guards would be nice.
Have a blast!
Trish

"How did it get here so fast?" said Becca.

"She must have sent it before we left."

Trish. She didn't have a clue what was going on with Dana,
but she was true blue.

"Shall we?" said Tom, getting up.

"Do we have to?" Ben said.

Chase was pushing the wheelchair. "Don't worry," he said as
they headed out to the street. "They've got some neat things."

"What," Ben grumbled, "statues without heads?"

"How about a chair made out of AK-47s?"

"Are you joking?"

"Throne of Weapons, they call it."

Ben compressed his lips and nodded. This might be worth
a look.

The sun was bright and Ben's corny father started whistling
"On the Street Where You Live."

"Dad?" Ben said.

"What, son?"

"Could you *not* do that?"

The British Museum was as close to a palace as the little
New England family had seen, and they spent the first minute
standing in the Great Court and staring up at the glass-covered
atrium. Even Ben was impressed. After a huddle, they decided
to head in different directions and meet in the upstairs restaurant at noon. Tom and Becca went to the Elgin collection to
check out the friezes from the Parthenon. Chase and Ben set off

for the exhibits of weapons and Viking treasure hoards. Dana wandered by herself, glad for the chance. Ever since yesterday's revelations in the park, she'd grown pensive, not part of the family commotion.

She looked around the gift shop awhile, checking out postcards. She picked out one to send Trish, and then poked her head into the library, a huge domed area that seemed the size of a football field, only circular, with shelves going up and up. Dana had her camera—there were apparently no restrictions about that—but couldn't think of an original way to photograph the place and decided not to try.

She resumed wandering. A few minutes later she found herself, with others, in front of a big chunk of rock covered with incomprehensible scribbles. *So this*, she thought, eyes widening, *is the Rosetta Stone.*

Dana took out her camera and prowled around the mysterious object. How did you photograph the most famous rock in the world? The flat front of it, she knew, contained the same message in three languages, one of them Egyptian hieroglyphics, which no one knew how to read until this stone fell into their laps, so to speak, and they could compare the languages they knew with the one they didn't.

There in the dim hall, alone in the surround of tourists, Dana found herself falling into one of her semidream states. Her present life was slangy and plain as day. Before that—hieroglyphics.

Or was there an even earlier language, a third lifetime she had yet to contact? The thought stopped her, like a stranger's hand on her shoulder, cautioning her not to go further. She knew that the fragmentary memories of her existence as Hannah, in the 1700s, had done nothing to end the nightmares or her terror of enclosed spaces. What of the wounded boy behind the altar? How did he fit into Hannah's world?

Dana circled around the back of the great stone and was struck by what she could only call its nothingness. It was the chaos before history, she thought with a shiver, a choppy sea at night, dark and meaningless, without the scratch of human experience to make sense of it. She raised her camera. Suddenly she knew how she would photograph the Rosetta Stone.

"There you are!"

She jumped at the sound of the voice just behind her. It was Chase.

"You shoulda been there," said Ben, looking up from his wheelchair. "We saw the Lindow Man."

"The little man?" said Dana, smiling. What a relief to see the two of them!

"No." He shot a look of appeal at Chase.

"Lindow," Chase repeated.

"Yeah. He's this guy who's been in a peat bog for around, what?"

"I think they said two thousand years."

"Yeah, two thousand years. It's great!" Ben was breathing hard, trying to take in enough air to keep up with his sentences. "They hit him on the head with an ax."

Dana laughed. "Who did?"

"I don't know," said Ben. "His friends. And then they strangled him."

"Some friends."

"And they cut his throat."

Dana raised an eyebrow at Chase. "*This* is what you showed him?"

He smiled and shrugged. "When it comes to museums,

Ben's pretty tough to win over," he said. "But there's always a way."

His words were casual, but they struck Dana. "What did you say?" There was something about the way he looked, there in the dimness.

"I have no idea. Should we be meeting your parents?"

She checked her watch. "We have a few minutes. What about that Throne of Weapons you talked about? Want to show me?"

"Yeah!" said Ben, taking two extra breaths. "You're going to *love* it!"

Chapter Eight

Portobello Road

DANA AND CHASE HURRIED UP THE STEPS FROM the tube station at Notting Hill Gate to find the streets jammed and a warm wind blowing. Most of the people seemed to be heading toward Portobello Road. Dana and Chase followed along, past street musicians and panhandlers, soon reaching the market with its festooned storefronts and outdoor stalls. Trays of rings, pendants, and bone-handled dinner knives gleamed up at them, such a profusion of riches and junk that Dana had trouble taking it all in. Brass bicycle horns with rubber bulbs hung in rows above an array of beer mugs sporting the likeness of Prince Charles, complete with the ears. Ceramic spaniels stood beside silver-plated tea cozies. Antique cameras abutted plastic champagne buckets. It was all dazzling and exciting and, Dana realized, strangely familiar.

"Do you like any of these?" said Chase, nodding at a line of carved ivory barrettes.

"Sure. I don't know if they'd be any use in my crazy hair. . . ."

"I like your crazy hair."

"Liar."

The smile faded on Dana's lips. Before her, at a turn of the street, stood a white marble statue of a woman—a sudden, heart-stopping stillness in the swirl. She was wearing a long Victorian dress, white as chalk. Her eyes were closed, her arms half-raised before her. Long white ringlets snaked down to her waist.

"What is it?" said Chase, seeing Dana's frightened look. "What's the matter?"

"It's . . . *her.*"

"Who? Oh, that!" He laughed and took out a coin and dropped it in a box at the statue's feet.

"What are you *doing*?"

"Wait."

Slowly, as Dana watched, the statue's hands came together in prayer position. Then the whole statue turned toward Chase and slightly inclined its head.

Chase bowed in acknowledgment. He smiled at Dana. "Haven't you seen street performers before?"

Dana looked hard at the statue. It was a live person, a girl like herself, painted white from eyelids to toes. "My goodness!"

"What some people will do for pocket change," Chase said, taking Dana's hand and leading her on through the crowd.

Dana found herself glancing back. *But I dreamed of her,* she thought. *She was a statue!* Fear started worming through her.

"What about these?" Chase nodded at a display case of cameos and carved carnelian brooches.

Dana squeezed through the crowd to see. "They're more my grandmother's style."

"I guess. Pretty, though."

They went on to the next stall. Thin gold chains with pendants.

"Isn't your birthday coming up?" he said.

"Three weeks."

"Well . . ."

She flashed him a smile. "You want to buy me a present?"

He shrugged.

"That's so cute! Let me see if I can find something expensive."

He crossed his arms.

There really were some nice things, in among the hideous stuff. Dana started looking carefully. Despite her remark about her grandmother, she found herself much more attracted to the old things than the new.

"You don't mind me rooting around like this?" she said.

"Go ahead."

After a few minutes, she found herself skipping certain displays and spending whole minutes in front of others. It was as though she were looking for something specific but didn't know what. She only knew what it wasn't.

She then came to a stall that specialized in small antique pieces. A short man with gray hair and a comb-over grinned up at her, showing a missing side tooth. There was no reason the hair should begin to rise along her neck, but suddenly she felt afraid. This place was too familiar. Holding on to Chase, she glanced back over the crowd.

"What?" He felt her grip on his arm.

"I don't see him," she murmured.

"You don't see who?"

She forced a laugh. "The man who wasn't there."

He frowned. "Have you been watching a lot of Hitchcock flicks?"

"I guess." But when she looked down at the display case again, the fear rushed back. She was almost afraid to turn the pieces of jewelry over, in case they were really insects.

Don't be stupid, she told herself, but she knew stupidity had nothing to do with it. She glanced at the upper right corner of the case and gasped. A flap of green velvet half-covered a pin of some kind.

She started to reach out for it, but then hesitated, trembling. She glanced around. A woman in a florid dress stood just behind her, trying to see over her shoulder. No sign of a man in a dark coat. And Chase was beside her. Good old Chase.

Dana started to reach out again. The display case was a large one and she had to lean forward. At that moment a man's arm brushed quickly past her and grabbed the pin from under the flap of material.

Dana gasped. She whirled around.

It was Chase. "Are you okay?" he said, seeing her panicky look.

"Ah . . . I . . ."

He held up a small silver object. "Is this what you were trying to reach?"

She swallowed and nodded.

"You need longer arms, kiddo. Here." He dropped it into her hand.

Speechless, Dana stared at his open smile and clear blue eyes, then at the plain-looking locket in her hand. It was a silver oval, dented, with a design of some kind engraved on the front. She tried opening it. No good. It was stuck closed and missing a catch.

"Does this open?" she asked the little man behind the counter.

He held out a wobbly hand. "Let me see." He tried it, then shook his head. "I don't want to break it."

"How much?" said Dana.

Chase gave her an odd look. "You want that old thing?"

"Eighteen pounds," said the vendor.

Chase snorted. "Forget it."

Dana shot him a glance. "I *need* it," she whispered.

"She's got good taste," said the old man. "It's a fine old piece."

"It's worn down and it doesn't even open," Chase declared.

"Fifteen pounds. Final price. You don't want it, fine."

Dana looked up at Chase. "For my birthday?"

He shook his head, laughing. "Why not?"

They hurried away with their prize and ducked into a doorway to examine it. "Is that a coat of arms?" She was squinting at the faint design on the dented cover.

"Let me see." He turned it over several times. "Hard to tell. Looks like this thing's been through hell."

"Maybe it has."

He looked puzzled. "So how come you picked it, from all the other stuff?"

"I don't know."

"I mean, it doesn't even open."

She gave him a helpless smile. "I know. You're right."

"Well," he said, shrugging, "happy birthday."

She seemed not to hear. She was rubbing the locket with her thumb. "Amazing," she said under her breath.

"What is?" He touched her chin with his finger and made her look at him. "Do you want to tell me what this is about?"

She paused only a moment. "It's mine," she said.

"I know it is. I gave it to you."

"No," she said. "It's *mine*."

He stared at her harder than he meant to while her words sank in. "Dana, you know that's not . . ." He broke off. Many strange things were possible, he was learning. "How do you know?" he said finally.

"I dreamed about it."

"We should write Sprague about this."

"Soon as we get home."

"This stuff's getting a little scary, if you don't mind me saying."

"No kidding." She kept stroking the silver case with her thumb.

"So," he said, a little too heartily, "you want to see some more stuff while we're here?"

"Not really." But then, as she looked around, she thought she caught sight of a man in the crowd making his way toward her. A hat shaded his face, and he was wearing a raincoat, although it was sunny out.

"On second thought," Dana said, grabbing Chase's arm.

"Oh, good."

"But let's hurry up." She thrust the locket into the front of her jeans.

"Hey, look," Chase said, sighting an awning with a big sign, GLINDA THE GOOD WITCH. "I sort of remember this place. It's an indoor arcade."

"Let's do it," she said without thinking.

The entrance was aswarm with shoppers and gawkers, stumbling in and out like drunken bees in a hive. As they approached, Dana wasn't so sure it was a good idea. The man she'd glimpsed before had disappeared—just another sightseer.

"I don't know," she began, but Chase was already pulling her inside. "It looks kind of crowded."

A narrow aisle wound through a warren of indoor stalls, one wedged next to another, glittering with wares. Once Dana was inside, all she could do was inch forward and try to avoid elbows and low-hanging signs. Someone stepped on Dana's foot, but she didn't have room to turn around. She smiled bravely at Chase and held his hand as he made his way forward, but she recognized the beginnings of panic in her stomach. No way forward, no way back, no way out!

"Hey, Chase, let's get out of here."

"We will. We just have to follow the aisle around. It takes us out the other side."

"I don't think . . ."

He didn't seem to hear her, and the gabble of talk made it hard for her to think. A line of sweat beaded her forehead as her feelings of claustrophobia grew worse.

"I can't do this!" she said, louder.

"What? Oh." He tried to see over the heads around him. "It's easier to go forward."

Dana's breathing was growing shallow, and she found herself panting. The aisle seemed narrower than before, the bodies walling her in. She touched the locket through her jeans, for luck.

"Excuse *me*!" said an irritated woman when Dana stumbled into her.

"Say, are you all right?" said Chase, finally getting a good look at Dana's face.

She shook her head, unable to speak.

"Hold on to me!" He forged forward, calling out, "Sorry, excuse us, coming through!"

The bodies resisted. Their warm breath made Dana dizzy. The whole arcade began turning slowly, like a golden carousel. "Help," she gasped, but no one heard her. Chase was pulling her ahead, but it was hard to keep her footing with the world swirling. It spun faster now. Her throat ached as if someone's fingers were around her neck.

"Just a little farther," Chase called back to her.

Dana leaned on a display case of cutlery to keep her balance, but she must have leaned too hard, because the case upended and sent knives, dessert forks, and demitasse spoons showering to the floor. The last thing she remembered was a silver crummer lying next to her face. She must have cut herself, because she felt a sticky warmth working down her cheek. Grit from the floor bit her forehead. Then everything went black.

Chapter Nine

The Portrait

"LEMME SEE." BEN PUSHED BACK HIS BLUE BASEBALL cap and squinted at the locket. He rummaged in his backpack and came up with a small magnifying glass. There were all kinds of things in there, from playing cards to magnetic checkers.

"What do you think, Sherlock?" Chase said.

"Coat of arms of some kind," he said in his high, woodwind voice. "Hard to see."

"That's why we brought you in on the case."

"It's rubbed pretty smooth," Ben said. "You can see the escutcheon easy enough."

"Of course," said Chase. "What's an escutcheon?"

"It's the, you know, the shield. But it's hard to make out the charges."

Dana came out from the café carrying coffee for herself and Chase. Ben still hadn't finished his ice cream. "Any luck?"

"Wish I had my books with me," Ben said.

Chase pulled his laptop from under the table and opened it. "Would this help?"

The boy's eyes brightened. "Let me see that."

Being a smart, wheelchair-bound eleven-year-old, Ben Landgrave had long since turned into a computer whiz. It was his freedom, his legs. Within a couple of minutes he was scrolling down hundreds of coats of arms.

"Well, it's obviously English," he murmured after a bit, "so we don't have to worry about Irish or Scottish or Welsh."

"How do you know?" said Dana. "Never mind."

She caught Chase's eye. He gave her an approving purse of the lips. This was just what Ben needed—to be needed.

"Wish I could make out the motto," he said, squinting through the magnifying glass. "But it's from the north of England somewhere. Middle to north."

"Good going!" Dana said.

He shook his head. "Dana, do you know how many armigerous families there are in the north of England?"

"How many *what*?"

"Families with coats of arms."

Chase scratched his cheek. "That's Ben. He couldn't tell you who the president was during the Civil War, but he knows a word like armigy . . . ?"

"Armigerous."

"What do you say," Dana interrupted, "about getting this to a watchmaker or somebody and trying to open it up?"

Ben looked up from the screen. "Good."

It wasn't easy finding shops open on Sunday, but Chase located a jeweler near the Strand. Dana's mother wasn't happy about letting her daughter go out again so soon after the "incident," as she called it. Mrs. Landgrave had been badly upset when Dana walked into the hotel yesterday evening with blood oozing from her forehead, and she accused Chase of negligence. Didn't he *know* Dana had a problem with closed-in spaces?

The cut had looked worse than it was, and Dana's dizziness

hadn't lasted long, once Chase got her to the street. All that remained by this morning was a dark mark angling above her eye.

The Strand was a longish walk from Russell Square, but the sun was warm and Dana and Chase took turns pushing the chair. Ben was in one of his talkative moods, going on about "fesses" and "gules" and "ordinaries." Dana tuned out the heraldry talk pretty early on. Walking ahead, she found herself touching the locket through the material of her jeans. Her mind began to drift over half-formed images, and she walked right past the jeweler's shop, wedged as it was between an espresso bar and a haberdashery. Chase tapped her on the shoulder. "We're here."

She felt like an intruder, stepping inside. The place was narrow, bright, silent, and empty. After the noise of the Strand it felt airless as a glass booth. She got the feeling that the round-chinned man behind the counter liked it that way. A blond fellow in his softening thirties, he gave one of those smiles that grown-ups turn on kids they don't care for. The look turned suspicious when Dana pulled out the locket. "Where did you get this?"

"Where?"

Chase spoke up. "We were in Portobello Road yesterday."

"He thinks we pinched it," Ben said under his breathy breath.

Dana pulled the receipt from her back pocket. "Here."

The man flushed. "I believe you. It's not that."

"We'd just like you to open it," said Dana in a flat voice. "If you don't mind."

He turned the locket over several times. "A nice piece. Very old." He felt along the worn edge. "The catch, of course, needs replacing."

"How old?" Dana said.

He pursed his lips. "That's hard to say."

"A century?"

"A *century*? I doubt this has been *opened* in a century."

She could feel her heart beat harder.

"It looks fused shut. Let me see what I can do." He turned and disappeared into the back.

"More than a century," Dana murmured.

"A lot more, maybe," Ben said.

They looked around. Squadrons of thin gold watches, pins, and necklaces gleamed at them from the safety of locked display cases. Ben wheeled his chair up to a row of silver compasses.

Dana was eyeing a pendant. "How much is four hundred and twenty pounds?"

"I'd tell you," said Chase, "but why spoil your day?"

The jeweler was gone a long time. Finally he returned—*burst* in, you might say, like a magician making an entrance. Something had happened to him. His face was flushed and his eyes bright, the former condescension forgotten. "You'll want to take a look at this!"

He laid the open locket down gently on a square of blue velvet.

Dana's breath caught in her throat. Looking up at her was a miniature portrait of some kind. She looked closer. It was a boy!

"Oh!" Ben said, peeking over the top of the counter.

"I'd say," said the jeweler, "that whatever you paid for this in Portobello Road, you got a bargain."

"Fifteen pounds," Chase said, his eyes narrowed on the portrait. "I thought it was high."

"I'll give you a hundred for it."

Dana hardly heard. Something about the tiny painting

struck her like a blow to the chest. A curly-headed boy of not more than ten looked calmly out at her—at her alone, it seemed—with large clear eyes and the suggestion of a smile. A flight of lace encircled his neck. His short jacket, worn carelessly open, revealed a many-buttoned white vest beneath. This was clearly someone who knew his importance.

"He's beautiful!" she breathed.

"And beautifully depicted," the jeweler put in. "Look at the detail. And the condition!"

"I suppose that's what happens," Chase said, "when you don't open something for a century or two."

"In the darkness all that time!" Dana mused. She picked up the locket to examine it more closely.

The shopkeeper stepped back. "What do you say to my offer? I'm quite serious." He smiled, though it wasn't something he was good at. "It's not every day you stumble onto a hundred pounds."

Dana shook her head. "I want to keep this." She couldn't stop staring at the boy in the oval frame. The hint of a smile on his face seemed to say he agreed with her.

"All right, why don't we make it a hundred and fifty? That's ten times what you paid."

"You don't understand," she said softly. "It's mine."

"I'm sure it is. The thing is, I'd like it to be mine."

"I don't think so."

The man sighed so heavily his chin wobbled. "All right," he said. "Two hundred. But that's as high as I can go."

Dana looked into the man's face as if he were talking in a foreign language.

"Are you hoping for a better price? You won't find it."

Ben, from his wheelchair, pulled on his sister's pants leg.

"I'm not looking for a better price," she said.

"Three," he said quickly, before he could stop himself. "Take it or leave it. I've got to make *some* profit."

"Dana!" cried Ben, his eyes big.

"What, Benny?" She cupped the back of his head tenderly with her hand.

He kept silent.

Chase turned to the jeweler. "I don't think she wants to sell."

"But—"

"Why don't we leave it at that?" Chase said.

The man looked at Dana uncertainly. It was hard to accept that this strange-looking girl with the cut on her forehead and out-of-control curly hair was refusing his way-too-generous offer.

"I'm wondering, though . . . ," said Dana quietly. She held out the locket.

"Yes?" said the man anxiously.

"Do you think . . ."

"Yes?"

"You could fix the catch?"

At lunch Dana was aware that the boys weren't looking at her. Ben was concentrating his attention on a large macaroon, while Chase stared out the window at the Royal Courts of Justice across the way. Dana herself had left her egg-and-tomato sandwich largely uneaten. Her latte was cold.

"You think I did the wrong thing," she declared.

Ben looked up at her, then took a bite of the macaroon. "Three hundred pounds."

"I *couldn't* sell it, Ben," she said. "It's my only clue."

"Clue!" He spat the word out.

"Easy, Ben," said Chase. "She has her reasons."

Dana pulled the locket from her jeans and clicked it open. The strange boy peered out at her from his place of concealment. "Are you sure," she said, turning to Ben, "you can't figure out anything more about the coat of arms?"

He shrugged, but then gave in to curiosity. "Let's see." He wiped the crumbs from the blond wood counter and pulled out his magnifying glass.

Chase looked over Ben's shoulder.

"Looks like one of those animals," Ben said, focusing on the figure at the top of the shield. "Maybe a griffin or something."

"What's that?" Chase said.

"A griffin? You don't know much, do you?"

"Watch it."

"Well, the front part's an eagle. See the wings? And the hind part's like a lion."

"I don't see the hind part."

"I don't either." Ben kept scanning the picture with his feeble magnifying glass.

"I've got an idea," said Dana. "Remember when we were at the museum? I was wandering around and there was this huge library."

"That's right," said Chase. "The Reading Room."

"Maybe they have some stuff about this."

He nodded. "Is it open on Sundays?"

"Let's find out."

Suddenly they were all energized, and they hurried out to find a telephone. A red call box stood at the next corner, but they couldn't make it work. Even Chase, who was best at this sort of thing, found English pay phones baffling.

"Never mind," said Dana. "Let's just grab a taxi and go. If it's open, it's open."

"Right," said Chase.

Minutes later they were tucked in a cab jolting along Kingsway toward the museum.

To call the immense circular library a "reading room" was an example of British understatement. Dana gazed upward past several book-packed balconies to a domed ceiling whose round skylight radiated out into gold and ecru and Wedgwood blue. She paused on the outer ring of this great spiraling space. The idea of just going over to somebody and asking about a dented little locket was more than she could do.

But Chase was made differently and barged ahead, pushing Ben past gray-padded desks to the curved information area in the center. He caught the eye of a librarian. "Excuse me," he said brightly.

She was an efficient-looking woman in her forties, her blond-gray hair in a pageboy cut, held back on one side by a clip. Her assessing eyes had already scanned the three of them.

Dana took courage from the woman's light blue silk scarf, which she hoped was a sign of imagination, or at least tolerance. Slowly she extracted the locket and laid it on the counter.

At once the woman's eyes softened. "Oh," she said. "Interesting!"

A *blue-silk response*, thought Dana, relieved. "We're hoping you can help us figure out the coat of arms."

"Oh, yes. My goodness." She opened a drawer on her side and pulled out a considerable magnifying glass. "It's worn almost smooth."

"Is that a griffin on the top?" Ben piped up.

His wheelchair was lower than the counter, and the woman had to lean forward to talk to him. "A what? A griffin?" She looked through the glass. "No," she said slowly. "You see those wavy lines? I think they're flames."

"Flames?"

"So it would be a phoenix, not a griffin."

"The bird that gets burned up!"

The woman smiled. "Exactly. And do you remember what else?"

"What else?" said Ben. "Oh, it comes back from the ashes."

"Very good! Well, you hardly need *me*."

"Oh," said Chase, "we definitely need you."

"We're trying," Dana explained, "to find out what family this comes from."

"I see." She plied the magnifier. "Well, it's English."

"Northern England," said Ben.

"Do you think?"

"Look at the engrailed line."

"Really? You don't think it's invected?"

"*You've* got the magnifying glass."

Dana looked from Ben to the librarian and back. It was like watching a Ping-Pong match.

The woman looked closer. "You may be right. Well, that would narrow things down. How many phoenixes could there be in the north of England?"

The kids looked blankly back at her.

She nodded and narrowed her eyes. "What do you say we find out?"

The woman went after information like a ferret after a vole. When the dust from a dozen old tomes had settled, she'd narrowed the search to three candidates, which she jotted onto a note card.

A narrow-faced man came frowning up to her and spoke briefly. She nodded.

"You'll have to take it from here, I'm afraid," she told Dana, handing her the three names.

"You're not going to abandon us now!" said Dana.

"You shouldn't have any trouble. Try Pevsner."

Blank looks.

"Nikolaus Pevsner? *The Buildings of England?* I'd start with the two volumes on Lancashire."

With that she was gone. The angel of heraldry was leaving them to their own devices. Fortunately, it wasn't hard to find the Pevsner series. "Cheshire, Sussex, Dorset," said Chase, reading the spines. "Ah, here we are."

He looked up the first name, then the second; but neither coat of arms was similar to the design on the locket.

"What's left?" Dana said.

Chase glanced at the notecard. "We're looking for Breen Hall."

And there it was. Pages and pages. Built in the twelfth century. Expanded in the fourteenth. Landed aristocracy. Family persecuted in the sixteenth. Famous for a tapestry. Castle and grounds taken over by the Borough of Bendelfin in the early twentieth. Now run as a museum.

At the head of the chapter stood the coat of arms, the phoenix clearly defiant in its burning nest. It matched the locket perfectly.

Beneath the escutcheon was the motto: *Le vraye renaist.*

"The what?" said Dana.

"Looks like French," said Chase. "Let's ask."

The angel in blue silk was gone, but Chase flagged down an

elderly European man—Belgian, they found out—who'd been shelving books.

"Middle French," said the little man, passing a hand over his bald head. He pronounced the word "meedle."

"And it means . . . ," said Chase.

He wobbled his hand back and forth. "More or less, 'The troot comes back to life.' Someting like dat."

"The truth . . . ," said Dana slowly.

"Comes back. Comes to life again. More or less."

"Thank you!" She looked at Chase. There was a gleam of tears in her eyes. "This is it."

"Look," said Ben. He had opened the volume to a section of black-and-white photographs in the middle. Among them was Breen Hall, like a great capital E laid sideways. Dana peered over his shoulder. It was not an elegant place, or majestic the way she'd thought castles should be. It was massive and dark and cold. Its castellated turrets rose like fists against an overcast sky.

She glanced at the others, her mouth set. "I'm going there."

Chapter Ten

North

GETTING PERMISSION FROM HER PARENTS WAS not as hard as she'd feared. Dana's dad wasn't a city person, much as he'd enjoyed poking around old bookstores in the West End and perching atop double-decker buses while tour guides barked through microphones. He was more than ready to get out and explore the country. Dana's mother, her mind filled with presentations and new connections, would stay behind. She didn't seem unhappy at the thought.

A flurry of phone calls from the hotel set everything up. Early Tuesday morning Tom Landgrave and the kids taxied to Euston Station, where they boarded the train to Preston, several hours north. Dana was wearing the precious locket on a silver chain borrowed from her mother. She fingered it as the train howled along past industrial towns, then suburbs, then farms.

Her dad, beside her, glanced over. "Mind if I have another look?"

She pulled the locket over her head and passed it to him, clicking it open.

"So this is what the ruckus is all about." The thing looked tiny in his calloused hand.

"What do you think?"

"Sharp-looking kid," he said, squinting at the miniature. "Not sure I'd trust my daughter with him."

Dana frowned. "What do you mean?"

"He thinks he's somebody."

"He *is* somebody. I just don't know who."

He handed it back. "I'd stick with Chase."

Dana smiled and looked behind her. Her brother's wheelchair took up too much room, so Chase was hanging out with Ben at the back of the car. They were playing double solitaire on the laptop.

"He's all right," she agreed.

"And you really think," said Landgrave, handing the locket back, "this thing has to do with you?"

"I know it sounds crazy."

"I don't know. I guess I never gave much thought to that sort of thing."

"And yet you're interested in history."

"Oh, yes."

"Well, maybe past lives are just an extension of that."

He frowned, not getting it.

"Maybe," she said, "reading about history is just a step away from remembering it."

"And you're remembering it?"

"Small patches."

He shook his head. "Funny. I used to be able to help you with your homework. Now you're way beyond me."

"You still help me, Dad. All the time."

They reached Preston by mid-afternoon, only to find they faced a two-hour wait for the connection to Bendelfin. They spent the time browsing the newsstand and eating cold sandwiches on soggy Italian bread.

"For this they took out my trake?" Ben scowled at a floppy pickle slice. He could eat almost anything now if he was careful.

"Come on," said Chase, "let's fire up the laptop. I'll teach you how to lose at Twenty-one."

"I'll teach *you* how to lose!"

Dana thanked Chase with her eyes.

"Hey," he said, checking his e-mail. "Something for you."

It was Sprague, answering yesterday's message. Dana had reported their discoveries at the British Museum and their plans to head north. The usually calm doctor sounded strangely excited.

> I knew you were a girl of talents, Miss Landgrave,
> but you have surprised even me. About Breen Hall
> I know nothing, except that destiny takes you
> there. What I would give to see that locket! Write
> to me after your visit.

Chase threw Dana a look. "The old snapping turtle seems to be warming up."

"He considers me an interesting case."

Finally the train to Bendelfin was ready to board. It was only two cars long. Tom and Chase hoisted Ben and his wheelchair into the rear car, and before long they were pounding along through the countryside.

As the sun sank into a bank of darkening clouds, Dana held the map open on her lap, keeping track of the stops. It was evening when the conductor came by, calling out, "Bendelfin Central." Fields gave way to fog-blurred houses as the train slowed, gave a lurch, and let out an exhausted hiss. Chase and Tom lifted Ben's wheelchair down while Dana did her best to keep an umbrella over them. Little could be seen beyond the platform—some weedy grass and scraggly ailanthus trees beside the tracks. Then she made out, at eye level, the roofs of houses, the upper windows lit, and realized that the town lay below the station, down a flight of stairs. Again, Tom and Chase carried Ben in his chair, like royalty. They set him on the slanted sidewalk under a streetlamp that, just at that moment, clicked on, holding them in a funnel of light.

Tom spotted a taxi garage across the street and started toward it when suddenly, several brown-skinned men burst out of the building, looking, in their rain slickers, like great, bedraggled birds. Even their speech, Dana thought, had a birdlike squawk to it. She didn't, in fact, recognize it as English. It turned out to be English with a Pakistani accent. One of the men, nodding vigorously, started slinging their luggage into the trunk of a decrepit car. The wheelchair had to be collapsed and wedged in, while Chase and Tom, thoroughly wet, deposited Ben carefully in the back seat.

The cab swerved in a semicircle, then careened down the slick street and away from town, while amber beads swung wildly from the mirror and the radio blared out what sounded like belly-dancing music in Urdu.

"Are we sure this is the right town?" asked Chase.

"Are you sure this is the right *country*?" said Ben, hiding his head in his arms.

Bendelfin was surrounded by hills and narrow roads that shouldn't have been two-way but were. The driver's approach to the problem of zigzag turns was to accelerate, punching through the fog on pure faith. By the time he skidded to a stop in front of the vine-covered inn, everyone's heart was beating like a tambour.

Things got better after that. A plain-faced teenager, daughter of the owner, checked them in while an enormous orange cat lay on the counter watching with half-closed eyes.

"We're not in Cheshire, are we?" Chase whispered, eyeing the cat.

"Watch if he disappears," Dana said.

Far from disappearing, the cat followed along as the girl led them down the corridor. Because of Ben, their accommodations were on the ground floor, in earshot of the clattering kitchen and the laughter of men in the bar. The rooms were large, though, and looked out on the back garden. Dana had the smaller of the two by herself, with a separate entrance. Tom and the boys shared the other. By the time they'd unpacked and Tom had helped his son with his bathroom needs, everyone was in an improving mood. Dinner in the candlelit dining room was a thing of wonder, topped off with still-warm chocolate cake. Later, Tom helped Ben back to the room for the exercise routine, which had to be done several times a day. It involved working the legs and arms to stimulate circulation and prevent sores. That left Dana and Chase to go off by themselves. There wasn't a lot for young people to do, but they did find a billiard table in a dark-paneled room downstairs and played a few games. Neither of them was any good at it, but Chase managed to get her to laugh, which was a good thing. On the stairs back to the main floor Chase paused. "Hey, you," he said, and drew Dana in for a kiss.

"Mm," she hummed.

"You taste good," he murmured.

"You just like my cherry lipstick."

"You're right."

"Everything's food with you, isn't it?"

"Can I have seconds?"

She gave him seconds, generous ones, and was considering thirds when a lady with fluffy hair came by. They abruptly broke off and held hands down the corridor to their adjoining rooms.

"Tomorrow's the big day," he said.

She nodded, frowning at her shoes.

"Nervous?" he asked.

"Terrified."

He held her against him. One thing about Chase, he knew when to shut up. She slipped her arms around his waist. "I'm glad you're in the next room," she said.

The orange cat had appeared from somewhere and was rubbing against their ankles, making furry figure eights. Chase kissed the top of Dana's head, then her nose, then her lips.

"Night, kiddo," he said, and turned to go in.

"Hey," she said. She reached her arms around his neck and kissed his smile. "Didn't you want dessert?"

The smile faded as the kiss deepened. Finally she broke away, her heart thumping.

"That's all you get," she breathed.

He held her, his face barely an inch away. "You sure?"

She was still deciding how to answer when his lips grazed hers. "No fair," she whispered.

The next few minutes were a blur.

Chapter Eleven

The Altar

A BUNCH OF LILACS STOOD IN A DRINKING GLASS on Dana's side table. The same syrupy smell came from the garden just outside her partly open window. It was kind of an old-lady place, but cozy. She thought she had a good shot at a night's sleep without bad dreams.

After an hour or so, it began to look as though she'd have no dreams at all. Her mind was racing about tomorrow. It didn't help that the wind had picked up and was shaking the window.

Dana clicked on the light and pulled the locket from the drawer. The calm, slightly amused face of the mysterious boy was looking straight at her, posing a question she could not answer. All she knew—and it was immense—was that she knew him.

She knew him.

She laid the locket on the nightstand and killed the light. A stray branch scraped the side of the house. Shadows of bushes wallowed across the ceiling. They made her think of a fluttering coat, or cape, and she remembered her dream of the man following her through the outdoor market. Someone, she felt, was following her even now, leading her, misleading her.

Her eyes began to close. At least Chase was in the next room. And her sensible father, a man with his booted feet firmly on the ground.

She must have fallen asleep. A sound reached her, different from the branch against the house. A soft thump, the creak of a drawer. Dana's eyes flew open. She didn't dare turn her head. Barely breathed.

For a long time she heard nothing. Then, softly, something. A thin sound, like a small object being pulled across a smooth surface.

Dana's stomach wrenched with fear. Someone was in her room! She was *not* imagining it. Slowly she reached a hand down beside her bed and felt around for a shoe. She gripped it tightly. Not much of a weapon.

There was another scrape, louder, and then a distinct thump.

"Who's there?" she shouted, reaching over and snapping on the light. She looked around wildly, her shoe raised. "Where are you?"

He must be behind the chair. "Come out of there. I'm warning you!"

The door swung open from the next room. It was Chase, with Tom Landgrave right behind. "What's going on?" Chase said, starting toward her.

Dana still held the shoe high, ready for anything. "Careful! Somebody's in here. I heard him."

Chase glanced around. He went to the closet, waited a moment, and yanked the door open.

No one.

"My locket!" Dana cried out suddenly, her voice almost a wail. "It's gone!"

"What?" Tom hurried over to her while Chase crossed to the window. It was open only a few inches. Did an intruder have time to climb out and pull the window down behind him?

"Dana, are you sure?" her father said.

"It was right here on the nightstand."

It was not there now. Not in the drawer, either.

"Could it have dropped?" said Chase on his hands and knees, looking under the bed.

"What's going on?" came Ben's thin voice from the other room.

Tom called back. "It's okay, Ben. Dana lost her locket."

They had run out of places in Dana's small room. Dana knew it and saw the doubt on her father's face. Lowering her shoe, she had a thought she did not express. What if it was someone from the past? Someone not part of this world? A ridiculous idea, of course. It was one thing to remember the past. It was another to be burglarized by it.

Dana sat on the edge of her bed and dragged her tote bag over. She hadn't looked in there.

"Ow!" she cried out. Something stung her hand and a hissing scream issued from inside the bag.

Her father stood stunned. Chase slowly approached.

"Is it a snake?" Dana whispered.

Chase peered in. Staring up at him, still hissing, was the round orange face of the terrified cat.

"My God!" Dana cried.

Chase took the bag and upended it. Out thumped the cat, who raced past, leaped up on the window seat, and out the window into the yard. Dana's wallet, sneakers, Tampax, and socks also fell out. And then the locket.

Three large people stood staring at one another.

Chase was the first to smile.

By morning the rain had cleared off and a bleary sunlight filled the glassed-in porch where they took their breakfast. Dana, who'd gotten two hours' sleep around dawn, was going on nervous energy and felt wide-awake.

Tom poured himself a second cup of coffee without looking up from the brochure he'd picked up at the desk. Breen Hall Art Gallery and Museum, the castle was called, now that the Borough Council ran it. It opened at ten.

The only problem was they had no way to get there except by the taxi service from hell. Ben almost refused to go, but then decided to tough it out. He wasn't about to miss out on a castle. Eventually a driver arrived, shorter, heavier, and older than the first man. Tom emphasized to him that there was no hurry; in fact, there might be a bonus for driving slowly. The man nodded and grinned. Then he turned up the music and took off like a shot down twisting, slippery roads, skittering through a stone archway into Breen Park, as the grounds to the castle were called. The cab accelerated through pastureland dotted with sheep and finally came in sight of the great hall itself, its distant towers pronging the sky.

The car lurched to a stop in the circle drive and everyone staggered out. Ben didn't say anything, but he was shaken. Dana could see his hand trembling as his father settled him into his chair.

While the driver haggled—apparently he had heard the word "bonus" and expected one—Dana walked off a little way by herself. She was too close to take in the whole building. Seen from the front, the facade blocked out the sun and most of the sky. A minute ago, when they were racing through the park, the distant castle had seemed a dark crouching animal. Up close, in its shadow, she felt its pounce.

The taxi U-turned and sped off like an angry wasp, and the travelers trudged to the entrance. From the look of things, the drawbridge hadn't been lifted for a century, and the moat was now a pond, the fearsome defenses of the past reduced to the picturesque. Carved on an outer wall was the familiar coat of arms of the Breens, age-darkened and surmounted by a crude rendering of a phoenix. Chase caught Dana's look and nodded as they passed inside.

A dozen people had arrived before them and were milling about the souvenir counter in the entrance hall. Dana stood taking it all in, her eyes trying for the ceiling. There were many grander castles in England, but this was her first, and it was grand enough.

Nothing struck her as familiar, or not yet. Without thinking, she fingered the locket hanging from its silver chain.

An elderly gent, dark-suited and -tied, lifted his deeply seamed face to Tom Landgrave. "May I help you, sir?"

"Oh, we just want to wander, I think."

"Of course. You're free to go anywhere that isn't roped off."

There were a number of velvet ropes to contend with, but the visitors picked their way along. They discovered that each of the main rooms had been remodeled in the style of a different historical period. There was the Regency Room, in the oldest part of the Hall, whose red walls, gold-fringed drapes, and gleaming surfaces made Dana think of the inside of a romance novel. The vaulted, gold-bordered ceiling looked familiar, but everything else seemed oddly new. Old but new.

"I could get used to this," said Ben, staring up.

"Could you, Benny?" said Dana.

A tour guide was just leaving with a small group, and she caught his eye. "When were the walls painted this color?"

"Last year, miss." He gave her an odd look. This was not a

question he got from teenagers. Generally they wanted to know where the bathrooms were.

"I mean originally."

"Oh," he said, "I can't say. Sometime after 1814, I would think."

She took that in. "What color were they before that?"

"Haven't the foggiest. You might ask the curator. Short chap. He's somewhere about."

"I will, thanks."

They moved on to other rooms, the Victorian Room, the Renaissance Room, all of which struck Dana as familiar, but somehow wrong. The Breens, her father had learned from the brochure, had been great collectors. Different generations had collected different things, ceramics, gems, paintings, even old manuscripts, and many were on display. To a history buff like him they were fascinating, to Dana a distraction. They prevented her from seeing what was there.

Leaving the others before a display case, she went on ahead. The day had started with the promise of revelations and was ending as a sightseeing jaunt. If that was what she'd wanted, she needn't have left London.

A moment later Dana forgot all such thoughts. Up a low flight of steps and past a marble eagle, she found herself in the West Hall, face-to-face with a floor-to-ceiling Renaissance tapestry. Its rich red background immediately captured her. She couldn't stop staring.

Several tourists were milling in front of the great tableau, but Dana barely noticed. She was deep in a fiery dream filled with kaleidoscopic images: strawberries and lions, rabbits, hunting dogs, pomegranates, magpies, a goat, a panther, part of a forest, part of a castle. And scattered over the whole scene: a myriad of tiny flowers.

Her mouth formed the word Millefleur, a bit of French she didn't know she knew, meaning "thousand flowers."

But it was the human figures that gripped her: the soldiers, the lady, the mirror she held, her maids, the nobleman, the hunter.

The hunter! Dana moved closer, ignoring the tourists. Half-hidden behind a flowering tree, the figure held up a bow, arrow-less, as if he had just made his shot and was sure of his mark.

Dana reached out and gently touched the face.

"We don't want to touch the tapestry, miss." The voice was crisp.

She turned. A surprisingly short man, not more than five foot two, was watching her with narrowed eyes, his bald head bony and beaked. He was not in a guard's uniform—in fact, he wore a corduroy jacket—but he was obviously in authority.

"I was just . . . ," she began.

"*The Allegory of Time* is more than four hundred years old," the man said, his face smooth and impersonal. "We don't touch it."

"I'm sorry," she said. He was right, of course. "It was just the hatching . . ."

"Excuse me?" The man tipped his bald head to the side, like a teapot.

"The lighter-colored wool within the darker colors . . ."

"I know what hatching is," he said. "I was surprised *you* know it."

"Oh." Dana looked down, thinking. "I suppose I'm surprised too. Is that gilt wiring, worked in with the wool?"

"It is, yes."

"Really makes it pop, doesn't it?"

"Pop?" The little man shook his head. "How does it happen that you know so much about this?"

"I really don't know anything about it. Oh," she said, nodding toward the right side of the tableau, "but I do know who that guy is."

The eyes again narrowed. "Who *who* is?"

She pointed, careful not to touch.

"The hunter, yes."

"That's not what I mean." Dana's heart was beating hard. She had to speak, but she was afraid. "I mean," she said, her voice low and shaking, "I know *who* he is. It's a self-portrait."

"What?" The man's eyes widened. He noticed that several people were listening, and he moved away a few steps, cocking his head at Dana. "Could I speak to you over here a moment?"

She followed but didn't take her eyes from the tapestry.

"If you don't mind my asking," he said in an undertone, folding his arms, "what makes you think it's a self-portrait?"

Dana gave him a glance, then turned back to the fantastic scene before her. What was she supposed to say? That she *remembered* it?

"It's not in the guidebooks," he said quietly.

Again she was silent.

"We'd love to put it in, but it's just a theory some of us have."

"It's not a theory. It's true."

Now he was silent. "Tell me," he said finally, "do you have any theories about what he's shooting at? There is no arrow in the scene."

"Not what."

"Excuse me?"

"Not what. Who."

The man's eyes flew to the tapestry, his glance shifting from person to person. "You don't mean . . ."

"Yes." She nodded toward the lower left-hand corner, where

a man in a black cowl appeared to be bending forward over a patch of darkness. "Him."

The little man stared a moment, then broke into a smile. He seemed almost relieved that she was wrong. "No, no. The priest is leaning over the baptismal pool."

"Well, not a priest exactly."

"Not a priest? What do you mean? There are many unanswered questions about this tapestry, but that's not one of them."

She looked at him and then down at her feet. "Maybe you're right."

"Yes, well . . ." He stuck out his hand. "Forgive me for not introducing myself. I'm Graham Dunn. I'm the curator here."

"Hi."

"And you are?"

"I'm Dana Landgrave."

"Tell me. How did you become an expert on sixteenth-century Flemish tapestry? You look so young."

"People tell me that."

"Where have you studied?"

"Portsmouth."

"Really! I've heard they're good in the biosciences, but . . ." The teapot tipped again. "Do they have a department of Renaissance studies?"

"Oh, I don't think so."

"Lovely town, Portsmouth. I don't get to the south of England often, but when I do I always try to stop there."

South of England? Dana was confused.

"Have you been to Breen Hall before?" he continued.

She gave a shrugging smile. "First time."

"Well, you must let me show you around. The tour guides are good, but there are many crannies that aren't on public view."

"All those velvet ropes."

He laughed. "Yes. Quite."

She gave him one of her rare smiles. It made her almost beautiful. "I'd like that very much."

"That's fine!"

Dana's eye caught a hand waving from across the room. It was Ben, with Chase pushing.

"Hey, Dana!" Ben called out. "Where ya been?"

Graham Dunn swung the narrow boulder of his head in the direction of the voice. He seemed startled by Ben's sweatshirt, emblazoned "Portsmouth Clippers."

"Oh," Dana said, "would you mind terribly if we took my family along?"

"Ah," he said, taking in the two boys, and Tom Landgrave making his way behind them. "Your family."

The curator, it turned out, could laugh at himself. If he felt any chagrin at the realization that Dana Landgrave went to a high school, not a university, and in New Hampshire of all places, he didn't let on. In fact, he seemed to take a liking to the Landgrave clan, and to the dapper Chase Newcomer.

There were problems getting Ben around, but with Chase and Tom carrying the wheelchair up the narrow stairways, they were able to negotiate most of the back passages and catwalks. They even got behind the workings of the great clock in the tower. Ben was much impressed by the spools of thick rope and many-toothed brass wheels in the gearbox, although he had to cover his ears when the outsize contraption gave a warning whirr and began bonging the hour.

Ben seemed to feel at ease with the curator, who was nearly his own size, and pelted him with questions. He especially wanted to know about a sarcophagus, presumably containing a mummy, that some Eastern potentate had presented to a nineteenth-century Breen. Had anybody X-rayed it? Ben wanted to know.

Dana paid only slight attention. What struck her most was a hole in the floor, barely two feet square and covered now by Plexiglas, through which one could see into the "priest's hide"— a tiny room where fugitive Catholics were hidden during the persecutions of the sixteenth and seventeenth centuries. No food or water, except what could be lowered to them. How many, she wondered, had died there, or been dragged out by their hair?

When the Landgraves again emerged into the main galleries, led by the affable Dunn, Dana was in a somber mood. Breen Hall, with all its art and artifacts, was not a happy place. Terrible things had happened here.

Dunn led them into the family dining room, pointing out its mullioned windows, marble hearth, and the long table gleaming like a lake. Somehow Ben got him into a discussion about the family's coat of arms.

"That's the later design you're speaking of," said Dunn. "From the eighteenth century. Have you seen the early version? It's carved in the paneling above the confessional."

"You have a confessional?"

"Haven't you seen the chapel yet? You should."

With that he led them down a dim corridor that opened dramatically into the light-flooded Breen family chapel. Long devoid of pews, the narrow room drew the eye straight to the white-marble altarpiece, some eight feet tall and set on a platform of intricately carved rosewood. Through tall windows the morning sun glittered on the high-relief carvings of Mary and the infant Jesus, of Joseph and Saint Anne, bathing them in spectral fire.

Dana hung back. She felt a chill go through her.

"What is it?" said Chase.

She couldn't speak at first. The voices of Graham Dunn and Ben faded from her hearing. They were with Tom by the west wall discussing why the old coat of arms was so much less intricate than the newer one. Finally Dunn noticed that Dana and Chase weren't with them. His voice trailed off.

Dana laid a hand on Chase's shoulder to steady herself. She seemed hypnotized by the glowing marble figures.

"Is something the matter?" said Dunn, coming over.

She turned to him. "Has this," she waved a hand toward it, "this altarpiece ever been moved?"

He gave it a glance. "I don't think so. Not since it was installed."

"Installed when?"

"That would be, what, the 1580s sometime. I can look it up."

"Then he's still there!"

Dunn stared at her, catching the note of fear in her voice. "What are you saying?"

There was no way to avoid this. She took the locket from around her neck and placed it in his hands. He turned it over several times, tracing with his fingertips the design in the silver.

"Miss Landgrave," he said, frowning, "where did you get this?"

"Never mind. Open it."

Dunn turned it around again till he figured out the catch. Suddenly the cover sprang up. "My God," he breathed.

"Yes."

"It's him, isn't it?"

"I think so."

"This is incredible!"

"Move the altar."

"What was that?"

"Move the altar!"

Dunn met Dana's look. "I can't do that. What are you talking about?"

"He's back there."

"Who?"

She held up the locket and stared at Dunn fiercely. *"Him!"* she cried. *"Me!"*

Chapter Twelve

A Velvet Shoe

"COME WITH ME, PLEASE." GRAHAM DUNN TURNED and led the Landgraves and Chase quickly down a corridor to a door marked "Staff Only." He had his key out and escorted them through a suite of high-ceilinged rooms filled with filing cabinets and desks piled with papers. A young woman looked up in surprise from a computer screen as they swept past to a book-lined office in the rear.

Dunn clicked the door shut, then sat on the edge of the large captain's desk by the window and folded his arms. Dana noticed that his feet didn't reach the floor.

"Miss Landgrave," he said, "I think you need to tell me what you know. What you *think* you know."

"You won't believe me."

"Try."

She shook her head. "I know you won't believe me. You don't have to. All you have to do is move the altarpiece."

He looked at her as if she were a text he was puzzling out. "It's not so easy. We'd need equipment. Equipment costs money, which I'd have to justify to the council. What would you suggest I tell them?"

She sighed heavily. What did she know about such things?

Tom Landgrave spoke up. "Excuse me, Mr. Dunn. I know this sounds odd, but I'd probably do what she says."

"Can you give me a reason?"

"I can't. But Dana . . ." He looked over at her. "She seems to sense things. She found that locket and she got us all up here."

"It sounds, frankly, like a hoax. What, William Breen, the missing heir to Breen Hall, lost to history since 1583. . . . It's too much!"

"So that's his name," Dana said in a soft voice.

"Don't tell me you didn't know," said Dunn. "You know everything else."

"I didn't."

"I find that hard to believe."

Tom Landgrave splayed out his big hands in helpless agreement. "All I can say is my daughter doesn't lie. I don't think she ever has."

"And what," Chase spoke up at last, "would be the point of a hoax?"

"I haven't any idea."

"There *is* no point."

"Well, then," said Dunn, sounding with his smoothly sanded voice like a judge who'd like to be lenient, "she is simply imagining things."

"Excuse me," Dana said sharply, "if you don't mind, I'm standing right in front of you. Please don't talk about me as if I weren't here."

He shot her a surprised look. "Quite right. Sorry. But you know, I'm right in front of you, too, and you're not telling me anything."

"All right," she said, "I'll try." But even now she hesitated.

He waited.

"I've had dreams."

"Dreams."

"I knew you wouldn't believe me."

"No, no, go ahead."

"I've seen this same altarpiece maybe a dozen times. And I saw this boy." She took out the locket.

"This is getting wilder and wilder."

"You asked, so I'm telling you. The boy was behind the altar and someone was pushing it back toward the wall, shutting him in."

"And who was that?"

"I have no idea."

"Well, what did he look like?"

Dana closed her eyes. "What did he look like," she murmured. "He had a beard. A narrow face. His nose . . ." She shook her head slightly, her eyes shut tightly. "Crooked somehow. It's hard to explain."

"Go on."

"That's all. Oh, and he had a mark. Almost like a dent in his forehead."

"A dent, you say?"

"It seemed that way."

Graham Dunn was silent. He was silent a long time. Finally he slid off the desk and went to a tall file cabinet, stepping on a stool to reach into the top drawer. He came back with a folder and sat in the swivel chair.

"Open it," he said.

Dana turned back the blue cover. A reproduction of a time-darkened portrait lay before her. She looked at it for long seconds, puzzling over the bandage on the man's head. Ben wheeled himself up to the desk and looked at it too.

"Not him," she said.

"You're sure."

She nodded.

"Look at the one underneath it."

Another photocopied reproduction, this time of a long-faced, sorrowing man in his forties. There was a mark on his right temple.

"That's him," said Dana.

"Yes?"

"Absolutely."

Dunn nodded. "If you had said the first man, I would have sent you packing. He was a Saxon soldier wounded in Silesia."

"The second man?"

"His name was Paul Bertrand."

She gave him an uncomprehending look.

"He was a Belgian tapestry designer. You were just admiring his work in the West Hall."

Everyone was silent.

"The hunter in the forest," Dana breathed.

"Well, who knows? It's possible. The hunter does have a mark on his forehead, just there. Did you notice? It's what started us thinking it might be a self-portrait."

"It is."

He gave the blue folder a slap. "I don't understand how you can be so sure of yourself."

"It *is* a self-portrait," Dana said, her voice rising. "And that isn't a pool."

"*What* isn't?"

"You said the priest was kneeling beside a baptismal pool."

"He *is* kneeling beside a baptismal pool!" His voice had risen to match hers.

"It's a *hole*!"

"A what?"

"He's been struck by the arrow and he's falling down into Hell!"

"Impossible! Where's the wound?"

"I don't care. That's what it is!"

Dunn stared. His mouth hung partway open for several seconds before he remembered himself.

"So," he said, centering the folder carefully on the desk, "can you all come back tomorrow?"

Tom Landgrave stood up. "Of course."

"Come directly to this office. I expect the chapel will be closed to the public."

Dana's dreams that night were a jumble. Something about running down stone hallways, shouting men in pursuit. And she seemed to remember falling. Hurting herself. Shouts coming nearer. She woke up with her heart beating wildly.

Night was turning to hazy dawn as she climbed from bed and went to the window. The intense green of the lawn calmed her, and the coloring-book hues of the tulips. The lilacs were a muddle of purple shadow.

What if they found nothing?

She had sounded so confident talking to the curator yesterday, but what did she have to back up her claim? A dozen dreams, a dented locket, and a vivid imagination.

This could be pretty embarrassing.

She turned on the bedside lamp and opened the locket. In the shadowy room, just now lightening into day, the boy seemed vividly alive. That, at least, was reassuring.

Do it for him, she thought.

It was late morning when they arrived. Graham Dunn had left word with the woman behind the souvenir desk, and she led them to the private offices.

"You can't imagine the trouble this has caused us," said Dunn briefly when he caught sight of Dana and the others.

Seeing Tom Landgrave's extended hand, he remembered his manners enough to shake it. But his mind was running. "Getting the equipment into the chapel was not fun. Shall we go? They're almost ready."

A young assistant named Martha went with them, carrying a clipboard. A pleasant, broad-faced woman, Martha gave Dana an encouraging smile. "This is exciting."

Dana didn't reply. Her heart was making too much commotion.

"I've never seen the curator like this."

Dana managed to nod.

"Things don't happen around here very often," Martha continued in an undertone, her eyes bright.

"No?"

"You could say they don't happen for centuries."

Chase quietly took Dana's hand as they emerged from the corridor into the bright chapel.

"Wow!" Ben exclaimed.

"A little different from yesterday," said Tom.

The great altarpiece was swathed in heavy cloth and secured with ropes. On either side sat two orange machines the size of snowplows, their engines grumbling. Despite the open windows, the smell of exhaust was strong.

Dunn checked the ropes one last time. Then he spoke to the foreman, who nodded at the workers manning the lifts. These men were not arty types, but locals in smeared workclothes brought in at the last moment. Or that's how Dana read them. They reminded her of the guys who worked with her dad on the sewer lines.

At a sign from Dunn, the motors roared and the hydraulics groaned, raising the sculpture several inches into the air. Then the machines backed away slowly and lowered their cargo onto the tarpaulin-covered floor.

The curator, with Dana close behind him, hurried to the altar's heavy wooden base. It stood four feet high and was set into a shallow recess—impossible to see behind. This base would have to be moved too.

It took several minutes to cover it in cloth and reset the block and tackle. Dunn again checked the ropes before giving his nod. Then the engines groaned and the ropes grew taut.

"This is it," Dunn murmured.

Dana forgot to breathe.

With a shudder, the heavy structure rose six inches from the floor. The machines pulled it a little way into the room before setting it down.

Dana's arm felt blindly for Chase's supporting grip as she stared at the dust-strewn area where the altar had stood.

"Oh," moaned Graham Dunn.

What so transfixed them was a bit of trash mixed with some swatches of blue cloth piled against the wall. Or that's the way it looked, until one noticed the shinbone—fleshless and gleaming white—poking from a velvet shoe.

III

The Door

Chapter Thirteen

The Karma Thing

TRISH ROTH AND DANA WERE LEANING AGAINST the rail with a hundred others, waiting for the bulldozers to knock down the castles. Actually, very few castles had been built in this year's Master Sand Sculpture competition. That would be considered pandering to the crowd. Instead, a full-size Ford convertible, with driver, all made of sand, sat before them on the beach, along with a giant dolphin, a ten-foot-tall woman, and several elaborate monsters. There was even a giant family, realistic to the last toenail, shown digging with a shovel and pail.

They were all of sand, and to sand they would return. The bulldozers revved by the water's edge.

It was hot on the boardwalk, and Trish had on her blue whale-watchers cap. She had a lot of body to protect, all of it fair, and she wore a terry cloth wrap over her one-piece. "It was a good one this year," she said, squinting at the dazzling beach. "You missed something."

Dana grunted, sipping her frostie. The contest had ended several days ago after a frantic three days during which sand sculptors from around the country had formed, carved, watered, and smoothed their creations. It drew thousands of extra tourists, and Hampton Beach was crowded enough during normal times: the souvenir joints, arcades, and hot dog vendors besieged by heat-struck teens, sometimes five deep, waiting their turn at the mustard dispenser. Dana was glad she lived in Portsmouth, a safe car ride away.

"I can't believe I used to enjoy this," she said.

"Enjoy what? The contest?"

Dana gave a general wave. "The whole scene. The bulldozers could take the whole boardwalk."

"Miss Grump over here."

"I'm glad to see you, though."

A great cry went up from the crowd, part cheer, part dismay, as the machines set to work pushing down the enormous figures. "A shame they couldn't just leave them up," said Trish, giving the neck of her flowered bathing suit a tug.

They watched in silence. "See any kids from school?" Dana said.

Trish shrugged. "The usual mall crawlers."

"Any Gianna sightings?"

"She snubbed me a couple of times in Newington. We tend to go to the same movies." Trish looked over at Dana. "You haven't told me very much about your trip. How was it having Chase along? Was it fabulous?"

"Yeah, fabulous."

"I ran into Bingo last week. She was *totally* jealous."

Mary Bing. Dana hadn't thought of her since that day at the Friendly Toast when she'd flirted with Chase. Dana was getting used to girls flirting with her boyfriend, sometimes right in front of her.

"Maybe she should move on," Dana said.

"Easy for you to say." Trish gave her a quizzical look. "Sure you're okay? You seem different."

"How?"

"I don't know. Did something happen?"

"A lot happened." Dana tossed her cup in a trash can.

"I mean with Chase."

"Aren't we curious."

"Of course we're curious."

"Trish, there's more to life than boyfriends."

"I know that," she said, then paused. "Like what?"

"Good point." Dana took refuge in the banter. How could she tell her friend how much more there was? How many deaths, births, griefs? "Want to take a swim?"

"Okay. Give me a chance to work on my lovely sunburn."

The girls kept to the boardwalk till they were far enough from the shops that there was room to spread out. They held the rail as they stepped down, their flip-flops slapping on the splintery stairs.

Trish set her things on the sand. "You know, you can tell me things."

"I know."

"I'm not sure you know."

Dana gave her an honest look, her first in a while. "Trish." She paused. "I want you to keep liking me. I don't have that many friends."

"Why wouldn't I like you?"

"Because you'll think I'm a lunatic."

"Maybe I already think that. Ew! Look at that!" Trish's eyes narrowed. She was staring at something crawling in the sand.

Dana laughed. "I think they call that a hermit crab."

"Can we move?"

"He isn't interested in you. He's just looking for a shell to crawl into."

"Well, he can look somewhere else!"

They moved a few feet away. Trish looked around suspiciously. "Anyway," she said, settling down on the towel.

"Anyway," Dana agreed.

"I'm not trying to push. Well, that's not true."

"Just stay my friend." Dana stared out at the water, steel colored under the afternoon sun. "So," she said, giving the girl a shove, "anybody want to get wet?"

Morton Sprague had grown a beard. It was the first thing Dana noticed when she walked in, and it was a shock. Hardly anybody she knew had a beard, especially one so narrowly trimmed, a dark, downward-pointing dagger crossed by a mustache, like an old-time villain's. It improved Sprague's appearance, hiding his pockmarked cheeks, but it also made him look like someone from a different century.

"Is this another shrink thing?" said Dana, sliding into the chair.

Sprague's fingers flicked his chin. "Do you like it?"

"You're trying to look like Freud, right?"

"Nothing so interesting. Just a mundane midlife crisis. You'll be going through one in about thirty years."

"I'll grow a beard?"

Sprague leaned back in his leather chair, smiling expectantly. There was no way Dana Landgrave was going to get his goat today. Or his goatee. "So," he said, "show me what you've got."

"What do you mean?"

"The locket, Miss Landgrave! The locket! What do you think?"

"I left it home."

His eyes flickered momentarily but then calmed. "Why do I doubt that?"

"I don't know. Why do you?" But her eyes were giving her away. "Oh, all right." She reached for the silver chain inside her T-shirt, clicking the locket open as she handed it to him.

Sprague took it in his hands eagerly. "My goodness," he murmured, pulling off his glasses, rubbing them on his tie, and placing them back on his nose. "So this," he said, "is the boy you've been dreaming about all these months?"

"His name is William Breen. He disappeared in 1583."

"And turned up last week," Sprague finished. He looked at her over the top of his glasses. "And you've convinced yourself somehow that it's a portrait of—you?"

"Who else?"

Sprague set the locket down with exaggerated care, as if it were a tiny cup filled above the brim. "Who else? *Anyone* else. Do you know the chances of something like this happening?"

"I thought you didn't believe in chance."

He stroked his beard to a point. "A good thing I don't." He narrowed his eyes on the portrait, as if trying to psychoanalyze its subject. He shook his head in wonder. "You know," he said, "many years ago—I told you this—I tried to learn about one of my own lifetimes. I failed, mostly. But you, Miss Landgrave! It's like you dived to the bottom of the sea and came back with sunken treasure!"

Dana was not used to compliments from this strange man. It made her feel odd. "But now that we've got it," she said, "what do we do with it?"

"*Use* it," he answered quickly. "Use it to get back there again."

Dana saw an image of rat-gnawed bones and rotted silk. "What if I don't want to go back there again?"

"What do you mean? Of course you do!"

"I don't think so."

"Do you want nightmares the rest of your life? We have to find out what's causing them!"

She knew he was right, but something about him put her off. His intensity made her think he was interested in more than her nightmares. "You're not writing about this, are you? For some shrink magazine?"

He smiled. "What makes you say that?"

"I don't know. I always used to think you were putting up with me. Now all of a sudden it's like I'm a big deal."

"You are a very big deal."

"I'm a screwed-up kid."

"You're a screwed-up kid who happens to have a direct pipeline to two former incarnations. I'd call that a big deal."

She was silent.

Sprague waited.

"If you don't believe in chance," she said, changing the subject, "then how do you explain how I found the locket?"

"Good point," he said. "Have you heard of the word 'karma'?"

"Oh yeah. The karma thing."

"Any idea what it means?"

"Bad luck?"

"It's Sanskrit. Loosely, it means cause and effect. Every action has a reaction."

"What goes around comes around."

"Right. We see it all the time. Throw a ball against the wall and it'll bounce back and hit you in the nose. But they say it applies to the unseen world, too. If something was done in a past lifetime . . ." He lifted his hands.

"It might hit us in the nose in this one."

"Exactly."

"But how could it . . . *find* us?"

"That's the question, isn't it?" He stroked his mustache with the side of his finger. "What if karma's not just an idea, but an actual force, like attraction and repulsion?"

"Sounds kind of out there to me."

"I know. That's why I don't talk about it. My colleagues . . ." He wiggled his hand. "But what if we're *drawn* to certain things because we were involved with them before?"

"I'm drawn to photography," Dana said irrelevantly.

"Yes," said Sprague, taking her up. "But they didn't have photography in the seventeen hundreds, so you were a painter then. It's the same impulse."

Dana frowned in thought. "What about people?"

"What about them?"

"Could the people who are in my life now . . . ?"

"What do *you* think?"

Dana felt her heart starting to beat heavily, a slow thrumming in her chest. "I think," she said, "that would be very scary."

"Scary? Why?"

"*Why?* Look at this picture." She reached out and gave the locket a little push. "We found his corpse behind the altar!"

Sprague nodded. "Yes," he said, "that's right."

"Don't you see? Somebody I know is a murderer!" Dana paused a moment, realizing. "*My* murderer."

The usual schedule was to meet once a week, but at Sprague's suggestion they met the next day. The doctor assured Dana's parents that he would not charge them for the extra time.

He was feeding the turtle when Dana came in. "Want to help?" he said.

"Sure," she said doubtfully. "Oh my God, he's gotten huge!"

"Here." He pulled out a tray of plastic-wrapped goldfish from the mini-refrigerator. "Take one."

Dana didn't know which was creepier, the prehistoric-looking turtle, now almost two feet across, or the goldfish morgue.

"Hold the fish by the tail. Not too close."

Dana dangled the tiny corpse a few inches from the turtle's maw. No reaction. "How long do I—?" Suddenly she screamed as the beast lunged, its body boiling out of the water, and tore the fish from her fingers.

"Yeah, you can't get too close."

"What a horror!"

"You don't care for Id?"

"Id? That's his name?"

"Private joke."

"Why do you *keep* him?"

Sprague shrugged. "He's useful. He reminds me of what we're dealing with."

She looked to the snapper for an explanation, but he had turned back into stone.

"The Unconscious, my dear. It's powerful, ferocious, and not very pretty."

"That would be Id."

"Usually it keeps to itself, but it'll jump out at you when you least expect it."

She gave him a narrowed look. "Why do I get the feeling you planned this?"

"What do you mean?"

"This little scene just now."

"Who says you're not smart?"

She stared at Id. Nothing. He might have been a statue. "Yesterday you were saying I had to get back to my earlier life-

142

time. Are you telling me now that you *don't* want me looking into the past?"

"No," he said, "I'm telling you to watch out for your fingers."

"Isn't that what I have you for?"

"I think we *both* need to be careful." He folded his large arms, hugging himself. "Do you think you're ready?"

"I've got to be."

"There's material here you're struggling with. Until recently you didn't even know there *was* this other lifetime."

"Well, now I do."

"You were keeping it from yourself. There may be a reason. Have you thought what would happen if you actually found out who the boy's killer was? What if it's someone in your present life?"

Dana's mind scampered over the people she knew, one possibility more appalling than the next. Gianna? Trish? Her brother? *Chase?*

"And of course," he went on, "this person would have no recollection whatever of doing anything wrong. In which case, what would you have accomplished, except to torment yourself?"

"I'm tormenting myself *now*," she broke out.

Sprague watched her.

"I have nightmares. I can't sleep. I *have* to find out." She looked at him with wild appeal. "Don't I?"

"Do you?"

"Yes!" Her heart was beating hard. "Yes, I do."

Sprague looked at Dana with his heavy, sad-lidded eyes. But there was a spark in them. She realized he'd been hoping for this answer.

"Very well," he said. He gestured at the recliner, and she switched over to it while he lowered the blinds. "I'll try. But we'll be jumping back *two* lifetimes. I don't need to tell you this is unexplored territory."

"I know."

"It's up to you how deep you go. Do you remember your safe place?"

"The swing set in the backyard."

"If you run into trouble you can always go back there in your mind."

"Okay."

"Remember we used your mental image of Traxler to jump you back into that lifetime?" he said, taking a chair beside her. "I'm thinking we might use the portrait in the locket to jump you back to the life before that."

Dana nodded, closing her eyes. "Go ahead."

Sprague began the induction.

When she was deeply in, he asked her to look at the locket. She opened her eyes with difficulty.

"Do you know this boy?" he said quietly.

"Yes."

"Did you know him before this lifetime?"

Slowly she nodded. "Yes."

"I want you to go back to that time, in a lifetime before this."

She frowned. Her head moved back and forth.

"Are you back there?"

Dana's eyes closed more tightly. Sprague waited.

"Is something the matter?" he said.

"I can't."

"What is it?"

"There's like a wall. I can't get past it."

"That's all right," he soothed. "You don't need to do it if you're not ready. Do you need to go to your safe place?"

She seemed not to hear him. Her expression began to change, her brows tightening. Her mouth twisted into what looked like anger.

"Miss Landgrave, where are you?"

"Hateful man!" she spat.

Sprague's eyes widened. A momentary fear flicked across his face. "Who are you talking about?"

"Him!" she sneered.

Sprague seemed not to know what to say. "Where are you?" he asked.

"Back hall."

"Who is with you?"

"He's coming down the stairs."

"Who is?"

She sneered. "Uncle Gavin."

"Traxler?"

No answer. She was back in her lifetime as Hannah. Unable to reach the fifteen hundreds, she had stumbled out into the seventeen hundreds.

"What is your name?" he said, to make sure.

"You know my name perfectly well."

"Yes, of course." Dr. Sprague laid a hand over his chin and gently stroked his soft new beard. He had to be careful. He must not lead her. He must keep his suggestions neutral. "I would like you to look around you. What do you see?"

"I see . . ."

He watched in amazement as a tear formed at the corner of her eye.

What she saw—what moved her so strongly just then—was a trembling flower, a rose, red as blood. Really, it was the trembling more than the flower itself that struck her. It was in

James Pickerel's hand. He had brought it for her. He had just asked her to marry him.

Boots clumped on the stairs, and a moment later Gavin Traxler appeared before them, swaying slightly.

"What's this?" Traxler's eyebrows lifted into an arch, the better to help him focus. "For me?" He yanked the rose away from Pickerel, the thorns tearing the young man's fingers.

"Uncle," said Hannah, "please leave us."

"Oh, no," he said in his grand voice. "This is too rich. The footman asking for my niece's hand in marriage. That *is* what I'm seeing, isn't it?"

Pickerel clasped his hands before him to hide the blood that had begun dripping from his thumb. "It is, sir."

"Your impertinence astounds me," Traxler exclaimed. "You know I am Miss Traxler's guardian, yet you failed to ask my permission."

Pickerel's face was naturally serious, with a mournful downward tilt to his lips, but he was not without spirit. "I intended to, sir, just as soon as I knew Miss Traxler's feelings."

"Miss Traxler's feelings. Noble of you. Forgive me if I suspect another reason. You knew I would never give my consent!" Traxler closed his eyes tightly and opened them wide to clear his vision, which seemed to be giving him trouble.

"Uncle," Hannah spoke up, "I ask you to stop talking this way right now."

"Listen to her!" he said wonderingly.

"I'm not a child. I'm thirty years old. I can make my own decisions."

Traxler smiled. "Well said, my dear! Bravo!" One hand held on to the banister to stop his swaying. The smell of tawny port was on his breath. "Of *course* you may make your own decisions. Decide away. But consider what you're doing."

"I know exactly what I'm doing."

"Yes, quite so." He waved his hand languidly to dismiss the thought. "But have you considered how you'd live?"

"What do you mean?"

"Young Pickerel here is counting on entering the family and sharing in the general prosperity. Quite a step up for him, you must agree."

"That's not true," said James firmly, "and it's not fair."

"Let me finish!" Traxler snapped. He turned to Hannah. "But his schemes of wealth are in vain."

"I assure you," Pickerel began, "I had no intention—"

"Traxlers don't marry servants. Sorry to speak so directly, but they don't. Even plain, thick-legged, maiden-aunt Traxlers don't marry servants."

Hannah's jaw tightened. "Have you someone else in mind for me?"

"Of course not. Who would marry you?"

Hannah knew she had to keep her temper for James's sake, and probably for her own. "So then," she said evenly, "for appearances' sake I must marry *no one*."

"Don't underestimate appearances. I'm a painter. Appearances are everything."

"You give, at least," she said bitterly, "the *appearance* of a painter."

She could see from the way he stiffened that the thrust had hit home.

"And what do you mean by that?"

"Only," she said, picking her words carefully, "that I'm not entirely without use to you. I don't think you'd throw me out so quickly."

Traxler reddened. "You speak like this to me? In front of a *servant*?"

Hannah was silent. She had never raised her voice to her uncle. Usually she was tongue-tied before him.

"Pickerel!" Traxler swirled around to the footman. "Now that you realize that this scheme of yours will get you nothing, I'm sure you'll have no objection to withdrawing your offer."

James drew himself up. "Sir, money is not the only motive for marriage. I love your niece."

"Very pretty. And very selfish, since marriage to you would condemn her to a life of direst poverty."

Pickerel looked at Hannah. His confusion was pitiable.

"Let me be as clear as I can," Traxler went on, warming to his work. "If she marries without my consent, I will no longer support her. I took her in. I can turn her out."

"All right," Hannah shot back. "Go ahead."

"Perfect. And of course your mother goes with you. My own fault for taking in poor relatives."

"You wouldn't!"

"Wouldn't I?"

How she wanted to defy him! How she wanted to tell him that she and her mother could do without his stingy generosity. But the truth was, she wavered.

Traxler turned to Pickerel. "As for you, you are dismissed. You may gather your belongings and leave this house."

He stood uncertainly.

"Now!"

Hannah's head was bowed and tears rolled down her cheeks.

"Don't," said James, reaching out to her and squeezing her hand. "We'll find a way. There's always a way."

"You can find your way *out!*" Traxler barked.

Pickerel gave Hannah a long look, then bowed briefly to Traxler and turned to leave.

Hannah couldn't watch. She kept her eyes on her uncle's face. What appalled her was not his sternness but the little smile that kept breaking through. "Why," she said in a low voice, "are you so cruel?"

"Is that what you call someone who saved you and your mother from the poorhouse?"

"You did that," she answered quietly. "And you've made good enough use of us ever since."

"As I should. Those who eat my bread must do what they can to earn it."

She gave him a straight look, aware that she was not afraid of him. Not anymore. In the general pain of the moment it was a touch of relief. "And what is your plan for us now? Are we to continue eating your bread?"

Her uncle regarded her curiously. Even with all the wine he'd had, he recognized something different about her. "I haven't decided," he said. "In the meantime, there are two portraits upstairs that need backgrounds."

"I'll take care of them."

He nodded. "Then I will say good night." He started along the hallway, catching his balance once, and disappeared into the book-lined parlor.

The house was very quiet. Hannah looked down at her hand and was puzzled to see that it was smeared dark red. *James's blood*, she thought, remembering that he had grasped her hand.

The rose!

She saw it lying in the corridor, stem crimped, petals strewn, where Traxler had dropped it, and went to pick it up. The red smear on her hand, dry now, was so much darker than the petals. How would she paint that?

Hannah stood alone in the dim silence. Candles glowed in their sconces.

Clenching her teeth, she suddenly jammed the thorny stem into the base of her thumb. She gasped, but pushed the thorn even deeper before letting the stem fall. She had no tears to shed, only a detached fascination as she watched a droplet of new blood bulge up, mingling with the old.

The color burned into her eyes. She would never forget it.

Chapter Fourteen

Revenge

THAT NIGHT DANA SPENT A LONG TIME BY THE window, unable to sleep. The distant river sounds comforted her, and the occasional groan of a truck crossing the bridge to Badger's Island. Their very indifference to her confirmed there was a real world out there, an existence outside her mind. The session with Dr. Sprague had upset her badly, and she'd left in a daze, wandering aimlessly through the park and watching the waterbirds in the mill pond till almost dinnertime.

How was it possible, she wondered, to feel such a welter of emotions—loss, fury, tenderness, hatred—over events she'd had no memory of before today?

Later, back home, Dana had helped get Ben ready for dinner and answered her parents' questions with monosyllables. Since returning from England, everybody had treated her oddly, as if she were a fragile object. Her mother, always so quick and sharp, had almost stopped pestering her to clean up her room or dress "more appropriately."

Ben had gone quiet around his sister, sending her sidelong glances when he thought she wasn't looking. Probably Dana's father had changed the least, but she sometimes caught a look of puzzled admiration in his eyes, as if she'd revealed some unsuspected talent, like pitching no-hitters or playing the oboe.

Even Chase, good old Chase, seemed different. Always a joking, loyal, shoulder-hugging, kiss-stealing love, he was more careful around her, uncertain where he stood. She didn't know where he stood either.

That evening, Dana sat in her rocker with her feet up on the bed trying to make a dent in her summer reading list. But every few minutes she found herself glancing up from her John Knowles novel at the poster over her bed. It was a remarkable two-by-three-foot reproduction of the great tapestry in Breen Hall. She'd bought it at the castle's gift shop and carried it home in a bulky cardboard tube. Since tacking it up, she found she couldn't stop looking at the thing. The glowing reds drew her eye like a sunset.

She tented the paperback over the arm of the chair and stood up. What was it about that tapestry? Her goose-necked reading lamp was pointed down, so the poster was largely in shadow. Even the shadow reminded her of something, but she couldn't at first remember what. Then it came to her: *Hannah.* The muted, shadowy tapestry that Hannah had painted as a background for one of Traxler's portraits! How had Hannah Traxler known about this sixteenth-century tapestry? She'd lived two centuries later!

The jangling phone made Dana jump. She didn't want to talk to anybody. On the other hand, she was afraid of being alone. She picked up.

Chase.

Usually she was excited to talk with him, but now she felt oddly constrained. She couldn't confide. There was too much to say and no easy way to say it. Toward the end of their brief conversation he asked if anything was wrong, and she said no, she'd just hurt her hand. She glanced up, then, at the mirror over the bureau and noticed she was not holding the phone in her hands, but had it pinned between her lifted shoulder and her ear. Her hands, she saw, were gripping each other, her right hand rubbing her left.

"Gotta go," she said breathlessly, and hung up.

Without thinking about it, Dana had been squeezing the base of her thumb, trying to work out a growing ache. It wasn't a sharp pain, and her skin was smooth and unbroken. Later that night the ache became more bothersome, and she went downstairs and took a couple of aspirin.

You are way too suggestible, she told herself.

Above the bed, the tapestry glowed like a wound.

She dragged a summer quilt over to the window seat and settled down, listening to the river sounds. Around four, she drifted to sleep.

As soon as Becca Landgrave saw her daughter's hand the next morning, she put in a call to Howard Stingle, the dermatologist who'd treated Ben for poison ivy two summers ago. He was booked, but said he could fit Dana in at two. Dana didn't fight the idea. The ache she'd felt last night had turned visible, concentrating into a small red dot, tender to the touch.

Dr. Stingle, a slim, smooth-smiling, sandy-haired man, bent over her hand for several minutes.

"Spider bite?" suggested Dana hopefully.

"It's not like anything I've seen. Mind if I do some tests?"

He did several, one of which had to be sent out to a lab for analysis. In the meantime, till the results came back, he gave her something for pain and covered the wound.

Reaching the street, Dana stopped in at Starbucks and called Sprague on her cell. Their next appointment was three days away, but she asked if he could see her now. By late afternoon she was entering his office.

"What happened to your hand?" he said after Mrs. Robyns had closed the door.

Dana glanced at the oversize Band-Aid. "Oh, I don't know. Just protecting it. It's been hurting."

Sprague looked at her through half-closed eyes. There was no hiding from him. "Let me see it, please."

She peeled away a corner of the bandage, revealing a small red circle on the fleshy base of her thumb.

He pulled off his glasses and examined the wound. "How did this happen?"

"That's what's so weird. I didn't do anything! It just started aching last night, and by this morning there was this spot."

They exchanged an alarmed look. "First," he said, rubbing his forehead lightly with his fingertips, "we need to eliminate the obvious. It doesn't really look like an insect bite." He paused. "Of course, that's not my area."

"I just saw a dermatologist."

"What did he say?"

"He doesn't know." She paused. "It's where it *is* that bothers me."

"It bothers me, too. This is either the most amazing coincidence . . ."

She didn't answer. She'd had all these thoughts herself.

"Is it tender?" he said.

"Stingle gave me some pain medicine."

"Did it help?"

She shook her head.

"Medicine, Miss Landgrave, is for physical pain, not metaphysical pain."

"So then you *do* think . . . ?"

"I don't know what to think."

She swiveled slowly in her chair.

"Conceivably," he said, "there could be some crossover between the past and present. What we've done in these sessions is open a door. I suppose the question is, did we close it after us?"

"Meaning?"

"Did some part of who you were, part of your life as Hannah, follow you back to the present?"

Dana bit her lower lip. "You're creeping me out."

Sprague launched himself onto his feet and went to the window. "Maybe we should put a stop to this business right now."

"How?"

"I could hypnotize you and instruct you to forget all about that lifetime."

"Repress it?"

"In effect, yes."

"I have a better idea," said Dana, moving over to the recliner. "Why don't you hypnotize me and take me back there and see what happened next?"

"Not a good idea."

"It's the only idea, unless I want years of insomnia and bad dreams. You said so yourself."

"It wouldn't be ethical. It would be like experimenting on you."

"A little late to think about that."

Sprague sighed. "I shouldn't have started in the first place."

"But you did start. Mom asked me today how I hurt my hand. Somehow I couldn't tell her it was a little thing that happened two *centuries* ago!"

"Probably it didn't. Probably it's a skin condition I don't know about."

"Right."

Sprague was silent.

"So what do we do?" she said.

"I don't know."

"Can you cure my hand?"

"I don't know!"

Dana shot him an angry look. "You don't know very much, do you?"

"I told you before. This is uncharted territory."

"Yeah, and we're right in the middle of it without a compass. Look, Doc, you can't chicken out now. We've got to go ahead."

"Actually, we don't."

"No, we do."

Sprague gave one of his rare smiles. "I don't think I've given you enough credit, Miss Landgrave," he said. "You're a brave girl."

"Let's just say I don't have a lot of choices."

"Maybe not," he said, sitting down in the straight chair beside the recliner. "Maybe not."

"So. We go ahead?"

"All right. But I want you particularly to remember your safe place."

"The swing set in the yard."

"Don't forget that. You can go back there any time you sense the least danger."

"Got it."

"All right. Lie back now."

Dr. Sprague began his usual induction. It took Dana a few minutes to get over her anger at him, but soon she fell under the spell of his voice. As she stepped slowly down the curving stairway in her mind, the details of her present life began falling away. Near the bottom, she heard the doctor's voice saying, "I wonder if you can remember your life as Hannah Traxler."

Slowly she nodded. Her lids remained lightly closed.

"That's very good. Are you in that life now?"

"Yes."

"May I call you Hannah?"

"Of course."

"Hannah, look to your right. You will see a door. Do you see it?"

"Yes."

"I would like you to walk through that door. It will take you into your life."

"All right."

She approached a dark door with old brass fittings and turned the latch. With no particular surprise she found herself entering the studio at the top of the house at Lincoln's Inn Fields. A woman sat at a glass-fronted secretary in the alcove, her lined face framed in a linen cap. She did not look up from her account books. No hellos today. Hannah felt obscurely guilty but couldn't remember what she had done wrong.

"Good morning, Mother," Hannah said, passing into the main room.

Prudence Traxler gave a grunt and continued her work.

Across the large, light-filled studio Hannah saw a canvas and went to it, judging the work with half-closed eyes as she prepared her palette. She worked in silence, sketching in a Corinthian column twined with ivy. *Nothing like an ancient temple for a modern society matron*, she thought, looking into the saucy eyes of the portrait, a certain Lady Breen from up north in Lancashire somewhere. She'd been here all last week for her sittings. Now it was time for Hannah to complete, and in some ways rescue, her uncle Gavin's work.

Traxler was becoming famous, if a rural woman of leisure had heard of him and come all the way to London, escorted by her dour husband, to have her portrait done. No one suspected Hannah's part in all this; but she was the ghost in the painting, the mist over the background river, the sheen on the gold fringe, the gleam of the moistened lip.

And *she* was being told whom she could or could not marry? By *him*?

An almost imperceptible shuffling on the stairs preceded the arrival of Halsey, the Traxlers' butler, carrying a tray with a cup of chocolate. He set it before Prudence Traxler, along with an envelope.

"From my brother?" she said.

"Yes, madam."

Halsey retreated as soundlessly as he had come while Mrs. Traxler slit open the letter. She read the message and thumped it down. "I cannot believe that man!" she said, twisting off the last word as if tearing off the end of a baguette.

"What is it, Mother?"

"Two pair of women's gloves. Kidskin, small, with pearl buttons, no less. It would seem your uncle has found himself a new mistress! And look: a new plate-warmer for the front kitchen! What, may I ask, was wrong with the old plate-warmer? He gets these ideas, with no consideration of cost."

Hannah thought it best to keep silent.

"Your father was the same way. Utterly reckless! But he didn't have the income to support it."

Hannah hoped her mother would not bring up the two months her father had spent in the King's Bench Prison for his debts. It was from those days that Prudence Traxler had learned to "sharpen her pencil," as she put it, and calculate every penny.

"It's good," Hannah ventured, "that Uncle Gavin has you to do his books."

"If only he'd *listen* to me!"

"But he does, eventually."

Prudence conceded a nod. "Eventually. Otherwise he'd have ended up like your father."

"You saved him, Mother."

"So have you."

"Quite the little elves, aren't we?"

Prudence set her pen in the stand. "I suppose," she said, "you don't know how close you brought us to disaster."

"I?" Hannah lowered the easel.

"All this business about Pickerel. I can't believe it!"

Hannah felt her anger start to rise. This was a tender subject. "Mother, it was an honorable proposal of marriage from an honorable man."

"From a pauper!"

"Is poverty a crime? And what about Uncle Gavin's parade of mistresses? What should we call that?"

"His business."

"And whom I marry is *my* business, Mother. It's personal!"

"Personal? Having something to eat is personal. Having a roof to keep the rain off our heads is personal. Your uncle was ready to throw us out on the street!"

"That was a bluff."

"You don't know him. He's perfectly capable of acting foolishly."

"He'd regret it."

Prudence pushed her chair back and stood up. She was too

agitated to sit. "Regret it?" she said. "Yes, a year from now, when he found his paintings were not so much in demand and his expenses had outrun his income. But he doesn't think a year ahead. He doesn't think past teatime!"

Hannah rubbed her hand where the thorn had wounded it. "What did you tell him," she said, "to keep him from sending us away?"

"I begged. I'm ashamed to say it."

"Oh, Mother! *He* should beg. He should beg on his knees."

"Not likely. I'm just grateful I have a talent for numbers."

"You're a wizard."

"You too have a skill he can make use of."

"He'll never admit it."

"No, he won't." She started to turn away, then paused. "Just don't mention that Pickerel business again. Do you understand?"

Hannah said nothing.

"I was able to save us once. I don't know if I can again." With that Mrs. Traxler went back to her writing table; but she was too upset to work. She put the ledger away, picked up her chocolate— now cold—and started downstairs, the cup rattling in its saucer.

Hannah watched, suddenly afraid, as if the last ship had sailed and left her on an uninhabited island. Uninhabited, that is, except for the parrot in the corner, staring at her now with pirate's eyes.

This, then, was the place she would serve out her life sentence. No chance of love, no hope of escape. Even her mother, it seemed, was one of her jailors.

Hannah sank to her knees. "James," she whispered. "James."

He had been her friend, her encourager, her wonderful man, driven away like a leper for the crime of what? Lacking a few guineas? While her uncle . . . !

Suddenly she understood whom those beautiful kid gloves were for. Last week Hannah had watched him with his new client, Lady Breen. The woman, pretty in a florid sort of way, had blushed and laughed as he'd adjusted her clothes for the sitting. He paid particular attention to her ample décolletage, in order, as he said, to show off her charms to greatest advantage. "Your descendants," he'd told her in his smoothest tones, "must be shown what they have to live up to."

Tiny hands. Large bosoms. Yes, Hannah mused, those gloves would fit perfectly.

As she thought of this, and of her own lost chances, her anger mounted to a kind of shaking fury. There was something outrageous about her position. Lavishly talented, she was forced to waste her gifts immortalizing a matron's bosoms, impressive though they might be. Her real task, she knew, was to help raise her uncle, a man of middling abilities, to the rank of artists like Gainsborough or Traxler's great friend, Joshua Reynolds. Was no one to pull this man *down*?

Hannah remembered a recent dinner party during which Sir Joshua had lamented the problems he was having with the poor adhesion of paint. In fact, he'd said ruefully, when one of his assistants was bringing a portrait back to the studio for relining, part of the face had dropped from the canvas onto the street. It had to do, Reynolds thought, with too great an admixture of wax and Venice turpentine in his impasto. The story had struck Hannah forcibly. If so great an artist as Sir Joshua made mistakes, she would have to be extra careful of her own materials.

But what, she thought suddenly, if she were to be *less* careful? In fact, careful to be less careful?

She dismissed the idea as unworthy. There was something fiendish about it. But fiendishness has its devilish attractions, and the thought quickly returned. It was not to be denied.

Her hand darted out for a knife, and she quickly scraped the paint from her palette. She then went to the supply closet, her heart clumping so hard that her hands trembled, and pulled out new pigments, oils, turpentines, and wax.

This would take all her skill. It would take whatever artistic genius she possessed. It would be her greatest achievement— a masterpiece that would grow wrinkles and cracks while its buxom subject was still young. It would wither while she bloomed.

And Hannah would apply these deadly skills to all of Traxler's pictures she could lay a brush to.

She would ruin him!

Chapter Fifteen

Click

DANA LOITERED AT THE BOTTOM OF DANIEL Street, staring out at the gull-skimmed water while evening traffic whined overhead, crossing the bridge out of town. The last sunlight held a weakening warmth as the breeze picked up, lifting the edge of her hair. A perfect day. The only problem was that she was in it—a person so vindictive that she would destroy a man's career, his reputation, and his livelihood. Dana knew she had her faults, but until now she had not suspected that she was capable of vengefulness.

She was not a good person.

Obviously, Traxler was not either. He was considerably worse. Whatever happened, he had it coming in spades. But that it would come from *her*, that was the surprise. She had thought better of herself.

Slowly she made her way home. She'd suffer through dinner, then retreat to her room. That at least was her plan; but as she climbed the wooden stairs to the front door she heard the sound of laughter. Weird laughter. Ben.

Dana came in, and everyone turned to look at her. They were smiling. Had somebody won the lottery?

"Come over," said Ben, turning his wheelchair to face her.

"What?"

"Look at my toes."

His bare foot was propped on the footrest.

"What?"

"Keep looking." Ben frowned with effort, biting his under-lip, and a moment later the big toe moved. Just slightly, but it moved!

"Oh my God!" said Dana.

Ben beamed. "I'm going to beat this thing, big sister."

She went and hugged him hard. "Yes, you will, Ben. This is wonderful!"

"I felt it tingling yesterday. I've had that before, but this time it was stronger. So I've been kind of working on it."

"I've put a call in to the doctor," said Becca. "We're going to build on this. We'll get him into a really good PT program."

Dana nodded. The physical therapy they'd been doing in recent months had to do with moving his legs and arms manually to avoid "contractures" and "spasticity." And of course to keep him from developing sores from staying in one position. They'd just about given up on trying to restore muscular control. Now they would try again. Full-court press.

For the next half hour, Dana was actually happy. No one had thought to make dinner, so everybody was improvising sandwiches, after which there was chocolate cake from the Market Basket—generous hunks for everyone, washed down with milk, or, in the case of Becca, with tiny cups of espresso.

Ben is so good, Dana thought, watching him laugh, his mouth full of cake. *Let this really happen. Let it not be a false alarm.*

Thinking about Ben made her think about herself, and her smile drained. She excused herself and climbed to her room, where she called Chase and asked if he could meet her tonight.

He hadn't heard from her much in the past week and said yes right away.

A half hour later they were strolling along the boardwalk in Hampton Beach. It was nearly dark, and the social scene was in full swing. Reflexively, Dana had brought along her little digital camera, and she took several shots as they waited in line for frozen custard in waffle cones and later listened to a rock band with large speakers blasting out last year's hits. They wandered on, away from the lights.

The big news was Ben's breakthrough, but it was clear Dana had something else on her mind. She put off bringing it up, instead quizzing Chase on how his job was going. His dad had gotten him work as a gofer in the TV station's editing room. It didn't pay much, but it helped replenish his checking account, which had been badly dented by the trip to England.

A muffled boom made them look up. A great chrysanthemum of sparks, the start of the evening's fireworks, opened suddenly over the ocean, followed by a commotion of gold and red and blue, punctuated by loud *rat-a-tats*. Chase and Dana leaned against the railing to watch. Dana framed a couple of shots through the range finder, but didn't bother pressing the shutter. Cliché.

"So," Chase said, turning to her, "how's the old reptile?"

"Do you mean Sprague or the turtle?"

"Either."

"He's got a beard." She watched the twitch of his smile. "Not the turtle," she said.

"I figured."

She was summoning her courage. "I found out some things about me I don't like. Turns out I'm not such an angel."

"Want to tell me about it?"

"It doesn't matter, except . . ." There was no good way to do this. "Except it made me think maybe we shouldn't see each other so much."

In the weak glare of the fireworks his face looked pale.

"I mean . . . ," she began. She faltered.

"Hey!" boomed a big voice behind her. "It's the *artiste*!"

Dana swung around and found herself facing a sunburned Gianna Belkin, her red hair flaring. Beside her sauntered Dave Mastin, the school's debate champ, and another kid Dana didn't recognize. If there was one person she didn't want to see just now . . .

"I heard you were in England," the girl said. "The Queen holding up?"

Dana shrugged. "So what's going on with you?"

"Oh, big things. Jerry here is building me a website." Gianna nodded at the short kid beside her.

"No kidding." Dana looked at Jerry. He was one of those squirrelly kids you never notice.

"It's going to be the go-to place for all the kids in town," Gianna went on. "It'll be huge! You gotta check it out."

"I will."

"Hey, Chase." Gianna gave him a little half wave.

He nodded. "So what's it about? The website."

"Winners and losers. Who's in, who's out. The best of, the worst of."

"All right," he said slowly, trying to visualize.

"Best pizza place, worst pizza place. Who's cool, who's geeky."

"I get it."

"Should be up and running in a couple of weeks."

166

Dana frowned. "Why would you bother? You graduated. You're out of here."

"Oh," said Gianna, "this is way beyond high school. I'll be taking on everybody."

Mastin laid an admiring hand on her shoulder. "She's going to be the mayor of this place one of these days."

"And I suppose," said Dana, looking at Gianna, "you'll be the one deciding who's on the list."

"Me and Dave here, and a few others."

"Scary."

Gianna smirked. "That's the idea. Scare the pants off people. They'll have to check the website every day to know if their life's worth living."

Dana raised her camera and took a quick shot.

"What's that about?" Gianna demanded.

"The future mayor."

"Dave's just kidding around."

"Also," said Dana, "I wanted to catch the look on your face."

"What look?"

"Self-satisfaction, mostly."

"Yeah? You just wait."

Click.

"Cut that out!"

Dana nodded. "I wonder where I'll be on that list of yours."

"Oh, you!" Gianna laughed angrily.

Click!

"Yeah," Dana said, looking to check the image, "that's what I figured."

"Give me the damn camera!" Gianna's large shoulders humped up like a linebacker's as she came toward Dana.

Click!

Gianna's sneer was inches away.

Click!

"I'll break that camera over your head!" she yelled in Dana's face.

Click!

Dana dipped her head to avoid the fist that Gianna was bunching and unbunching. But in the end the blow didn't come. Gianna's eyes hardened. "Just stay out of my way, Landgrave."

"I'd like that."

"I mean it." She turned and headed off with her entourage down the boardwalk toward the lights and rides. Dana and Chase watched in silence.

Chase raised an eyebrow. "Have you ever thought of a career in combat photography?"

Dana took a deep breath, then another, to calm herself.

"I don't think I've ever seen you like that," he said.

"You didn't know I could be a witch?"

"I wouldn't call you—"

"Didn't know I could hurt people?"

They started walking. They didn't talk for a long time.

"She sure has it in for you," Chase said at last.

"Who can blame her?"

Chase shot her a puzzled look. "Wait. She takes credit for your work, then accuses you of something you didn't do, and you can't *blame* her?"

"Not really. She's taken credit for my work for hundreds of years. It's second nature."

He looked as though he hadn't heard her right. "You know who she *was*?"

"Yes, and I know what I did to her. She has a perfect right to hate me."

Chase stared out at the dim beach and the black water beyond. "Does this have anything to do . . ." He was having trouble finishing the sentence. "With what you were saying before?"

She nodded. "I don't know who I am anymore, and I'm afraid to find out."

"Well, *I* know who you are."

"I don't think so."

"Hold on." He laid a hand on her forearm. "I do know you. I've known you for years. There's nothing you need to be afraid of."

"You're wrong! If you knew what I did to Gianna—she wasn't Gianna then, she was a painter named Gavin Traxler. I ruined her life—*his* life. God knows what else I've done!"

"I'll take my chances."

Dana found herself close to tears. "You shouldn't. You don't know!"

"I know enough."

"No, you don't!" She was frantic to make him understand. "You used to tell me there's always a way," she cried, "but there *isn't*, James, there *isn't*!"

Chase was silent. He looked at her strangely. "What did you call me?"

"What do you mean?"

"Just now. You called me James."

She lifted a hand to her mouth. "Oh, no," she moaned.

"Who is James?"

"James Pickerel. He was . . ." She shook her head and started away from him at a fast walk. She broke into a run.

Chapter Sixteen

The Block

DANA TRIED TO BE ENCOURAGING DURING BEN'S first PT session, but she wasn't a bit of help. She winced at her brother's groans and frowned to see his gritted teeth and trembling arms.

The physical therapist was a short, pleasant-faced woman with a shiny black braid, olive skin, and large brown eyes. Her name tag said RENATA, and her Spanish accent was so strong it made Dana smile.

Renata certainly knew what she was doing. She had brought her portable equipment to the house and was putting Ben through a series of resistance exercises up in his room. One of them involved a two-foot-long rubber band that he held in his hands and looped around his feet. The idea was to pull on it with his arms while pushing with his feet. But the feet didn't want to cooperate.

Dana stood in the doorway.

"Hey." It was a quiet voice behind her. Chase. "How's he doing?"

Her heart gave a little jump. "How'd you get in?"

"The front door was open."

"Well," she said, nodding at Ben, "at least he's not giving up."

"Gutsy kid."

She gave him a little smile and looked down. She didn't talk about it, but she was glad Chase had ignored her halfhearted attempt to break up with him. She didn't know what she would have done if he had taken her at her word.

"Let's take him out for an ice cream afterward," he said.

"I'm supposed to see Sprague."

He nodded. "Well, maybe I can take Ben and we can meet you later."

She reached impulsively and touched his cheek with the back of her still-bandaged hand. "How come you're so nice?"

He leaned forward and gave her a brief kiss. They looked at each other frankly.

"Why do you bother?" she said.

"It's something to do."

The therapist came over to them.

"Is he ready?" Dana said.

"Jes." She gave a glance back. "I don't think he like me so much today."

Dana looked at her brother. He was still breathing hard.

"He not going to like me even more tomorrow."

"I know he's determined to do this," Dana said.

The woman nodded. "He better be."

A few minutes later Dana was leading the way through town while Chase tried to make light conversation. She was glad he was pushing the wheelchair. It would have been hard for Dana. Her hand hadn't been getting better, and it hurt her to grip anything.

Ben wasn't talking. It had been a discouraging morning, harder than he'd bargained for, with minimal results. He was able to move the toes on his right foot, and of course he had some use of his arms, but that was about it.

"Hey," said Dana, "let's head down Mechanic Street and see if Dad's there."

Ben shrugged.

It was a sharply focused morning, warm verging on hot, and she could see the glint of sweat on her father's bare shoulders from half a block away. He looked up and plunged his shovel into a mound of yellow dirt.

Dana waved.

"Must be nice," he said, "having nothing to do. Want to give me a hand?"

Dana gave him a mercy laugh. "You can't afford me," she said, as Chase pulled the wheelchair up to the chain-link fence.

"What are you working on?" Chase said. The site had widened and deepened since he'd seen it last.

"Oh," Tom said, pulling off his hard hat to wipe his forehead, "we've got to replace the stone box. It's a shame. It's been here since the seventeen hundreds. A beautiful thing."

Ben muttered, "A beautiful sewer."

His dad looked at him. "How did it go this morning?"

Ben shrugged.

Tom glanced at Dana, who gave him a "don't ask" look. "Ben," he said, "don't get discouraged. It's just the first day."

"Okay." He was turning his chair away.

"No, I mean it. You're going to make it. You're a beautiful kid."

Ben looked back at his father. "You think sewers are beautiful."

It was dim in Sprague's office. The air-conditioning was on the blink, so the doctor had drawn the curtains to cut down on the sunlight. His little desk lamp glowed feebly.

They were talking about the dream she'd had the night

before. "So, what do *you* think it means?" he said, loosening his blue and silver tie and undoing the top button of his shirt.

"Guilt, obviously."

"Wouldn't be surprised. But what do you have to be guilty about?"

"Probably what I did to those paintings."

Sprague ran his finger around the inside of his collar. "That was two hundred years ago."

"But I only learned about it the other day."

"Any idea why your mom would be in the dream? I mean, it was Traxler who was the bad guy, no?"

"Yeah."

"Yet it was your mother that you, shall we say, dismembered?"

Dana looked up sharply. "I didn't do anything! It just happened."

It had been a terrible dream. She'd heard her mother calling from upstairs and found her in the bathroom putting on makeup. The more she put on, the more cracks began appearing on her cheeks and forehead. As Dana watched, horrified, a small piece of her mother's chin broke off and fell into the sink. Becca's face was coming apart.

Dana woke up strangled with fear.

"It didn't 'just happen,'" Sprague replied. "It was your dream."

"I can't help that!"

"If you can't, who can?"

She rounded on him. "Are you saying I want to hurt my mother?"

"Do you?"

Dana got up and walked behind her chair. "That's crazy."

"Okay." He waited a beat. "Is that why you're getting up to leave?"

"I'm *not* getting up to leave," she said with some heat. "I'm just getting up."

"And putting a chair between us."

"Why would I hate my mother?"

"Which mother are we talking about?"

She circled the chair but did not sit. "What do you mean, 'which mother'?" She felt a droplet of sweat work its way down from her armpit under her shirt.

"There were two."

Dana stopped walking. She was in front of the aquarium. *He's right. There were two. Like one wasn't bad enough.*

"From what you tell me," Sprague went on in his insufferably calm voice, "your mother in your past life—let's call her Mom Number One—ordered you to give up the man you loved. You could say she ruined your life."

Dana stared at the turtle, which stared back at her. Prudence Traxler had sided with Gavin. What kind of mother would do that? "But why," Dana stammered. "I mean, my dream wasn't about her. It was about my mom in this lifetime."

"Aren't they the same?"

"I never said that!"

"No, but look at you. I just ask you a question and you're on the verge of bolting out the door."

"I am not!"

"Glad to hear it."

Dana glared at him. Then she came around and plunked herself into the chair. "Man, it's hot in here!"

He didn't reply.

"When are they going to fix that air conditioner?"

Sprague was silent.

"So, okay," she said, "what if they are the same?"

"It could explain a few things."

"Like why Mom and I don't get along?"

He shrugged.

"Or why she's mad that I don't give a damn about math?"

"It may go deeper than math."

"Like what?"

"There must have been consequences, don't you think," Sprague mused, "when those paintings started falling apart?"

Dana frowned. She wished she could remember.

"I mean, not only for Traxler himself, but for you and your mother."

A realization began to take form. "You mean," Dana said, "he wasn't the only one I ruined."

He raised his heavy brows, waiting for her.

"When he went down, we *all* went down," she said quietly. It wasn't a question. It wasn't a memory. It was an inevitable fact. "So," she said, "it seems I'm an even crappier person than I thought."

"I'm not saying that."

"You sure know how to make a girl feel good."

"Not my job."

"Good thing."

"So what are we going to do about it?" His eyes widened.

"*Do* about it? Two hundred years later?"

"Better late than never."

"That's crazy. Mom has no memory of this."

"No conscious memory, no." He ran his finger around the inside of his collar again.

"Are you saying I should tell her?"

"I'm not saying that."

"Well?"

"She wouldn't believe you, anyway. Our sessions are not about her. They're about getting you straight with yourself."

Dana looked down at her hands.

"You came to me," he said, leaning forward on his elbows, "with certain symptoms you wanted help with. Insomnia. Nightmares. Claustrophobia."

"So?"

"And an *unbelievable* amount of guilt. About what we don't know for sure. This business with Traxler and your mother is part of it. But I doubt it's the whole thing."

"Seems like plenty to me."

"Yes, it is. And we need to look at that. But there's that other lifetime, the one you have been blocking out, except that it keeps leaking into your mind through your dreams."

"Yes," Dana murmured, "the dreams."

"You want to get rid of the nightmares, but you're afraid to face what's causing them."

She was used to his being direct, but this was brutal. She gave him a desperate look. "What *is* causing them?"

"Ah," he said, leaning back in his chair and making a cage of his fingers. "For that we have to go back—what was the year, 1580-something?"

"But I can't! We've tried! It's blocked out!"

"Who's blocking it out?"

"Who?"

"Yes. Who is blocking it out, Miss Landgrave?"

"I suppose I am."

"Bravo. And who can unblock it?"

She looked at him with a sinking heart. "I don't know how!"

"How?" Sprague's eyes glittered. "I will tell you how. You have to be *willing*, that's how!"

"I *am* willing. I'm here, aren't I? Ow!" She had been gesturing and hit her bandaged hand against the back of the chair.

Sprague's face softened slightly. "Yes, you're here, and you were willing to go to England. You allowed yourself to be guided to that marvelous locket. You followed its lead to the castle. You discovered the boy behind the altar. When you think about it, you really have been very brave."

She looked at him with surprise. She hadn't thought of her trip to England that way.

"But now," he said, "at the last moment, when you are at the edge of the diving board, your nerve has failed you."

"I'm doing my best."

"Jump!" he cried. "You must jump, Miss Landgrave!"

"I can't!"

"You're the only one who can!" A line of perspiration gleamed on his forehead. She stared at him, unnerved by his intensity. It was as if this had to do with him personally and she were just his instrument, a probe he was sending back in time. But it excited her. He was right. She *had* been holding back.

"I'll do it."

"Will you? *Will* you?"

She could feel her heart beating.

That afternoon they tried and failed. Then they tried and failed again. She would go under, but something kept her from regressing.

"Maybe we're trying too hard," she said.

"Maybe you're still resisting."

He was right. She was. She didn't know why.

"Don't worry, my dear," he said finally. He had never called her "dear" before. "We'll get there."

"I'm hopeless."

"You are a prodigy. But even prodigies have to practice. We'll try again next time."

"You aren't giving up on me?"

Sprague lowered his lids to halfway. He shook his jowls just a fraction. "Never," he said.

Chapter Seventeen

The Priest's Hide

IT WAS STILL DARK AS DANA PEDALED HER OLD Schwinn to Pierce Island. She was getting used to predawn excursions when even the cats were sleeping. Dana had two cameras around her neck, the nifty little digital and her dad's heavy Nikon. She liked to have both, in case.

Stopping on the east side of the island, she set the bike on its kickstand and sat in the grass, looking back at the town she'd spent her life in. Only a few lights trembled in the water. She zipped her windbreaker. Nearly five, she saw, checking her watch. Except for the dew and the breeze she could have been sitting in a theater waiting for the curtain to go up.

And then it did go up. Nothing hurried, night lifted grandly away and the dawn came on, gilding the steeples and rooftops. What picturesque shots she could take, if she were interested in the picturesque. But she'd learned to leave that to the makers of postcards. She was after different game.

She couldn't have said what it was, exactly, but she always knew when she found it. Her photography teacher had remarked on her "unusual eye." Dana wasn't sure it was a compliment. Unusual, odd, weird. She'd heard all these adjectives applied to her in the last few years, mostly by other kids, and she felt hurt every time. But somehow, after England, the opinions of others

179

didn't matter so much. Or maybe she was too sleep-deprived to care.

She'd gotten two hours last night. Was Sprague right? Was she afraid to sleep? She'd told him she was willing to confront the past, but part of her had no intention of letting the past back into her mind. Hannah Traxler's life was different. Upsetting as it was, it was allowable. But not the lifetime before that.

She'd read about repressed memories in psych class, but until now it was just a unit to study for a test. She'd never thought it could happen to her. Dana had a double problem. Not only had she repressed her past, but she was now in a different body. Her twenty-first-century brain cells would hold no traces of her sixteenth-century life. *No wonder people forget their past lives*, she mused, focusing the Nikon on a distant light.

That was Miss Edwards's house, she realized. What was she doing up so early?

No, to remember her past, she'd somehow have to leapfrog into a nonphysical state, what people called the spirit, or soul. She had no idea what those words meant.

She did know some things. For one thing, her visions were real. If the body behind the altar proved nothing else, it proved that. Which meant the soul was real, a permanent self that carried over from life to life. Or that's how it seemed this morning, sitting in dew-soaked jeans, changing the Nikon's 50-millimeter lens for the telephoto.

But how do you access that self?

Be willing, Sprague had said. *Get out of the way. Jump.*

Miss Edwards, now that Dana had magnified her through the telephoto, was padding around her kitchen in an old blue robe. The window was a rectangle of yellow set in a black cutout of a house against a blueing sky. Dana pressed the shutter. Then pressed it again when she saw a gray and black cat jump up on the counter.

Wait. For this she should be using the digital camera. She'd want to manipulate the image later on the computer.

She zoomed in. Old Miss Edwards had seized the cat and lifted it up before her, then brought it close till they were nose to nose.

Click.

The following Tuesday Dana woke at ten, having dropped off to sleep around six in the morning. Renata would be coming any minute, she realized, for Ben's PT session. She swung her legs out of bed and pulled on her jeans, then went in to see if Ben was getting ready.

To her surprise, she found his room dark. He was still asleep, his breath rumbling in his throat. "Hey, kid. Up and at 'em."

Ben groaned but didn't really wake up.

"Come on, Benny."

"I know." Ben's eyes opened a slit, then quickly closed, as if someone were shining a light in his face. His body was shivering under the covers, and his face looked flushed.

"Hey, Ben, don't poop out. You've made a lot of progress this week."

"I'm not feeling that good."

Dana stepped over and took a better look at him. She felt his forehead. "You're hot!"

He didn't answer. His eyes were closed.

Dana ran for her mother.

Mrs. Landgrave took Ben's temperature—102 degrees—and called the doctor. He wasn't in, so she left a message. As long as Ben was on a catheter, fevers had to be taken seriously. Infections were common and could lead, in the worst scenario, to life-threatening septicemia.

An hour later, when the doctor called back, Ben's temperature had risen to 103. He immediately ordered Ben into the hospital. Dana went along in the van and stayed at Ben's side as he was transferred to a gurney and hurried off down the hall.

Once her brother was settled in, there wasn't anything for her to do but stay out of the way of nurses.

"Go on, dear," said Mrs. Landgrave.

"I can cancel my appointment with Sprague."

"No need. I'll call if anything comes up. Do you have your cell?"

Her mother was right. It was senseless to hang around. Dana went outside and tilted her head, eyes closed, into the sunlight, then started for the center of town. She regretted not taking her bike. It was quite a trek on foot, and by the time she'd reached Islington Street her T-shirt was sticking to her back.

The road curved upward and the white steeple of North Church hove into view. She held the sleeve of her T-shirt and wiped the sweat from her eyes and looked around. The street was nearly deserted, just a man up ahead stumping along in the same direction. He looked familiarly odd, Dana thought. The oddest part, now that she really looked, was his clothing, a theater costume for some old-time play, complete with tight-fitting doublet and—were those leggings? Boy, they had to be hot today! She was hot enough in her cut-offs.

And the way he walked, going easy on the left leg, coming down hard on the right. Dana sped up. She had to get a look at his face.

But as she sped up, so did he. He glanced behind him as he went and she caught a glimpse of an intense, bearded face with a mark on his forehead, a scar or something. Her eyes widened. She thought she knew him, but he wasn't from here—certainly not one of her teachers, or a friend's parent.

The man reached the church, pulled open the door, and darted inside. He was running away! Dana followed at a trot. *Bertrand*. The name came to her. *Paul Bertrand, the tapestry maker*. She yanked open the door and ran in. "Mr. Bertrand!" she called out, her voice echoing in the empty building. "Are you here?"

"May I help you?" said a quiet voice behind her.

With a gasp she swung around, to find herself looking into the mild, open face of Martin Scholes, the minister.

"Did you," she began, finding her voice, "did you see someone come in here just now?"

Even before Scholes replied she knew the answer. He had seen no one. The past was leaking into her life. This time it wasn't in a dream. It was in broad daylight.

"Let's think of this as a good sign," said Dr. Sprague, when he had her in the recliner, ready for the induction.

"A good sign? It's a sign I'm totally crackers."

"Or that you're finally ready. Do you have the locket with you?"

Dana pulled it out from under her shirt and clicked it open. The boy gave her a straight look. It seemed *he* was ready.

"Okay," said the doctor. "Now I want you to relax completely. Take a deep breath and let it out slowly. Good. Again."

Dana's eyes drifted closed.

"That's it. All right, let's begin."

It wasn't easy putting her under. She was still resisting. But

183

his voice, soft, low, reassuring, finally prevailed. As she descended the long curving staircase she let go, one by one, of her fears.

"I want you to look at the locket now," Sprague murmured. "Do you recognize the boy?"

She nodded.

"Who is he?"

"William."

"Do you see him now?"

Dana frowned.

"Miss Landgrave? Do you see him?"

"He's not here."

"Where are you?"

"We're climbing."

"We? You're not alone?"

"They're ahead of me. We're climbing the stairs."

Sprague paused, uncertain.

"Don't go in there!" Dana cried out suddenly.

"Where are you?"

Dana's eyes, still closed, winced tight. She began murmuring under her breath.

"What was that? What are you saying?"

"Stay quiet. Don't make a sound. Don't make a sound!"

"Who?"

She didn't reply. She was breathing quickly through her mouth.

"Dana, what's happening?"

She answered the doctor's questions haltingly, in torn phrases, sometimes almost inaudibly, to avoid being overheard. The men in front of her, a half dozen, most of them soldiers, had burst into the round stone room, swords drawn. Except for a table and several chairs, the place was empty.

"Thank God," Dana breathed.

"Thank God *what*? What's going on?"

Dana didn't immediately answer. Eventually, as the doctor kept prodding, she described some of what she saw.

The man in front of her, clearly the leader, strode into the room and held up his hand for silence. He was not facing Dana, but his stiff shoulders and the forward stoop of his head told her he was in a dangerous mood. With his black cape and tonsured bald spot he looked like a condor sensing prey.

Don't make a sound. Don't breathe.

Flames fluttered in the wall sconces, casting a glow on the figured rug. The leader took a torch and strode about the room, peering into corners. "The old man was wrong," he muttered. "No matter. We'll find them." He handed the torch to a soldier and started for the stairs.

Suddenly he stopped.

It was almost nothing. A little mewing sound, nothing more. The man in the dark cloak turned. His hand was raised for silence.

For long seconds there was nothing. Then it came again, muffled and faint, but unmistakable.

The man's head bent farther forward as he stepped quietly around the room. He paused by the wooden table and gestured to one of the soldiers to remove it. Dana's heart beat wildly as the man in the cape placed the toe of his boot on the narrow rug and slowly pulled it aside, revealing a trapdoor barely two feet square.

He nodded at another soldier, who strode over and yanked it open. A muffled scream came from below, and a thumping of colliding bodies.

The man nodded to the soldier with the torch. The light shone into the hole.

He turned to his men. "Bring them out," he said.

One of the soldiers wedged himself through the narrow opening and, finding no ladder, dropped into the darkness. A second soldier followed.

"Nooo!" A woman wailed.

A man cursed. There was a scuffle. A child was crying. A moment later the top of a ladder poked up through the hole, and the head of a priest emerged, his eyes wide with fear. A soldier yanked him up by his armpits. Next came Lord Breen himself, master of Breen Hall, his curling locks glinting in the candlelight. He was in his nightclothes, as was his wife, who came after. Finally, a young girl emerged, not more than seven years old, shielding her eyes. The two soldiers brought up the rear.

"Malveaux!" Breen whispered incredulously. "Not you!"

The man in the cape turned toward Breen, and Dana saw his face in profile against the torchlight, his thin neck, the long Frankish nose, the wisp of a beard, the smoldering stare. "Did you think I was one of you?" he said in a cold voice.

"You were my councillor! I trusted you!"

"I have no time for this," Malveaux said sharply. "Where is he?"

Breen seemed not to understand.

"The brat," snapped the other. "Where is he?"

"Who do you mean? What is this about?"

"About? It's about heresy! Deviltry! Papacy! Where have you hidden him?"

"Who? I don't understand!"

"Your son!"

Breen blanched. His cheek actually trembled. "He's not here."

"I didn't ask where he is *not!*"

"In France. He's in France."

"You lie! He was seen this morning by the servants."

"Leave him alone, for God's sake! You have me, John. Isn't that enough?"

"The child of a serpent is as dangerous as the father."

"Serpent? What has come over you?"

Lady Breen took a half step forward, her daughter clinging to her nightdress. "Leave my son alone!"

"If you cared for your son, madam, you would have renounced your Catholic heresies, as your queen commanded."

The woman was pitiable in her tears, her shoulders slumping. "Take me!" she cried. "Take me instead!"

In one swift motion, Malveaux unsheathed his sword and slashed the woman's neck, blood spattering her amazed face and drenching her bodice as her knees buckled. She was dead before her body struck the floor.

Breen stared. His little daughter, face white with horror, stood open-mouthed.

"As you wish, madam," Malveaux said simply, sheathing the sword. He turned to Breen. "Now, sir. Your son."

"What?" Breen seemed unable to hear or speak.

"Or would you prefer to see your daughter die first?"

A low, unearthly wail escaped the child's throat. Dana backed away, out of the room. "Get me out of here," she whispered.

"What was that?" said Sprague.

"Get me *out* of here!" Dana was in the stone corridor, still backing away, her hand trailing along the wall, when Sprague recalled her to the present.

Chapter Eighteen

Fun at the Mall

AFTER THE FIRST DAY, BEN WAS MOVED INTO A semiprivate room. Two days later the doctors decided the infection was under control, and he could go home. He remained on antibiotics, though, and was confined to bed.

Dana pulled up the wooden rocker and sat on its front edge, to keep it from creaking. "How're you doing?"

He looked at her sleepily. "Kind of mealy."

"You'll be all right." She was telling herself that as much as she was telling him.

He nodded.

"You got a friend visiting you," she said.

"Yeah?"

Dana motioned to a tall sixth grader who was standing uncomfortably in the doorway, wedging his fist into a first-baseman's glove.

"Hey," he said, coming in.

"Hey, Eric," said Ben, smiling.

They didn't know exactly what to say next. Dana got to her feet. "I'll be downstairs, guys."

"So," she heard Ben say.

"So."

"How's the baseball?"

"Okay, I guess. Make any more coats of arms?"

Dana looked back from the doorway and saw Ben shake his head.

"You were going to change out the falcon for a seagull or something."

"Yeah."

Eric socked his mitt.

Dana headed to the kitchen, where she found her mom and dad. Mrs. Landgrave was making a lot of noise with her espresso machine. "Want some?" she said.

"Sure." Dana slid onto a chair.

"Nice that Eric came," said Dana's dad, tilting back.

"About time," said Becca under her breath.

"That's all right," Tom soothed, glancing at the stairs. "At least he came."

Becca brought over two tiny cups and went back to make a cappuccino for Dana. "Say," she said, looking at her, "don't you have an appointment?"

"I called him."

"Wait a minute. I thought you liked this doctor."

Dana shrugged. "I thought I should stick around. With Ben and all."

"What do you mean? It's Saturday. I'm here. Your father's here."

"Ben might need me."

"That's ridic—" Mrs. Landgrave looked up and saw Eric Plante at the top of the stairs.

He slowly descended, holding his mitt against his chest. "Ben fell asleep," he said. He looked a little bewildered. "Is he going to be okay?"

"Of course." Becca spoke in her Voice That Cannot Be Denied.

189

"He's a lot better," Tom supplemented. "Should've seen him a few days ago."

Eric grunted.

"He's missed you," Tom said.

The boy glanced up the staircase.

"He doesn't talk about it much, but he has."

"Maybe," Eric said, "I could come back again?"

"That would be great. Sooner the better."

"Well," he said, his hand on the screen door. He let himself out.

The kitchen was quiet. Three people sat sipping their coffee, bound together by what they knew and didn't need to say.

The next Tuesday, when Dana called again to cancel, Sprague didn't accept her excuse. Ben had continued to improve and was even spending time with his coin collection. Dana could certainly get away for an hour.

"Well, actually," she said slowly, "I don't think I really need it anymore."

On his end of the phone, Sprague was silent.

"I mean," she said, rubbing her left hand with her right, "I'm sleeping a little better these days, and things are going pretty well."

"Miss Landgrave," Sprague resonated, "it's all right to be afraid."

"Afraid?" Her hand, now that she thought of it, was throbbing.

"I think you should come in again," Sprague went on. "If you want to quit, fine, your choice. But we need to clear up a few last things."

It wasn't easy to say no to him, his personality was so strong.

But then, she had a personality too. "I'm not sure I want to clear up a few last things."

"Well, I want it. Do it for me."

He was making it hard. She sighed. "What time?" she said.

August was starting hot, and Sprague's air-conditioning was still on the blink. When Dana arrived he suggested they pass through into the Athenaeum, which was exactly next door—and cooler.

Dana stood up, ready to go outside and around to the street entrance, but Sprague said there was another way. He led her past the receptionist and down a corridor to a locked door, which he opened with a key. To Dana's surprise, she found herself on the Athenaeum's second floor, in a cluttered back room not used by the members. The general public seldom got to use this building. It was a private, members-only library, a century old, housed in an elegant old building with lofty floor-to-ceiling bookcases, marble busts, and sweeping cornices.

"Morning, Bettina," said Sprague.

A bright-eyed eighty-year-old looked up from the card catalog. "Morton! You startled me."

"This is Dana Landgrave. I'm showing her around."

"Your first visit, Miss Landgrave?"

"Yes."

"We don't see many young people."

Dana smiled and continued on. "They just let you come in here?" she whispered as Sprague led her into the main rooms.

"I'm on the board. Since my office is next door, they let me come and go."

"It's fantastic," she said, taking in the high ceilings and book-crammed walls. Did anyone, she wondered, ever dust the top shelves?

"Let's go up to the balcony," he said, heading for the staircase. "There are a couple of easy chairs."

Dana followed dutifully, and soon they had settled themselves in flowered chairs by the front window, raising a faint cloud of dust motes. Far below them, Market Square clattered with outdoor cafés and honked with noontime traffic, but they were sealed off from it.

"So why do you want to quit?" Sprague said, getting right to it.

She shrugged. "I just don't think I need to do this anymore."

"Your problems are handled."

She rubbed her hand gently. "I think I can take it from here."

"How's your hand?"

She quickly took her other hand away. "Better."

"How are you sleeping?"

"Better."

"I see. Better and better."

"Look. You're not going to make me go back there," she said.

"I'm not making you do anything."

"Yeah, right."

"It just seems odd." He looked out across the square, choosing his words. "You manage to break the lock of a treasure chest," he said, "something you've been trying to do for months, and then you decide, no, you're not going to lift the lid."

"We did lift the lid. We lifted the lid last time. I don't need to see any more."

"You don't? Do you know who you were in that little scene?"

"Me?"

"Yes. You were watching it. You went into the room. But who *were* you?"

"I don't know. I don't care."

"Don't you?" He leaned forward, his eyes intense. "Everything depends on it."

"You just want to get me back there."

He looked around to be sure they were alone. He spoke in a low voice. "That's right, I do. I want to understand. Don't you want to understand?"

"I just want to live a normal life!"

"But you're *not* normal!" he shouted in a whisper.

"Thanks a lot."

"You're exceptional. You have an exceptional gift."

"I don't want it!"

"How long," Sprague pursued without mercy, "do you want to keep dreaming about that boy behind the altar? I think you need to know who you were in order to know who you *are*."

"What if . . ." She fumbled her words. "What if I'm afraid to find out?"

"I wouldn't blame you." He folded his hands in his lap. "Have you any idea who that man was? The man with the sword?"

Dana flinched, remembering.

"Malveaux, you called him. John Malveaux. I looked him up."

"And?"

"Quite a character. One of Calvin's agents in England. Do you know who Calvin was?"

"Not really."

"Have you heard of Calvinism?"

"Sort of."

"Do they teach you *anything* in that school of yours?"

"We're doing the Declaration of Independence."

"Well, our boy came a couple of centuries before that. He got everybody stirred up, even in a backwater country like England. He was especially tough on Roman Catholics."

"Yeah?"

"I'm just saying Catholics didn't have it easy. For a while they couldn't hold office. Just being a Catholic became a crime. Sometimes punishable by death."

"And the Breens were . . . ?"

"Catholic, yes. You saw the altar."

"I did see the altar."

"They were also on the wrong side of the political fence. They'd aligned themselves with Mary, Queen of Scots, against Queen Elizabeth. It was their death warrant."

He wasn't going to convince her. She didn't care what he said.

"And somewhere in the midst of all this history and blood and tragedy we find—who? Dana Landgrave, the happy-go-lucky teenager who just wants to be *normal*."

"What's wrong with that?" she said hotly.

He sat back in his chair, dust motes swirling. His jaw muscles were working. "Nothing at all. Go ahead. Live well."

"I will, thanks." She stood up.

He watched her stride along the balcony to the stairs. "Have fun at the mall!" he called after her. There was a sharpness in his voice that she had never heard before.

She didn't stop.

Dana stood watching the gulls swerve. The slap of water on barnacled rocks and the moan of traffic on the bridge above her made a mournful soundtrack for her thoughts. The breeze was warm, crisping the wavelets into points. She should have been happy. She had stood up to Sprague and refused the torment of ancient memories. She was free. Why didn't she feel free?

Dana turned and started up the hill. The street was steep and her mind flashed on the stone stairs of the castle and the soldiers going up ahead of her.

Why hadn't they noticed her? Was she someone of no consequence to them? *Was she one of them?* The thought made her stop right there in the street. A woman pushing a carriage almost bumped into her.

No, Dana thought. *That couldn't be.* She remembered the dread she'd felt thinking Malveaux might discover the trap door and the family cowering below.

So why did I do nothing to save them?

She walked on, past the post office and through Market Square, oblivious to those around her. Sprague was right. It did matter who she'd been. Everything depended on it.

"Miss Traxler! I say!"

Dana swung around. Across the square by the news kiosk an unusually dressed man was waving at her.

"Halsey!" she called back, smiling. She was always glad to see her uncle's butler, although she almost never encountered him in the street. As he started toward her, watching out for carriages and horses, she noticed how well he looked, his stride agile, his body forward-sloping as if hurrying to bring her something, or take something off her hands. Though old enough to be her father, he looked smart in his new periwig, green waistcoat, and leggings. *The London air must agree with him,* she thought vaguely.

Halsey came within a few feet of her and inclined his head in a bow. "Forgive me," he said, "but I couldn't help observing that you were unescorted."

"I hardly think . . ."

"Please, allow me," he said, inclining his head again.

"Oh, very well," she said lightly. "I was just . . ." She paused. "I was just going . . ."

The man called Halsey was nowhere to be seen.

"Going where, Button?"

Startled to her senses, Dana looked into Tom Landgrave's eyes. "Dad! What are you doing here?"

Landgrave took off his cap and wiped his forehead. "Taking a lunch break. But I just told you that."

"You did?"

"Are you okay?" His sunburnt face crinkled in a concerned smile. "You were talking kind of funny."

Dana's hand went to her mouth. "What did I say?"

"You called me some name. Hall?"

She shook her head in disbelief. "You must think I'm totally nuts."

"Never thought that in my life. Want to join me for lunch? Thought I'd hit the Friendly Toast."

They walked together to the restaurant and found a booth.

"I don't know what happened," she said. "I just saw this person. He was dressed in this weird old way they used to dress, and I thought, I mean he looked like . . ."

"Like what?"

"He reminded me of you."

Landgrave tapped his lips with his finger. "Was he an okay guy, this man you saw?"

"I *loved* old Halsey, Dad. He was . . ." She paused, remembering. "He was loyal to me when other people weren't."

"Well, that's good, then."

"Yeah. It's very good."

Halsey. She smiled. She hadn't thought of him in, well, centuries.

The waitress came and Tom ordered his usual cheeseburger and Coke. Dana was too confused to think and ordered the same. It amazed her that her father never pushed for more information. He seemed to accept her visions as true, or true for her. He didn't even ask if she thought he'd been Halsey in his past life. That was somehow not his business.

His business was being her father, and Ben's. How different he was from the pushy, sarcastic Sprague, who was never satisfied and had to know everything, no matter the cost.

They had a good, easy talk, first about her, then about Ben's slow progress.

"His friend Eric came back again, you know," her father said.

Dana lit up. "That's great. Just what he needs."

"Seems they're working on some project."

"The coat of arms?"

"Couldn't tell you. My kids are way beyond me."

"Oh, right."

"Good thing I don't mind."

Dana grabbed an oversize fry as they got up to pay. "Dad," she said when they were out on the street again, "I don't know what to do about Dr. Sprague. We're getting into some pretty weird stuff."

"Weird how?"

"Like seeing you just before and thinking you were Halsey."

Landgrave nodded, watching the sidewalk.

"I mean Halsey's a lovely man and all," she continued, "but he's dead. Been dead a while."

197

"I see what you mean."

"Sprague says the past is a door that swings both ways." She looked over at him. "Things from the past are starting to follow me back here."

Tom met his daughter's look briefly. "And that scares you."

"It scares the heck out of me."

"What are you going to do?"

They were starting down the hill to the construction area. "I was hoping you would tell me," she said.

"I think if anyone knows the answer, you do."

"I don't know the answer to anything."

"Maybe," he said slowly, pausing by the entrance to the site, "you know the answer but you just don't like it."

He went through the gate and secured it with a twisted wire. "See you at dinner?"

She hadn't gone far up the street when she turned suddenly. "Dad!" she called. A truck roared by and he didn't hear her.

What was she afraid of? The street was nearly deserted, the afternoon sun blazing, yet she glanced between buildings and up at sun-blinded windows as if someone were watching. Someone who meant her harm.

That night Ben was well enough to prop himself up in bed and play checkers. Actually, he was well enough to play chess, but Dana wasn't any good at chess and they'd agreed to avoid humiliating her. At checkers she had a fighting chance, which didn't mean she was winning. Ben gave her such a sly look when one of his men was kinged that she told him to hold on and ran to get her camera.

"God, Dana! Don't."

"Come on. You had such a neat look."

"Well, now I don't."

She sat in the rocker and focused the Nikon. "Look the way you looked when your guy was getting kinged."

"How do I know how I looked?"

"Like you were getting away with something."

"Dana, are you going to play or not?"

"All right." She put down the camera and went back to losing for a while. "Did Eric come over today?"

Ben was concentrating. "Yeah," he said.

"Work on the coat of arms?"

"We finished that."

Dana moved one of her remaining checkers across the center into imminent danger. "So what bird did you decide on finally for the design?"

Ben double-jumped her. "Purple finch."

"Really?"

"Well, he's our state bird. And he's a spunky little guy."

"Like you?"

He shrugged.

She raised her camera. "Give me a spunky little guy look."

He yawned instead and looked up from the board. "I think I'm going to have to pack it in."

Dana watched him through the range finder.

"I didn't sleep so good," he said. "I had a nightmare or something."

"Oh?"

His eyes took on a distant look. She snapped the shutter. "Kind of spooked me."

"So, what was it about?" She wanted to keep him talking so that she could get a good shot.

"I don't know."

She waited.

"It was like I was trapped or something."

"Trapped?"

"Yeah. It was in a dark place, behind something heavy."

A fleeting look caught her attention and she clicked the shutter again, just too late. "Tell me more."

"I don't remember. Oh," he said.

The look on his face just then startled her and she forgot to press the shutter.

"Now I remember. My head was hurting. Like the worst headache I ever had."

Dana continued watching him through the camera, but she had forgotten she was taking his picture. She'd recognized the look in his eyes. It came and went, but when it was there, Ben was someone else.

He leaned back on his pillow and closed his eyes.

"Ben," she whispered.

"What?" he murmured, his eyes closed.

"Look at me."

He opened his eyes just a bit. She lowered the camera.

"Are you okay?" he said.

She stood up. "Yeah. Get some rest." She set the checkerboard on the chair and flipped off the light.

"Night," he said, but she forgot to answer. She stood in the hall outside his room, trying to catch her breath. The images were coming too fast. She put a hand on her chest. The look she had seen in his eyes was like a shot in the heart.

It's him. He's the boy behind the altar. And all this time I thought . . .

Dana's throat was dry. She was panting, panicked.

Then who was I?

The answer hit her so hard her legs buckled and she slid down the wall till she was sitting on her heels.

She was the man on the other side of the altar!

"Paul Bertrand," she whispered.

She was the one who'd pushed the altarpiece against the wall, despite the boy's pleading sobs.

She was the murderer!

IV
The Hole

Chapter Nineteen

The Den

"CHASE CALLED AGAIN." BECCA LANDGRAVE'S VOICE sailed up the dark stairway to Dana's room.

"Mom, please! I told you I can't talk to him."

"He's not giving up."

"Mom, no!"

Even from downstairs her mother's sigh was audible. "Whatever you say."

Dana's room was dim. The gooseneck lamp cast a half moon against the wall, and the castle-shaped night-light added its glow. Outside the open window the river was black, but Dana could hear its current and took comfort from the sound, like a shushing of silks down distant hallways. She herself was almost invisible, a shadow among shadows, curled on the window seat, a summer quilt wrapped around her. She hadn't left her room today, except to cross the hall to the bathroom a few times. If her mother hadn't brought up a sandwich and a glass of milk, she wouldn't have eaten.

Becca climbed the stairs and stood in the doorway looking at the lump that was her daughter.

"What?" Dana said.

"I want to take your temperature."

"You took it before. I don't have a fever."

"Why won't you talk to Chase?"

"I can't."

"Did he do something?" said her mother, leaning against the doorframe.

"I did something."

Becca was seldom at a loss, but she hesitated. "Can you tell me about it?"

Dana turned her red-rimmed eyes to her mother. "Actually, I can't."

"It can't be that bad."

Dana just looked at her.

Becca went over to the window seat and sat down, her slim arm encircling her daughter's shoulder. "I don't think I've seen you this bad since you had the whooping cough."

Dana felt odd. Her mother was not a hugger. She must be pretty worried. "I'm okay, Mom."

Becca stroked her daughter's head. "So," she said, "you're just going to stay in here by yourself?"

Dana shrugged against her.

"How about playing a game of checkers with Ben?"

Dana didn't respond.

"I mean, he's right in the next room."

"I can't do that."

"He's your little brother. He won't bite."

"No!"

Becca paused. Her daughter never refused to do something with Ben. "Can't you tell me what's going on?"

"I don't think so."

"Dana, I'm your mother."

Dana leaned her head against her mother's arm.

"Not much of one sometimes," Becca said, "but that's your tough luck."

"I know."

Becca looked at her again. "Are you crying?"

"No."

"Baby," said Becca softly. "Tell me."

Dana closed her eyes. "Just stay like this."

"Sure." Becca looked bewildered, but grateful to be needed. "I'll stay as long as you want."

Sometime in the next half hour they dozed off; but then, quite suddenly, Dana was awake, afraid she'd forgotten something.

She couldn't remember what it was, but it had to do with the tapestry. Slowly, to avoid waking her mother, Dana got up and stood before the poster. She realized she'd always felt there was something wrong, ever since her first visit to Breen Hall.

Something wasn't there.

There was so much that *was* there, including hundreds of tiny flowers raining down over the scene, that it was hard to think what might be missing. Her eye scanned the composition, from rabbits to hunting dogs, the distant castle to the ornate tent with its golden coat of arms. And the people: the woman with the mirror, the courtiers, Lord Breen himself on horseback, the hunter with the empty bow. Yes, and in the left-hand corner the man in black robes whom the curator insisted on calling a priest.

The man in black. Where was his wound? No wonder the curator didn't believe Dana when she said the man had been shot!

Where was the red thread woven into the black?

Dana stared at the picture. It was impossible to tell from the poster, but she was sure she was right. The man had been wounded. He was bleeding and about to tumble into the hole to Hell. Baptismal font indeed! This was not baptism but retribution!

She hurried to her desk and clicked on the computer. The curator, Graham Dunn, had given her his e-mail before she left and told her to contact him at any time. Well, the time was now. She tapped her message quickly. It was an order, really: Examine the man's black robe, search for irregularities in the weave, or any evidence of tampering. And please, get back to her right away!

Her mother stirred. "Oh," said Becca, "you're up. Feeling any better?"

Dana could spare her no more than a glance. "Tons," she said.

By the next day Dana couldn't stand herself. She had to go outside. Avoiding her usual haunts, where she might run into kids from school, she ducked into Warner House, the eighteenth-century manse that had been turned into a museum. She'd never been in there before, but immediately felt at home among the household objects of the seventeen hundreds. While a guide pointed out porcelain to an elderly couple, Dana remained in the parlor before a painting of a young, auburn-haired girl with a dove perched on her wrist. The image calmed her, and the face was wonderfully realized. No reliance on a *camera obscura* there. And the dress! The voluminous, ochre-colored silk was as fresh and richly textured now as it must have been when the paint was wet, back in the 1760s. Of course, the artist, a fellow named Blackburn, didn't have a subversive assistant working secretly against him, adding ingredients that would turn his work to mud in a decade's time.

Dana closed her eyes, rubbing her forehead with her fingers.

So, she thought, in the eighteenth century she'd destroyed a man's career. In the sixteenth, she'd murdered a child.

Was that possible? Had she murdered a child?

Who in God's name *was* she?

She didn't *feel* like a monster. In her daily life she felt no temptation to kick old ladies or disembowel kittens. And yet the memories were devastating.

While the guide led the tour upstairs to see the murals and squirrel-pattern bed hangings, Dana slipped out the front door. The late-morning sun dazzled her, and the heat struck her like a slap. Shielding her eyes, she saw before her the apparition of Chase Newcomer, feet planted before her on the sidewalk, a hand on his hip, aviator sunglasses in place, looking as though he were waiting to take her up in a biplane.

"I can't talk to you," she said.

"That's okay." He fell in beside her as she started up the street. Heat quivered off the pavement.

"Then why are you following me?" she said.

"I thought you weren't talking." He hurried to keep up with her. "Want to drop in at the Den?"

She didn't answer.

"My treat."

She looked at him without stopping. "I don't think I can be with you right now."

"Iced latte?" he asked, smiling.

"Chase."

"Come on." He steered her down a narrow, brick-paved alley past RiverRun Books to a tiny, tucked-away coffeehouse.

She stopped. "You don't understand."

"I stopped trying a long time ago."

"I'm serious."

He lifted his sunglasses to the top of his head. "Come on. I've got something to show you. I think you'll like it."

She didn't budge. It pained her to look at his open, "why not" smile. "I like you too much to see you anymore," she said.

He ducked his head reflexively, as if to dodge a blow. "I'm trying to follow the logic here."

"I know it doesn't make sense."

"Not a lot."

"I'm sorry. It's not you. It's me."

"I don't care who it is," he said.

"I tried to tell you before. I shouldn't be with anyone."

"Actually, you should be with me."

"Oh, God," she breathed. She closed her eyes as despair overtook her. "You give and you give. Why?"

"You think I do?"

"Yes, you do. You're always giving. You're always . . . wonderful. And I give nothing back."

"Okay, I'll let you pay for the latte."

"I'm not talking about that."

"In case you can't tell, I'm trying to change the subject."

She felt an ache in her throat and realized she was about to cry.

"Hey," he said gently, seeing her look. He pulled her against him, and for a moment she let him. But then she broke away.

"Chase, please. You're making this so hard."

"I'm trying to."

She looked in his eyes and saw he was not far from tears himself. "Don't do this," he whispered.

The ache in her throat was strangling her. Her eyes were hot. "Chase," she murmured, "just go away. Please!"

He stepped back, looking at her with something like fear. Then he glanced down and turned away. She watched him walk to the end of the alley and turn the corner. The urge to run after him was overwhelming, but her feet stuck to the ground. *Let him go. You have to let him go.*

Dana stood several minutes watching the shadows of leaves on the bricks. Finally the ache in her throat lessened a little. She tried to swallow and realized she was very thirsty. Maybe she'd get something after all.

She looked in the window, glad there were no customers, and stepped inside, standing by the counter till a man came out from the back wiping his hands on a towel. She remembered him, even his name, Tim, although she didn't come here often. With his graying hair, worn actorishly long, and his short-cropped beard, he gave the impression of a reformed hippie. A pleasant presence, with an easy way about him. She ordered a latte and watched him make it.

She could feel her heart beating. She recognized the feeling as fear. She had really done it. She had broken up with Chase. *Don't think about it.*

A line of simply framed eight-by-ten photographs hung along the wall. She got up to look. They weren't bad: black-and-white studies of household or backyard objects, from a rusted wheelbarrow to a colander filled with glistening blueberries. Good, clean work.

"Are these by someone around here?" Dana asked, sipping her drink.

"A fellow over in Newington."

Don't think about it, she told herself again.

"I'll probably have a new show up next month," he continued. "A kid came in today. Showed me some stuff by a friend of his."

Dana added more sugar to her drink. She was hardly listening.

"Take a look?" He pulled out a stack of four-by-five photos from a leather case.

Dana preferred her own thoughts, but she gave the pictures a glance. Her eye was immediately caught by the black silhouette of a house at dawn, a river vaguely rippling in the foreground, the sky brightening behind.

Her breath caught in her throat and hot tears sprang to her eyes—the tears she'd tried so hard to block before—as she made out a yellow-lit window and a woman in a blue dressing gown holding up a cat.

"You okay?"

She was not okay. She was a terrible crier. Her face went red and puffy as tears streaked her cheeks and her nose ran. "Chase," she groaned.

He had done this. He had done this for her.

She threw down some money and bolted out the door.

Chapter Twenty

Killers

"I THOUGHT YOU DIDN'T WANT TO SEE ME ANYMORE."

"I don't."

"But?"

"I have to know."

Sprague sat down again. He'd been up and down three times since she arrived five minutes ago. Why was he so twitchy? To Dana he didn't look well, not that she cared that much. She'd decided, not for the first time, that she didn't like him.

"After the first week when you didn't come back," he said, "I thought that was it."

"So did I."

"But here you are." He got up, went to the window, then turned to Dana. "How has the week been for you?"

Dana looked at him coolly. "Why do you care?"

He nodded. "Wasn't that great for me, either."

"Why? Because you couldn't finish your little experiment?"

Sprague resettled his large frame in the chair. He picked up a pencil and tapped the eraser end on the desk. "I would understand," he said, "if you resented me."

"You don't understand the half of it."

"Maybe not."

She was silent almost a minute. Sprague seemed to want to

get up, but he waited. "I broke up with Chase," Dana said at last.

Sprague's heavy-lidded eyes widened, then narrowed. "Do you want to tell me why?"

"I didn't think he should have to hang out with a murderer."

He heaved himself to his feet and went to inspect the turtle at the end of the room. It lay like a stone, half submerged. "And you're quite sure that's what you are."

"I dreamed about it enough times."

"If you're sure, why do you want to go back?"

"I want to know *why*."

He returned to the desk, standing above the desk lamp. The upward beam caught the tail of his beard, along with his nostrils and cheekbones, leaving his eyes in shadow. "What if you don't like what you find out?"

She looked into the shadow where his face was. "I'll have to live with it."

"All right," he said, nodding. "You have the locket?"

"Right here."

He gestured to the recliner. "Let's see if we can get this thing done."

It took a while. Even with the locket open in her hand, Dana had an impulse to veer into memories of her present lifetime. Unconscious avoidance, Sprague would call it. After several tries Dana, still in a trance, took refuge in her "safe place," the backyard swing set she used to play on when she was little. Sprague let her stay there, watching the leafy branches swoop close to the tips of her shoes, then recede, back and forth, with the comforting rhythm of a pendulum.

"Do you think you're ready to try again?" came Sprague's soothing voice.

The creaking chain and luffing breezes lulled her. "I like it here," she said, her Mary Janes tipping high, the sky showing through the leaves.

"That's good," he murmured. "You can come back any time you want. But just now I'd like you to take a look at the locket."

Crooking an elbow around the chain for balance, she held the locket up. There he was, young William, gazing out at her.

"Do you see him?"

"Yes."

"Are you ready to go there now?"

She didn't answer right away. Fear still held her. *For him*, she thought. *Do it for him.* She let the swing slow. "All right," she said.

"Very good. Now concentrate on his face. You can let your eyes close, if you want. You can still see him, can't you?"

"Yes."

"Even with your eyes closed."

Dana could see him better with her eyes closed. He was not a portrait but a person, his eyes flicking with recognition.

"Now," said Sprague quietly, "I want you to follow him. Let him lead you back to his world. I know you can do it."

She barely nodded. It was already happening. The boy was ahead of her, walking quickly up a broad staircase, not looking back. She found it hard to keep up, and he disappeared around a turn in the stairs. Only the sound of his footsteps told her he was still ahead.

But there were other sounds now, the thud of boots, men's voices, shouts. She reached the landing and found herself at one end of a long gallery lit by torches set in the wall. The boy was nowhere in sight, but the men's voices were louder. This was the second floor of the east wing, Dana realized, where the

Breen ladies, in quieter times, used to take their constitutionals when the weather was rainy.

A line of framed ancestors gazed down from the right-hand wall, above the doorways that led to the family's quarters. That's where the noise was coming from, a crash of heavy furniture followed by a woman's scream.

A door suddenly banged open and one of Breen's nieces, her black hair in disarray, burst out and raced past Dana down the stairs. Two soldiers ran out after her but stopped at the landing.

"She's not important," the taller of them muttered, sheathing his sword. "We'll get her later."

The other man, stockier, with thick brows, nodded.

The first soldier suddenly noticed Dana. "What are *you* looking at?"

Dana shook her head, speechless.

The short one gave a mirthless laugh. "He probably wants her for himself."

The other looked Dana up and down, then spat on the floor. "He wouldn't know what to do with her."

The men turned and went back into the room.

He? thought Dana, looking down at her hands and arms. They were a man's arms! Her amazement increased as she noticed the clothes. The embroidered vest and loose-fitting pants, ending several inches above the stockinged knee, were in the latest Elizabethan fashion for gentlemen, with blue silk showing through the slashings. The boots were of the softest leather, and a sheathed dagger hung from a suede belt.

Suddenly she remembered the man's name—Paul Bertrand—and in that instant was no longer herself, Dana Landgrave, a girl who would be born on another continent four hundred years in the future. She forgot her own thoughts and astonishment and felt only his. And to him, just now, one thing mattered: William, the young heir he had befriended during the past few weeks, while working out plans for the hall's renovation. The boy was hiding here somewhere, and that devil Malveaux was out to murder him.

Bertrand started down the gallery, flinching at every sound and glancing behind any object large enough to conceal a boy. There were several dark, intricately carved chests, and he lifted their heavy lids. No William.

Farther along the hall he came to another door and eased it open. It led into the bedroom of Lord and Lady Breen. A scuffling sound reached him, and he opened the door wider, slipping inside.

There was someone lying across Lord Breen's bed. Bertrand's breath caught in his throat as he realized it was old Breedlove, Breen's personal valet, his eyes staring. Bertrand looked away, fighting the urge to retch. The twisted coverlet was soaked in blood. *Who would do this? Why?*

He heard the scuffling sound again, coming from an adjoining room, and pulled his inlaid dagger from its sheath. He had never used the implement for anything more than paring apples and trimming his paintbrushes. He was an artist, a designer of tapestries. The tip of the blade trembled as he crept forward.

"Out of there, you little beggar," a man's voice snarled. "Now!"

Bertrand peered into the room in time to see a tall, meaty-faced fellow, sword in hand, dragging a boy from behind a curtain. The child, who couldn't have been more than ten, was dressed in a silk vest and a cape of maroon velvet—a miniature version of Lord Breen himself, even to the velvet shoes.

"Well!" the soldier crowed. "The young master!"

The boy gasped in pain as his arm was twisted behind his back, then cried out sharply as the man lifted him off the ground.

"I think I'll gut you like a chicken," he muttered.

"Stop!" Paul Bertrand cried out, brandishing his dagger.

In the brief moment the man looked up, the boy, in an agony of pain and terror, kicked wildly, catching the soldier in the groin. With a roar, the man dropped him, clutching himself. "You meddling ass!" he shouted and raised his sword to strike off Bertrand's head.

It was the end. It had to be. Paul Bertrand's puny knife, pretty as it was, fashioned of silver and engraved with his initials, was nothing against the swooping broadsword of this bloody-minded man.

The boy had started to scramble away when the soldier noticed and turned, deciding to kill him first. The blade had just begun its horrid descent when Bertrand hurled himself forward with a force he didn't know he possessed, thrusting the dagger to its elegant hilt in the man's stomach.

The sound the man made was horrible, an eruption of agony and surprise, but his sword continued its downward slash, passing young William's head and opening a livid gash in his forehead. The boy fell back with a sigh and the huge man, tottering for an uncertain second, collapsed on top of him.

Bertrand stood stunned in the suddenly silent room. A soft gurgling sound escaped from the soldier's throat, and then nothing more.

"William," Bertrand whispered, as if not to awaken the man. "William!" he said more loudly. Suddenly panicking, he rolled the soldier away and knelt, fearing the boy was dead. Blood had begun pooling around him, whether the boy's or the soldier's was hard to say. At least he was still breathing.

"Come on," Bertrand coaxed. "We've got to get out of here."

The boy remained unconscious. Bertrand lifted him, careful to cradle his head.

Suddenly he stopped, his heart seizing up as a door banged and male voices quarreled in the outer room. He pressed himself against the wall, the boy in his arms, as the door swung open.

"I *told* you there was nobody here!"

"Well, where is he, then? It's his head or ours."

"We'll find him. He'll be in a corner somewhere puking with fear, praying for the Pope to save him."

"It'll take more than the Pope," growled the other, heading out through the first room into the gallery. His companion thumped after him, and soon their voices grew fainter.

Bertrand hadn't realized how much he was sweating, or how cold he felt at the same time. He looked around, then laid the boy on the bed and tore off a strip of bedding, tying it around the wound. William moaned, his tongue briefly licking his dry lips. Outside the door more footsteps hurried past and thudded down the stairs.

Bertrand waited. With the boy again in his arms, he peered into the hallway. He had half a plan, remembering something Lord Breen had mentioned when first showing him around the place.

If only he could find it. Moving silently along the gallery, he felt the dark paneling for any sign of give. The wall seemed solid. He kept feeling his way along, trying the edges of the wainscoting with his fingers.

And then he found it. A panel he could get the tips of his fingers around and pull toward him. It creaked open, revealing a small alcove with a tightly circular staircase leading downward through a plunge of darkness. Old Breen had said it'd been built a hundred years earlier, at another time of persecution, a secret escape route to the courtyard below.

"We'll be all right now," Bertrand whispered to the unconscious boy. He started downward, spiraling into the dark. Several times he nearly lost his footing and grabbed at the invisible wall to catch himself. Down and down, as if drilling a hole to hell, he wound his way, trying to protect the boy's head from hitting the rough stones. Finally, when the blackness was total, he reached the bottom and felt along the wall in front of him, praying it was a door. His hand felt a thin metal bar, which he realized was a bolt. He slid it and gave the panel a shove. With a groan it opened, and he looked out at ground level into the early evening air.

Not ten feet in front of him a soldier stood in the grassy courtyard, his arms crossed and his back turned to him. He was talking to another soldier, who held up a torch. Bertrand could see other men with torches across the green.

Careful not to make any noise, he began pulling the door shut when a soldier happened to glance toward him. Their eyes met.

"Hey there! Stop!" the man shouted, starting forward.

Bertrand slammed the door and shot the bolt in place. In the darkness he could hear only his panting breath, and then the boom of fists from outside. He was sweating profusely. *What now?*

He turned, protecting young William's head as best he could, and started up the long stone spiral of stairs. He had to reach the top before the soldiers arrived above him or all was lost; but he couldn't hurry, because he couldn't see anything, and also because, carrying the boy, he was already breathing hard. He continued on, his arms aching and his breath coming in gasps.

Finally the stairs ended. It was pitch-dark on the landing as he listened. No sound reached him. Malveaux's men had either not arrived or were right there outside the wall waiting for the panel to open. With painful care, he pushed. The door creaked.

No one.

Bertrand glanced each way. *Quick!*

Out in a moment, he reached the broad stairway and was halfway down it before he heard the thud of booted feet coming from below. Glancing around desperately, Bertrand spied a fat urn in a shadowed niche and scrambled behind it, crouching over and tucking the boy's legs in as best he could. William seemed to be coming to. He moved his head back and forth, as if denying something, and let out a loud moan just as the first soldier came around the bend in the stairs.

Bertrand clamped his hand over the child's mouth.

"Hurry!" the leader was saying to those behind him. "It's just up here."

William groaned, twisting around to free himself. Bertrand held him tighter.

The men passed very close and continued up the stairs, all but one soldier, whose sword was out.

"Are you coming?" a voice barked from the upper landing.

"I thought I heard something."

"You're always hearing something."

"Just a minute!"

"If that fellow gets away . . ."

The first man was looking over the marble balustrade and didn't reply.

William twisted more violently now. Suspecting he was having trouble breathing through his nose, Bertrand lifted his hand from the boy's mouth for the briefest moment to let him draw in a lungful of air, then clamped his hand down again.

"We found the panel!" a voice called from upstairs.

The soldier lingered another moment, then started up at a run.

The stairway was quiet. Finally Bertrand took his hand away. "You're going to be all right," he whispered. "But you must be *silent*. Do you hear me?"

The boy's eyes were closed, and Bertrand couldn't tell if he'd heard him or not. Struggling to his feet, he hurried downstairs with the boy in his arms and cut through a connecting hallway to the wing where his tapestry would hang one day, if he lived to finish it. Called *The Allegory of Time*, it was to be Bertrand's greatest work, the capstone of his career. The design was complete, the Flemish weavers already contracted—the best in Europe. All he needed to do now was survive.

First he had to hide the boy. He took a corridor to the family chapel, currently in the process of renovation. Lord Breen, an ambitious man, was determined to make improvements to his ancestral home. The finest woodworkers had carved designs—including the family crest—above the new confessional, and stone carvers from Italy had created a white marble altarpiece, delivered just a few days ago and ready to be set in place. An idea came to him then, in a moment of inspiration. If the altarpiece wasn't too heavy to move . . .

Exhausted though he was, Bertrand clambered onto the rosewood pediment and lowered the boy to the floor behind it. "Don't make a sound!" he hissed, not sure whether William could hear him. "I'll be back for you."

He stood trembling before the altar, his body aching. "Help me, Mother Mary," he whispered.

With that he put his shoulder to the statue and pushed. He practically whimpered with the effort to move it. At last it shrugged forward an inch on its wooden base. Sweat stung his eyes as he pushed again. Another inch, then another.

He thought he heard a faint voice but dismissed the idea. Again he threw his weight against the stone.

Footsteps were coming down the corridor. Too late to hide! Bertrand crouched in the altar's shadow, keeping his head low. The footsteps continued past the chapel, and the voices diminished.

That was when he heard the moan.

He peered through the opening between the altarpiece and the wall but could see nothing. Fetching a candle from a side table, he squinted through the narrow space. His imagination again. He heaved his weight once more against the statue.

"No," came a weak voice from the darkness. "Stop!"

It was unmistakable. William!

Bertrand held the candle up and peered through the opening. The boy looked back at him, head bloody and eyes bleared, but alive. "Oh!" the boy cried. "It's you!" His eyes filled with grateful tears.

Bertrand was about to speak when he heard quickly approaching feet. Were they coming this way? He mustn't be found here!

"What's the matter?" the boy said, frowning. "What are you doing?"

No time. Bertrand again threw his weight against the altarpiece, which moved, then moved some more.

He tried not to listen to the boy, who weakly cried, "No! The other way!"

The space was almost closed.

"Don't," William moaned, his voice a quaver. "Please don't."

Another inch or two and the boy would be safe. His voice was barely audible, but his words cut into Bertrand's heart: *"Not you! Not you, too!"*

The altarpiece snugged into place.

Two pairs of footsteps were striding briskly in his direction. Bertrand looked around wildly, then pulled aside the curtain to the confessional and slipped in, just as boots clicked on the chapel floor.

"Shame, isn't it?" came a smoothly cultured voice. Bertrand recognized it at once: John Malveaux, Lord Breen's traitorous adviser. Bertrand crouched lower.

"Such brilliant artistry, so hopelessly misdirected."

Malveaux crossed in front of the altarpiece and stood beside the confessional. Bertrand felt the structure shudder slightly and imagined Malveaux was leaning against it, perhaps resting his elbow on the carvings. "Do they imagine God is pleased with this frippery?"

"I'm sure I don't know, sir," said a softer male voice.

"We live in an abyss, my friend," Malveaux declared. "An *abyss!*"

"Too true."

"An abyss of sin. We can never climb out! Our puny efforts are useless. Only God's grace can pluck us out. That's what these Papists never understand, with their writs and indulgences and pardons. Can God be bribed?"

"Of course not."

"Of course not! You are absolutely . . . Hold on a minute."

"What is it, sir?"

"Quiet!"

Bertrand tried not to breathe.

Suddenly the curtain was torn aside and Malveaux, candle

in hand, peered into the confessional. "Come out of there!" he barked.

Bertrand didn't move, his eyes closed, as if even now he might escape detection.

Malveaux's eyes burned. "Out, creature, or I'll kill you where you lie!"

Slowly Bertrand rose. Malveaux was a man of severity and sobriety, his head bald except for a monklike fringe above the ears and a sparse goatee fuzzing his chin. The smile that twisted his lips was as unsettling as it was unexpected.

"Why, it's the artist!" he said. "Are you here to give confession or to make one of your own?"

Bertrand stepped out. He gave a glance at the man's companion, a court official of some sort, round and ineffectual looking. No help to be expected there. "Sir," Bertrand said, turning to Malveaux, "it has been a little noisy here tonight and I thought it best to keep out of the way."

"In a confessional?"

"I am a man of peace. What better place?"

"Indeed, a man of peace could find no better place." Malveaux's smile faded. His eyes narrowed into twin accusations. "Your name, I believe, is Bertrand?"

"Paul Bertrand, yes."

"Well, Paul Bertrand, it appears I have something that belongs to you." He nodded to his companion, who pulled a shiny object out of a leather pouch. It was a dagger.

"These are your initials on the hilt?" said Malveaux, taking the knife and tapping the flat of the blade on his palm.

Bertrand did not reply.

"You'll never believe where I found it."

"Really?" Bertrand managed.

"Perhaps you could tell me, speaking as a man of peace, how it got there?"

Bertrand cleared his throat. "A small disagreement."

"What sort?"

"He wanted to whack off my head. I didn't like the idea."

"And what, do you think, gave him the notion to whack off your head?"

"You'd have to ask him."

"I would," said Malveaux, "but he is a man of few words."

Bertrand was silent.

"Fewer even than you."

Bertrand had no words at all. He wondered simply how soon his death would come and in what form. A sudden sword slash to the throat? A thrust by his own dagger?

"Tell me," said Malveaux, "was anyone else present during this disagreement of yours?"

"No, sir."

The man held up a thin finger. "Think!" he said. "It is easy to forget certain people. People who are small and insignificant. The person I am thinking of stands no higher than your waist."

Bertrand in that moment prayed. It was a brief prayer, not that he be spared from what would follow, but that he might bear it. That he not betray the boy.

"Come, Bertrand. Was someone there or not?"

The artist remained silent.

Malveaux sighed. "I have ways to improve your memory. You may not care for them, but I assure you they work."

Silence.

"Why not spare us both the trouble?"

Silence.

"Tell me, damn you!"

Bertrand said nothing.

Malveaux unsheathed his sword. "Very well, then. Come!"

Bertrand neither spoke nor moved. He looked into Malveaux's eyes. He needed to understand this man who, in all likelihood, would very soon torture him past endurance, perhaps past the edge of sanity. *Who are you?* he silently asked. *How did you come to be?*

Malveaux briefly returned the look, and what Bertrand saw in those seconds left him breathless. For beneath the coldness, beneath even the rage that underlay the coldness, was such profound sadness that it seemed to Bertrand impossible that the man could go on living. It was the bone weariness of having always to judge, to hate intensely and in secret. To kill for God.

Take me home, Bertrand prayed silently.

He was addressing the Virgin Mary, but somewhere, in some dimension, the words must have been spoken aloud, because an answer came. It was a strange answer: "I want you to count slowly backward from five to one."

Senseless, but orders must be obeyed.

"When you reach three," the voice continued, "you will begin to remember where you are."

Where who is?

"When you reach one you will open your eyes. Are you ready, Dana? Five . . . four . . . three . . ."

Gasping, Dana Landgrave opened her eyes and stared up into the mournful face of Morton Sprague.

Her eyes widened. "It's you!" she whispered.

He flinched, as though she'd suddenly slapped him.

She said it again, her voice louder and deadly certain. "It's you! *You're that killer, Malveaux!*"

Chapter Twenty-one

The Game Ender

THE SECRETARY, THAT NICE MRS. ROBYNS, LOOKED up in surprise as Dana bolted out of Sprague's office and into the hall, not bothering to take a mint or even say good-bye. Barging down the stairs, Dana hit the street running. She ran without direction, although some quiet and still-functioning part of her brain guided her away from places where she might meet others.

Instinctively she headed for the river, her old comforter, a presence that asked no questions. She had enough questions herself. *Even his beard,* she realized, *even that's like Malveaux's. Does he know that?*

She leaned against the fence, breathing hard, a pain knifing through her. A gull screamed and took off from a piling. Early rush-hour traffic howled on Memorial Bridge.

I trusted him. I trusted a killer.

Did he kill me, too?

The thought staggered her. She didn't know what to do with it. *What were the chances?* she thought. *What cosmically improbable odds that his past life would overlap with mine?*

Dana threw a stone into the swirling current. *No such thing as chance, remember?*

Yeah. She threw another. *The karma thing.*

She needed to talk to Chase. He was the only one who

understood. She could tell him the most remarkable things and he'd slip an arm around her waist and everything would be all right.

But she'd blown that now. Releasing a sigh, Dana started along Marcy Street in the direction of her father's work site. It would be good to see her dad at least. She arrived to find the place deserted, the workers gone for the day. That was quite a hole they were digging.

She stood, thinking about her father. *Here he is, replacing sewers for a living, and he's a happy man. Chase is like that too.*

It came to her why. They were just more interested in other people than in themselves.

Then there's me, center of the known universe.

She started up along Chapel Street. It was coming clear to her how much she'd lost when she gave up Chase. *I told him to go away,* she thought. *Twice.*

How could she *treat* him that way? To spare him. Yes, but he didn't want to be spared. And now she'd learned that she wasn't the monster she'd feared. Not worthy of him, maybe, but not a killer.

Thank God for that much.

She shivered, remembering the look on Sprague's face when she emerged from the trance. He'd looked as shocked as she was. *So he doesn't remember, then? Is that an excuse?*

She shivered and walked more quickly. Soon she found herself passing the alley with that little coffee shop, and she paused. On impulse, she felt in her hip pocket for the five-dollar bill she'd put there this morning, then ducked inside.

"Hey," said Tim, coming over. He was scratching his trim beard. "Feeling any better?"

Dana blushed. "You must have thought I was a crazy person."

"Not really." He smiled. "Those were your pictures,

weren't they? Your friend came in again the next day and told me about you."

"Did you tell him what an idiot I was?"

"I didn't put it that way."

She closed her eyes briefly.

"You still want to do the show?" he said. "It's not much of a space, but . . ."

"I'd *love* to do it."

Over coffee and an oatmeal raisin cookie, she worked out a general idea of what was needed and when Tim needed it, if they hoped to get the show up before Labor Day. She couldn't believe it was this easy to arrange.

"Don't expect a horde of people," he said. "But everybody who comes in will see it."

Dana glanced around and smiled. She was the only customer in the place. "That's just fine," she said.

Afterward, she stood in the alley trying to get a hold on her feelings. Within a half hour she'd learned something awful and something awesome, and she was a little dizzy from it all. Sprague was a demon. Chase was an angel.

She *needed* to see that boy. She wanted to thank him for setting this up, and she just . . . wanted him. He'd have to forgive her, that's all there was to it.

Late afternoon was edging toward evening, but he might still be in the park scrimmaging with some of the other guys, whoever could be rounded up for soccer practice. School didn't start for another two weeks, but he liked to get a jump on the season.

Dana set off in the direction of the South Mill Pond, feeling better now that she had something to do. Coming nearer, she could make out a commotion of boys in the distance, and a muddy ball arching into the air. A tall kid who might have been Chase was waiting to head the ball when it came down. Then everyone was running again. Dana could see there were spectators, mostly girls, along the side.

When Dana was close enough to make out individual faces, she felt a jolt of pride seeing Chase fake out an opposing player and boot the ball past the goalie. A general cry went up. That, apparently, was the game ender.

Dana started to hurry toward them when she saw one of the girls, jumping and skipping, loop a towel around Chase's neck and pull him into a big kiss. His arms went out in surprise, but he didn't exactly fight her off.

It was Mary Bing.

Bouncy Bingo.

Chase looked up with the stupid grin still on his face and saw Dana standing there.

Stung, she stared back. She turned slowly away.

Chapter Twenty-two

The House on Bow Street

SOMEHOW THE REST OF THE DAY PASSED, AND THE night, and the next day. Dana kept to her room. She didn't answer her cell the few times it rang, although she did check to see what number was showing. It wasn't his. Twice it was Trish's, but Dana couldn't bring herself to talk.

She kept busy working with photographs on the computer, adjusting the color, contrast, and cropping. She even got her courage up and called Miss Edwards about the picture of her and the cat. The voice on the other end went thin. It was clear she was miffed that Dana had been spying on her. In the end, assured that the picture was shot from a distance and no one could tell who it was, she gave Dana permission to use it in the show.

Another night passed. Blessedly, no nightmares, unless you counted the recurring image of Bingo planting that big open-mouthed kiss on poor, befuddled Chase.

You know he'll be back for more.

Dana had kissed him that way sometimes when saying good night, and a couple of times in the stairwell at school when nobody was around. But for everyday purposes, playful, flirty, edge-of-the-mouth kisses had seemed enough. Bingo had skipped right over that stage.

Next morning around ten, she heard a commotion and realized her dad was carrying Ben up to his room. They'd been out for a walk. She listened to their indistinct voices, then roused herself and went out in the hall. Tom was settling Ben into his wheelchair.

"How is it outside?" she said.

Tom nodded. "Good. You should get out."

Ben wheeled himself into his sister's room and looked at the prints she had laid out on the bedspread. "These are good."

"Thanks."

He nodded, then looked at her brightly. "I've decided something."

"What's that?"

"Don't laugh. I'm going to be walking by Christmas."

"That's great! Absolutely. Why not?"

"Yeah. Why not?"

"You're going to have a big, long life this time, Benny. You're going to be a grandpa with a white beard."

He gave her a quick look. "What do you mean, 'this time'?"

"Oh," she said, catching herself. "I didn't mean . . ."

"There was a last time?" His clear brown eyes homed in on her.

She hesitated. "You don't want to hear about this stuff."

"Was I cut down in a hail of bullets or something?"

"You really want to know?"

"I don't know." He thought. "Yeah, maybe."

"You didn't used to want to know."

"Maybe I'm different."

"Well," she said, "I can show you a picture."

His eyes rounded.

"Here." She took the locket from around her neck and put it in his hands. "Say hello to William Breen."

"*Him?* You're saying I was the kid behind the altar?" He clicked open the locket and stared at the boy's portrait. "How do you know?"

"I know."

"But *how?* You can't know."

She smiled sadly. "You probably know too. Didn't you tell me you had a dream?"

"You mean," he said slowly, "the one where I was trapped in a dark place. . . . ?"

"And you said your head was hurting."

"And you think . . . ?"

"What do *you* think?"

Ben looked around the room. "Wow," he whispered.

"Yeah," said Dana, giving his shoulder a squeeze.

The phone was ringing down in the kitchen. A few seconds later their mother's voice reached them from the bottom of the stairs. "Dana? For you. A Mrs. Robyns?"

"Who?" Dana dawdled down and took the receiver her mother held at arm's length.

It was Dr. Sprague's secretary, her voice hesitant. She knew it was a strange question, but did Dana happen to know where the doctor might be? She was only asking because he hadn't seen any other patients after Dana, and he hadn't come in the next day, or so far this morning.

Dana was surprised and not surprised. *Hope he jumped off the bridge,* she thought. "Did you try him at home?"

"I did, several times."

"I don't know what to sug—"

"It's not like him."

Dana felt a little irritated, but she couldn't discount the urgency in the woman's voice. "Maybe," she said, "you

234

should go around to his place and knock on his door."

"Yes, a good idea. Yes. Thank you. Good." She paused. "There's just one other thing. It seems silly, but do you happen to know anything about, I mean, turtles?"

"He hasn't fed Id?"

"Id, yes. No, he hasn't. And I'm, well . . ."

"Id creeps you out."

"I'm a little afraid of him, yes."

"I guess I could come in and help."

"*Would* you?"

Dana sighed. "I'll be over."

She couldn't believe she'd agreed to feed that repulsive reptile. She started to take back the offer, but the grateful Mrs. Robyns had hung up.

"What is it?" said Becca.

"I've got to go feed a monster."

Her mother nodded. "About time you got out of the house."

Dana entered the office to find Mrs. Robyns standing, as if, without Dr. Sprague there, she didn't feel quite right sitting down. Dana hadn't realized how short she was. Her sturdy middle-aged body, encased in sensible pants, was at odds with her fluttery politeness, as if she were a small tank that fired only flowers. Mrs. Robyns was particularly fluttery today.

"Thank you *so* much for coming, dear." She shook her head helplessly. "I don't know what I would have done. . . ."

"That's all right, Mrs. R. Let's see what we can do."

Mrs. Robyns led the way into the sanctum. No lamps were on, and even with the sun angling in the window, the office was dim as a church. The glowing tank in the bookcase gave out a moony light. They approached cautiously.

"Is he dead?" said Mrs. Robyns.

"I wouldn't poke him to find out." Dana opened the cabinet that hid the mini-fridge. "Dr. Sprague showed me once how he does this," she said, pulling out a tray with neat rows of dead goldfish. On a second tray sprawled an assortment of mice.

"Oh, my!" breathed Mrs. Robyns.

"I suppose you want me to do this," Dana said.

"Would you?"

Dana picked up a goldfish by the tail and held it well away from Id's anvil-like skull. The creature's eyes seemed as inanimate as pebbles. There was still a fair chance he was dead.

Dana dropped the little fish beside him and pulled her fingers away. "Last time he lunged at me. You need to be careful."

"I should say."

For good measure, Dana dropped in a mouse as well. The turtle didn't blink.

"That should hold him."

Retreating to the safety of the outer room, Mrs. Robyns was profuse. She wondered, though, if Miss Landgrave would be willing to do one more *huge* favor and go with her to see if the doctor was at home.

Absolutely not. No way, José.

She sighed. "Sure."

"Miss Landgrave, you are a lifesaver!"

She's more afraid of Sprague than she is of the turtle, Dana said to herself.

The women set off together, turning on Bow Street, which ran close to the water. They found the address, a two-story clapboard with peeling yellow paint. Something about the place seemed sad, uncared for, and neither woman was anxious to push the bell. Finally, Mrs. Robyns, as the adult, squared her shoulders and rang.

"Well, we tried," she said quickly.

Dana reached past her and gave the bell a second push, then went and peered in a window. No lights, just a dim gleam on a bare floor, the thick arm of an easy chair, and a shadowy bookcase. Scattered across the coffee table was a squirrel's nest of papers held down by an extinct pipe.

"Where else would he be?"

Mrs. Robyns shrugged expressively. "He'd have told me if he was going out of town. I schedule his appointments."

"Would he possibly be in the library?"

"The Athenaeum's closed for repairs for the next week. Old pipes or something. That's the only library he goes to."

Dana saw a flicker of fear in her eyes and tried to reassure her. "I'm sure nothing has happened to him," she said.

"I know," she said, not knowing at all. "He just seemed so upset when he left that day."

Of course he was upset. With any luck he'd be completely distraught. But suicidal? "Let's take a look in the back, while we're here," Dana said.

They edged around the house, along a scraggly sideburn of brown grass, to the unkempt yard where an old wooden deck chair sat rotting. Dana pulled open the screen door and squinted through a diamond-shaped window. A kitchen, empty. A kettle on the counter. A languishing geranium on the sill above the sink.

"This is a man who could use a wife," she said, standing aside to let Mrs. Robyns take a look.

"He was married once, I understand," said Robyns.

"He was?"

"He doesn't talk about it."

Dana gave her a sidelong look. "What have you heard?"

"Only that she was a very lively woman. A striking woman. That was years ago."

Sprague years ago. Sprague a young man with a lively wife. It was too much for Dana. She tried the wobbly door handle. To her surprise, it turned and the door groaned open.

Mrs. Robyns blinked. "We're not going in there."

"I think we have to."

"It's, I mean, isn't it breaking and entering?"

Dana looked at the half-open door beckoning like a tomb. "Well, we haven't broken anything, so it's just entering."

"We can't."

"You go on. I'll just take a look around."

"That's a very bad idea, Miss Landgrave."

"Do you have a better one?"

"We could call the police."

"And say what?"

Mrs. Robyns shook her head helplessly. She did that a lot.

"You don't have to wait for me. I'll be fine." Dana turned quickly and stepped into the house.

"I don't think . . ." But Mrs. Robyns's thought was cut short by the slap of the screen door.

The kitchen had a sour smell, as if food had been left out. Then Dana noticed the frying pan and plates in the sink, and the overflowing garbage can. She caught a glimpse of something moving and caught her breath as a large water bug skittered across the linoleum in front of her foot.

"Hello! Anybody home?" she called.

Dana saw Mrs. Robyns's face through the screen door and

gave her an okay sign, although she was not feeling okay at all. She went on into the living room, standing in semidarkness beside the coffee table, listening hard. Her foot scuffed a paper on the floor. Papers were all over the place, and books, she saw now, were piled on the side table. She picked one up: *The History of Everyday Life in Renaissance England*. She glanced at another: *Calvinism and Its Discontents*.

So he was a history buff. She set the books down, but the pile toppled and thumped loudly to the floor. Again she listened.

"Hello? Anybody here?"

She glanced back through the kitchen and screen door to the bright outside world as a swimmer might look back at the receding shore.

Mrs. Robyns had vanished. The realization came as a jolt, and Dana had to remind herself that she had told her to go.

Now what? Dana glanced up the staircase. She was trying to ignore the growing dread that chilled her. Was the menace she felt only her fear, magnified by what she knew about Sprague? Or was it present, palpable, here with her now in the dark house?

She put her foot on the first step, but then froze, hearing what sounded like the creak of a floorboard overhead. It was followed by a muffled clanking, and the grumble of something metallic being dragged across the floor.

Chains? Is there someone in chains upstairs?

Sprague's wife! Dana had seen horror movies like that. *Call the police!*

Her foot was already on the second stair, then the third.

"Hello?" she called out. "Dr. Sprague?"

She was almost to the landing when she heard a deep throaty growl. *Oh my God, he's got a dog up there. A big son of a gun.*

Suddenly snapping turtles didn't seem so bad. Dana gently pushed open a mostly closed door. "Dr. Sprague?"

A ferocious squall of barking sent her heart jumping in her chest. "Oh!" she gasped, stepping back. She was halfway down the stairs when she stopped herself. No dog had come boiling out of the room in wild pursuit, although the barking continued, as loud as ever.

It must be tied up. Chained up.

She turned and went back to the door and looked in. The barking continued nonstop, but she saw no sign of living creatures, great or small. And something about the noise was . . . unconvincing. Dana stepped inside and found the room empty. On the wall to the right of the computer screen was a small blinking light: an alarm with an on-off switch. She clicked it off and the room went dead silent.

Clever Sprague. He'd hooked up the alarm system to a recording of clanking chains and vicious dogs. Pretty effective.

So this was Sprague's lair. Sloppy bookshelves stood beside a worn leather chair and a dangerously wobbly lamp. No pictures on the walls or family photos on the side tables. Certainly no pictures of a wife.

You'd think he'd have nicer things, she thought. *He's a successful psychologist.*

Looking around, it was obvious that worldly goods weren't his focus. He had drive, but he was driven inward. Even Dana, no wizard at housekeeping, would have had that lamp fixed ages ago.

What kind of person lives in this kind of place?

Against the far wall stood an antique washstand flanked by two thick candles, partially burned down. Between them lay a

neither. Apparently, this morning had been quite enough excitement for her.

Dana now remembered other scenes in which the hero had used a credit card to finesse a lock. Dana didn't have a credit card. She did, however, have a library card, and she ran it along the groove between the door and the latch. The door was old, with lots of play in it, and the lock looked antique. She could feel the metal tongue retracting.

She kept wiggling the card, and something she did must have been right because suddenly the latch popped open. *Well, Nancy Drew*, she thought, taking a breath. *Ready for a little more breaking and entering?*

Dana had never been in Sprague's office alone and wasn't planning to waste time there. In and out, that was the idea. Crossing the reception room with its leatherette settees and old magazines, she went right into the consulting room. "Hey, Id," she said, eyeing the tank, "what's shaking?" She flipped on as many lights as she could find and leaned back against the desk. The books looked undisturbed, to judge by the dust; and the papers that littered the desk referred to some psychological conference being held next month—nothing special there. More promising was a beige file cabinet that stood against the wall, but it was locked. Maybe her own file was in there. What she'd give to have a peek at that! Dana opened the desk's flat center drawer and poked through the rubber bands and paper clips, looking for keys. She found one, but it didn't fit.

What does this open? she wondered, turning it in her hand. Then she remembered the door at the end of the hallway, connecting to the second floor of the adjoining building, which happened to be the Athenaeum. But the old library was closed.

They were fixing the pipes or something. That's what Mrs. Robyns had said.

That wouldn't stop Sprague from getting in.

Grasping the key, Dana strode out of the office and down the corridor to the unmarked door. She stood before it for several seconds, the key trembling. "What's the matter with you?" she muttered angrily. She slipped the key into the lock. It fit easily and turned with a click.

Again she hesitated. Was this smart? Dana thought of all she had learned about her therapist in the last few days—what he had done in his past life, what he might be capable of in this. She thought of the crucifix. Did she really want to be alone with him in a deserted building?

He's probably not even there, she told herself, pushing the door wide. But she knew this was exactly the sort of place he'd choose, if he wanted to hide out.

She moved through the library's storage area and out into the public rooms. Busts of the illustrious dead gazed down from high bookcases as Dana headed for the stairs leading to the wide, wraparound balcony on the top floor. She glanced up anxiously. The building was so quiet you could hear the dust settle.

The first step groaned under her foot, and she stopped. "Hello?" she called weakly. Then in a louder voice: "Dr. Sprague? Are you up there?"

The dead air muffled her words, as if she had never spoken. She continued up, trailing her hand along the banister, till she reached the landing. Remembering the last time she'd been here, she headed for the front of the building, where the windows were and the balcony widened out.

Suddenly she stopped short, her heart flipping in her chest

like a fish. Just a few yards before her, in an armchair, a heavy, hunch-shouldered man sat staring out the window. His back was turned, but she recognized the thick neck and worn tweed jacket. The floor around his feet was littered with books, some open and face down, and papers held under a half-empty bottle of cabernet and an open package of Fig Newtons. An old brown army blanket was bunched up on the other chair.

He didn't turn around. "Go away."

Dana remained silent.

"Why did you come?" He spoke to the window.

"I guess I was worried about you," she said, finding her voice.

"Wait a minute." Sprague turned toward her at last. He looked like hell. His heavy-lidded eyes, red-rimmed from weeping or lack of sleep, lifted to take her in. "You're telling me that Paul Bertrand is *worried* about John Malveaux?"

The sight of him shook her. Therapists were not supposed to have breakdowns. "We aren't those people anymore."

"Aren't we?"

She didn't answer. Maybe they *were* those people, in which case she should hate his guts. Maybe she did hate his guts. To judge from his reddened eyes, maybe he hated his own.

"I was looking for you," she said. "How come you came here?"

He turned back to the window as if there were something of great interest to be seen.

"Are you hiding?" she pressed.

"You could say that."

"Who from?"

He turned slowly and looked at her, his face a misery. "Who do you think?"

"I don't know. God? Satan? Me?"

"From *him*."

"Malveaux?"

"Don't say his name!"

She stared at his puffy face, his soiled cuffs, his disgraceful jacket littered with cookie crumbs. *He's mad*, she thought suddenly. *He's gone mad. Can you hate a madman?*

"Dr. Sprague," she said quietly, "why don't you go on home? You can't just camp out here."

He looked at her as if she'd suggested something outlandish. "He's there," he said.

She opened her mouth but hesitated. "You're saying that you're here and he's *there*?"

"He's everywhere."

"Malveaux's been dead four hundred years. He's just a memory."

"He's taken over the house, so I had to come here," he said, ignoring her. "Soon he'll take over this place, too. I don't know where I'll go then."

Dana again found herself without words.

"And don't look at me like that!" Sprague spat out suddenly. "You of all people."

She leaned back against the balustrade. She would have sat in the other chair but wasn't sure she wanted to be that close.

"The past keeps coming back," he continued. "You know that yourself. You've seen people from your past walking down Islington Street in the middle of the afternoon!"

"They haven't taken over my house."

"You haven't been at this game as long as I have."

Dana rested her hands on the banister to steady her balance. "What does that mean?"

He shook his head.

"No," she said, "this is interesting."

Sprague made a gesture, as if his hand were a broken flipper. "I first saw him thirty years ago. Didn't know the name. All I had were some disconnected images."

"Wait a minute," said Dana. "Are you talking about the regression you had somebody do. . . . ?"

"Yes."

"When you were being trained. . . . ?"

He clawed at his bearded cheek. "He let me alone for a while. He let me get married. He let me be happy."

"I heard you had a wife."

"Yes. But then the images started coming back. I'd see a man disappearing around a street corner as I approached. I'd wake up in the night beside my wife and I'd know he was in the room. He wouldn't show himself and he wouldn't leave me alone. He was jealous, I realize now. Jealous that I was happy." He frowned up at her. "I had no right to be happy, you see."

"I don't see."

"Finally he scared her away."

"*He* scared her?"

Sprague wasn't listening. "She didn't scare easily. She must have loved me very much."

"What happened?"

He closed his eyes as if to end the discussion. "Let's just say he succeeded."

"What did he do?"

"There were threats. You know how he likes to cut people."

"He . . . *cut* her?"

"She left before that happened, thank God. I saw no more of him for a long time. He'd gotten what he wanted."

"What he wanted . . ."

"To make me suffer as I deserved."

"How long did he leave you alone?"

"Until I saw you."

"Me!"

"You brought him back. I suppose he'd never left."

Dana had a sudden suspicion. "So how long, exactly," she said, "have you been using me?"

"From very early on," he answered right away.

"How early?"

"When you first came to me with that dream. You described the altar, and I recognized it. It was like a miracle. Of all the people in the world, *you* had to walk into my office!"

"The old karma thing."

"I *had* to find out more."

"But you couldn't get back there yourself, so you sent me," Dana declared, understanding now the doctor's insistence, his vehemence, the stake he had in her case. "I was to bring you back more pieces of the puzzle. I was your little errand girl!"

"Not very professional of me, I'm afraid."

"It was *rotten* of you!"

"It was the only way. I had to find out who he was and deal with him once and for all."

"Is that what you're doing here, hiding out in the library?"

"I didn't realize how strong he was. He can come and go at will."

Dana stared at a corner of the ceiling. "Did you ever," she said, "at any point, care about the problems you were supposed to be helping me with?"

"Not very much. I was too interested in my own."

Her eyes brightened with anger. "Well, then," she said, "I guess you found what you were after."

"Lucky me." Sprague's gaze lowered from her face till he was looking at nothing at all.

They were silent.

"You've started to remember things, haven't you?" Dana said suddenly, catching his look.

He seemed to waken from a daze. "What was that?"

"Things from back then. You've started remembering on your own."

He nodded. "Flashes mostly. More and more since our last session."

"The last thing I remember," she said, "I was being arrested by Malveaux. Do you happen to know if you killed me?"

Sprague gave her a glance before looking away. "He wanted to. I wouldn't let him."

"But you and Malveaux are the same person!"

"*Parts* of the same person."

"Wait," she said, trying to clear her head. "What are you saying?"

"Back then we didn't have the diagnosis of schizophrenia."

Dana gripped the banister she was leaning against. Behind her was empty space.

"Back then," Sprague went on with a weak smile, "you were either possessed by the Devil or inspired by God."

"So, tell me," she said, her voice hardening, "did you torture me?"

Sprague looked down.

"I see. But I survived, didn't I?"

"Of course you survived. You lived to make that red tapestry that nobody seems to understand."

"And I didn't give away the hiding place."

"The hiding . . . ? No, you didn't." He looked up at her,

raking his hair with his fingers. "That's where you found him, still hiding."

"Still hiding. Thanks to you."

"Thanks to me."

"Aren't you even *sorry* about this?" she flared.

"Of course I'm sorry! I'm sorry that being sorry doesn't help. I'm sorry that I don't have the *luxury* to be sorry!"

"The luxury!"

"Now that Malveaux is back, there are more important things."

"But he's just part of yourself. You can control him!"

"Can I?"

"Of course! You've lived this whole lifetime helping people, trying to be a good person."

"Malveaux would say he's a good person too. A man of God."

"He's insane!"

Silence hung between them.

"You're saying *I'm* insane," Sprague said quietly.

Dana stopped, confused.

"Physician, heal thyself," he said.

Again, silence.

"At least," he continued, "I'm sane enough to fear him. I see him around every corner. It's not only dreams. I saw him yesterday in that restaurant on Islington. Two nights ago I came home and found him sitting in my own house, in my room upstairs!" Sprague's eyes looked wildly into hers. "He was scraping at something with a metal file. He ignored me! Can you believe it?" Sprague began breathing harder as the memory came back. "I shouted at him. *'Get out!'* But he wouldn't. Finally he stood up with that horrible half smile of his and walked past me out the door, as if I wasn't there."

"The crucifix," Dana murmured.

He shot her a look of alarm. "How do you know about that?"

"I was there today, looking for you. Mrs. Robyns was worried and—"

"Mrs. Robyns? She was there too?"

"She asked me to help look for you."

Sprague's head had lowered to his chest and his eyes closed. Dana broke off speaking and watched. He seemed to be going deep inside himself.

"Are you all right?"

No response. Dana was starting to get nervous. "Dr. Sprague?"

At last his head lifted and his eyes glinted open. "She's a fool," he said, his voice quiet as a purr.

"Well, I wouldn't call—"

"A demented, godless fool." His voice, still quiet, took on an unpleasant edge.

Suddenly Dana's breath caught and her heart began speeding as Sprague got to his feet, a bear of a man, eyes flashing. He approached her, and she was again aware of the empty space behind her, and of the distance to the floor below.

"Was Mrs. Robyns in my room?" he said.

"No, she didn't—"

"Did she see the crucifix?"

"Really, she never went in. I was by myself."

"You said she was with you."

"No, I meant . . ."

His mouth twisted around his words. "She's a Papist, you know." He grasped the balustrade on either side of her, his thick arms forming a cage.

Dana's breath was coming fast now, her mouth half open.

251

"You should have seen her during Lent," he went on with a bitter laugh, "traipsing into the office each morning stinking of incense and cheap perfume."

Dana twisted helplessly as Sprague moved closer. He was inches from her, his sour breath in her face. She leaned back.

"What should we do about her, Miss Landgrave?" he said. His chest was now pushing against her.

"Sh-she's harmless," Dana gasped out, struggling to keep her balance.

"So heresy is harmless now?"

The weight of him was pushing her over the railing, her back arching. "Stop! What are you doing?"

"Don't you know? You designed the scene yourself."

In her panic, Dana couldn't think. "Designed?"

"The tapestry." His eyes narrowed dangerously. "The hole to Hell. Surely you remember."

She shook her head in denial, her stomach clenching.

"Now *you're* the one falling. How do you like it?" He leaned against her like a tilting wall. "*You're* the one going to Hell."

Desperate, she gritted her teeth and slapped him full across the face, at the same time shoving him back with all her strength. "Stop it! You can stop this! Stop it now!"

Sprague looked stunned.

"Don't let him do this!" she rushed on. "You're stronger than he is!"

Sprague blinked as if waking from a tumultuous dream. "What was I doing?" he said, looking fearful.

She stepped nimbly away from the railing. "You were scaring the hell out of me."

"I was?" He seemed to be reaching for a memory. Suddenly his eyes widened. "Oh, God," he whispered. "My God, I'm sorry!"

She was a good ten feet away from him now, within an easy dash of the stairs.

"So he's here, then." Sprague glanced around him. "I can't stay here."

"It doesn't matter where you are."

His eyes fell. "You're right, Miss Landgrave," he said. "There's no escape."

"That's not what I mean!" She wanted to shake him. It upset her to see him afraid. He was her doctor, after all. He was supposed to be strong.

"But it's true. I'm just a shell. He's the hermit crab that has climbed inside."

"Nonsense. You can stop him!" She felt a fierce pity, seeing him there, a dark bulk against the bright window. Still, she kept her distance.

"I've tried," he said. "He just *smiles* at me!"

"He's who you *were*, not who you *are*."

He looked at her with interest, and the tension in his heavy features eased a little. "You believe that, don't you?"

"I know it!"

"But you wisely keep your distance."

"Yeah, well . . ."

He took a deep breath and expelled it noisily. "I don't know what happened just now, Miss Landgrave. I'm truly sorry I frightened you."

Dana's breathing was slowing to normal. She worked her shoulders around. *Just a little tension here,* she thought. "Well," she said, "I gotta go."

"Of course you do."

She stood indecisively. "Will you be all right?"

He didn't respond right away. "I don't know. Anyway, he's not here now."

"You're sure of that."

"We'd know."

"I guess we would." She hesitated. It was hard to leave Sprague like this. "Well," she said, starting for the stairs.

He was back in the chair, looking out the window. She thought of the package of Fig Newtons at his feet. This was what he was living on?

Go, she told herself. *Quick.* But it was hard. *Look at him.*

"Hey," she said with false brightness, "why don't we get out of here? What do you say?"

He turned questioningly.

"Come on," she said. "I'll treat you to a latte."

"That's very kind, but I'm afraid . . ."

"I won't take no."

He hesitated.

"Trust me. It'll be good for you to get out."

Sprague frowned as though she'd asked a question too hard for him. Slowly he followed her around the curve of the balcony and down the stairs.

Chapter Twenty-four

The Wayward Arms

DANA HADN'T EXPECTED TO ENJOY HER OUTING with Sprague, but he was actually interesting, once he dropped his Dr. Weirdo role and talked like a person. During the half hour he spent at the Den hunched over a cappuccino and a glorious turkey sandwich, he seemed on vacation from himself. He even talked a little about his days in grad school at the University of Texas, Fort Worth—"The most productive time of my life"—and his research with hypnotism to treat autistic kids.

Dana was dying to ask if that was where he'd met his wife and what she was like, but she held back. She didn't want to risk it.

"You might look into psychology yourself," Sprague said, testing the edge of an oatmeal cookie. "You've got obvious talents in that direction."

"You mean I can be hypnotized at the drop of a hat . . ."

"I mean, Miss Landgrave, you have an understanding heart. And a forgiving one, apparently."

Dana frowned at the counter. Did she?

"Sometimes I'm not sure," he went on, "if I've been your therapist or you've been mine."

"That's easy," she said, returning the serve. "I've been yours. I just didn't know it."

Tim came over and slid the check on the counter. Dana

slapped her hand on it. "Tim, do you think I'd make a good shrink?"

He humphed. "I'd stick to photography if I was you." He saw Sprague's look. "You didn't know she's having a show? Opening's next week." He handed him a flier.

Sprague beamed like an uncle. "Well," he said, "I'm glad to see the tapestry maker has found a new trade."

"Yes, and Hannah, the long-suffering painter. You should come."

"I will try. I will certainly try, Miss Landgrave."

Despite a drizzle that had started shortly after nightfall, the little coffeehouse was packed, the crowd overflowing into the lanterned courtyard. Dana, who was not used to being the center of attention, found herself besieged by classmates she hadn't seen all summer and by adults whose names she could sometimes recall, sometimes not. It didn't seem to matter. They loved her pictures.

The show was good; Dana knew that. In the days since she'd taken Sprague here for lunch, she'd thrown herself into enlarging, matting, arranging, hanging. She thought of him often enough, but didn't go looking for him. She hoped he would show up for the opening.

No sign of him yet, but just about everyone else was here. She felt a little panicky, the first stirrings of claustrophobia, but managed to scold herself out of it. *These are friendly people*, she reminded herself. Among the friendliest were Ben and, behind him, her dad, pushing the wheelchair while fumbling a bouquet of fall flowers. "For you," he said. "From your mom. She had to be in Boston tonight."

Dana kissed him and gave her brother a shove. "Hey, Ben,

you're the one we should have a party for," she said. "You did a big thing today."

It was true. This morning, with no help from his PT coach, Ben had moved his right leg—only a few inches, but it was enough for shouts of jubilation.

The other hopeful event today was a brief e-mail from the curator of Breen Hall. "Do all Americans," Graham Dunn began, "issue commands and expect the world to jump? Well, I thought you'd like to know we are obeying. I've brought in a chemist to assist me in examining the tapestry, and we should be able to report our findings in a few days' time." He'd signed it, "Your humble and *obedient* servant, etc., etc."

It had made her smile. Was she really that bossy?

Live with it, Mr. Dunn.

Noticing Tim coming by with jingling glasses of chai, Dana leaned across the counter. "Say, where did all these people come from?"

"Not sure." He set a cup under the espresso machine. An assistant was taking down orders. "You should ask your friend there."

Dana turned, half expecting to see Chase, but instead there stood Trish Roth, saluting her with a raised coffee mug from across the room.

"Did you have something to do with this?" said Dana, working her way over.

"A little." Trish giggled.

"Tell."

"Are *you* the photographer?" A twiglike lady laid a hesitant hand on Dana's wrist.

"How are you, Miss Geller?" Dana felt a small triumph that she had come up with the name—after how many years?

"I always knew you'd do something wonderful."

"You knew when I was ten years old?" Dana turned a widening smile on her fifth-grade teacher.

"Are you Dana?" A tall woman in her forties interrupted. "I'm Josh Fenton's mom. I was wondering, are these pictures for sale?"

Dana glanced at Trish, who grinned back at her.

"Sure! Yes!"

More people came up. The odd thing was that everyone seemed surprised that Dana was the photographer. Who were they expecting?

Trish explained. She'd taken on the challenge of getting people to show up for the big night and figured the best way to do it was to create a sense of mystery, refusing to reveal who the remarkable new photographer was. She'd plastered the stores with fliers, but her biggest coup was getting on the local TV morning show—thanks to some string-pulling by Chase's dad, the station's news producer. A big man with easy eyes and thinning blond hair, Mr. Newcomer offered to do what he could. The next slow news day he called Trish in for five golden minutes of airtime.

A nice twist was the e-mail Trish got right afterward from Gianna Belkin, queen of the who's-in-who's-out website. Gianna wanted to know if this was something worth posting. If she'd known it was Dana's work, she might have trashed the show, but Trish managed to keep the artist's name secret. In the end, the much-visited website declared, essentially: Be there or be square.

What Gianna didn't know about were the half-dozen five-by-sevens of herself that Dana had taken on the boardwalk. Titled simply *Rage*, they showed the progress of Gianna's fury, ending with a truly ugly close-up just as she was yelling, "I'll break that camera over your head!" Everybody, the kids especially, crowded around, some of them laughing.

"That's the yearbook picture she *should* have used," snorted one smart aleck.

The other big attraction was an eleven-by-seventeen on the far wall. It was the image Dana had captured at dawn of Miss Edwards's house, with its one lighted window, the old lady in silhouette about to kiss the nose of a silhouetted cat.

And now, Dana noticed with alarm, here was Miss Edwards herself making her way through the crowd and waving a small piece of paper. An arrest warrant?

"Here," said the old lady, her face cobwebbed with smile lines and her eyes extra bright. "I hope this is enough."

It was a check for a hundred dollars.

Dana folded Miss Edwards into a hug, careful not to squeeze her little bones too hard. "You like it?"

Miss Edwards's smile crinkled like cellophane. "I'm going to have it framed and put it in the living room."

They were interrupted by a shortish man with a press badge dangling from his breast pocket. "So you're the mystery woman," he said expansively. "Chuck Hardin from the *Herald*. Mind telling me about yourself?"

Before she could answer, there was a commotion by the door. Dana couldn't see at first, but then the blazing red hair of Gianna Belkin appeared over the heads of lesser beings. Flanked by two of her National Honor Society henchmen, she stalked down the line of photographs like a drug-sniffing dog until she came to the *Rage* suite.

Her eyes narrowed, and even from where Dana stood a dozen feet away, she could see the girl's shoulders bunch up.

Gianna turned, scanned the crowd, and marched over to

Dana. That whole part of the room fell silent. The air between them was so charged that if a fly had flown past just then it would have been zapped.

"You rat!" Gianna murderously muttered.

Without warning her hand flashed out, stinging Dana's cheek with a loud smack, sending her staggering. Dana's reaction, totally unexpected even to herself: She laughed! She wasn't laughing about anything—just pure nervous combustion—but Gianna's face reddened. Somewhere a camera clicked.

"Nobody does this to me," she snarled.

Still, Dana couldn't speak. Another nervous titter escaped from her.

The place was silent except for the click of a camera. Both girls turned to see the man named Hardin firing away. "Thank you, girls. Could I have the spelling of your names?"

"Oh, crap," Gianna groaned, ducking for the door. She bumped Miss Edwards, nearly knocking the woman over. Dana ran to help, so Trish stepped in and talked with Hardin. He jotted happily in his narrow spiral.

It was all too much. Dana saw her chance and pushed the door open. A dozen people were outside, some under umbrellas, a few smoking under the awning. Dana walked into the alley, relieved to feel the light rain on her forehead. Her claustrophobia hadn't been bad tonight, she realized. Maybe she was getting over it. Her hand, too, was better, although it sometimes itched like crazy. The bandage had come off a week ago.

"Hey," a familiar voice called from the shadows.

She looked up sharply as Chase Newcomer stepped from under a tree. Despite his umbrella he was dripping, his khakis rain-darkened and his sneakers muddy.

He looked perfect.

You're not going to ask, she told herself severely.

"Quite a thing you've got going," Chase said. His hand flicked the water away from his brow.

You're not going to say, 'Where's Bingo?'

"Yeah," she said, "Isn't it great? Trish really went overboard."

"I can see that."

"Where's Bingo?"

"I have no idea. Was that Gianna I saw barreling out of there a minute ago?"

"I don't think she cared for the show."

He nodded. "I suppose not. I see that reporter's still talking to Trish."

Dana momentarily forgot her frizzing hair. "What do you know about the reporter?"

Chase charmingly shrugged. "I suppose I did call and give him a heads up."

"You told him to come?"

"I just said it might be worth his while."

"Why would he listen to you? You're a kid."

"I said I was Martin Sharpe."

"You said you were the *principal*?"

"I thought it might be pushing things if I said I was the mayor."

"Chase!" She was trying not to smile. No use.

"Well." He was turning to go. "Just wanted to say congratulations."

"Walk with me a little?" she said quickly.

He shrugged, holding the umbrella out for her to duck under. They ambled to Penhallow and turned toward the river.

"So where's Bingo?" she said.

261

"You keep saying that. I don't know. Probably perming her hair."

"Does that mean . . . ?"

He tilted the umbrella thoughtfully, watching the water sluice off. He held it upright again.

"I hope you didn't just blow her off."

"No, but you know. I just wasn't . . ."

"Ready?"

"Maybe next lifetime."

She gave him a playful shove. "Not if I have anything to say about it."

"Actually," he said, "you don't."

The rain was making an increasing racket on the umbrella and they ducked into a doorway. For a while they said nothing. A car moaned by.

"So, what have you been up to?" Dana said.

She was finding his shrugs less charming than before.

"I know I don't deserve it," she went on, "but have you forgiven me?"

"For what?"

"You know for what. For being a jerk. I'll never, *ever* do that again."

He glanced at her. "I know you won't."

This wasn't going the way she'd hoped. "I never meant to hurt you."

"I know that." He gave the umbrella a twirl. "And I know you wouldn't mean it the next time, either."

"I wouldn't *do* it the next time."

"How do you know? You might have another dream. You might remember another lifetime."

"Chase, what are you saying?"

He looked at her briefly, then away. "I don't think I can do this anymore."

Suddenly, out in all the wind and rain, she was finding it hard to breathe. "Are you breaking up with me?"

"I don't know if that's technically possible, since you already broke up with me."

She looked at him with fear. "Don't."

Something about her voice made him turn to her.

"Please don't," she said. "You don't know what's been happening."

"More dreams?"

A movement across the street caught her eye. It wasn't easy to see through the rain, but she could make out a man in, of all things, a cape, striding up the hill. She grabbed Chase's arm.

"It's Sprague!"

He squinted. "Does he always dress like that?"

"Shh!" Dana suddenly forgot her problems with Chase. She pulled him out into the rain. "We've got to follow him."

"Why do I have to follow him?"

"Because I need you."

They set out along their side of the street. The doctor, across the way, was a fair distance in the lead, heading away from the center of town.

"What do you care where he's going?" Chase vaguely protested, drawn along.

"Keep up!"

The rain was becoming unpleasant, pelting down on them, sizzling along the sidewalk. Still Sprague, caped but hatless, kept on. He walked steadily, not looking right or left, till he came to the approach to Route 1.

"Is he planning to walk to Boston?" Chase complained.

"Be quiet."

They were on the service road beside the highway. Up ahead a sign was blinking:

WAYWA D ARMS MO EL.

"What's a Waywa?" Chase muttered.

"Shh."

They saw Sprague pull open the glass doors and practically stumble inside, wet as a muskrat. Through the window they tried to make out his pantomime conversation with the desk clerk, while a puddle spread at his feet. He looked terrible, his forehead pasty and eyes bloodshot. After signing the register, Sprague handed the man a credit card and received a key card in return. Then he lumbered down the hallway, his cape resembling a wet brown blanket around his shoulders. In fact, Dana realized with alarm, it *was* a blanket. Her therapist was going around like a homeless person!

"What's this about?" said Chase.

She didn't answer. She was looking through the window at the dingy lobby, empty now except for the clerk, who'd gone back to his crossword puzzle.

"Is he shacking up with a girlfriend or something?" Chase said.

"If only."

"Dana," he said, turning her shoulders toward him, "could you please tell me what's going on?"

"Why? I thought you were breaking up with me."

"I know, but . . ." He stumbled to a pause. "I guess you're right," he said.

"Yeah."

"How serious is it?"

"I think he's having a breakdown."

"I can believe it." He scanned the lobby.

They turned and started back, the rain drumming on the umbrella. He kept glancing at her as they walked. "Do you think he's dangerous or something?"

She shrugged. "Not usually."

"What does *that* mean?"

"Not worth talking about."

"Dana . . ."

"Now don't freak. A few days ago he, well, tried to push me over a balcony."

"He did *what*? Did you call the police?"

"They wouldn't understand."

"What do they have to understand?" He seemed dumbfounded. "I can't *believe* you're following this man around in the middle of the night!"

"Why do you care?"

"*Care?*" The even-tempered Chase Newcomer, the amused, unflappable friend, had finally passed the point of exasperation. "Of *course* I care, for God's sake! Hey, can we get out of this rain? We need to sit down somewhere and *talk* about this!"

She smiled briefly at his outburst before forcing her expression back to neutral. "Don't I have to get back to the show?"

"Show?"

"Photography? My first show?"

He huffed out a sigh. "Well, come on, then. We'll talk on the way. And you can start telling me what's going on!"

Chapter Twenty-five

The Visit

THE RAIN INCREASED THAT NIGHT AND SWEPT right through the next day. The local news spoke of flooded streets and sump pumps. Dana's house didn't have a basement to worry about, but in her room a rubber bucket and towels were brought in to catch the drips.

Becca Landgrave came upstairs around noon and stood in the doorway. "I guess we can't put off that new roof much longer," she said.

Dana looked up. "Is it just my room?"

"There's a leak by Ben's window. Renata's making the best of it."

"She's here?"

"Nice of her, in this weather. She says she wouldn't miss one of Ben's PT sessions, now that he's beginning to get somewhere. How's lunch sound?"

"Good."

"Tofu burgers in ten."

On her way downstairs, Dana poked her head into her brother's room. He was on the massage table, grunting with effort.

"Keep going! Keep going! You're getting it. Jes!" cried

Renata. She threw a smile at Dana. "Your brother makes *torrrific* progress!"

Dana looked at Ben, lying back now with his eyes closed. "Nice going, Benny," she said.

He barely nodded.

"I think he's ready," Renata said brightly, "to sweetch to the hospital for his sessions. They have equipments, much better, and an exercise pool."

"You'll still be the PT?" Ben said.

"Oh, jes."

"Ugh."

"He really love me," Renata said.

Dana squeezed Ben's foot. "You're doing great."

He opened his eyes a sliver to look at her. "Another day in paradise."

Dana smiled as she headed down to face lunch.

Becca's cooking was as odd as ever, but her relationship with her daughter had improved. She hadn't been to Breen Hall with the others and wasn't convinced of Dana's abilities, but she did see there was something about the girl that was beyond her.

Dana was separating the sunflower seeds from her chicory salad when the telephone rang. It was Chase. "Are you planning to see him?" he said abruptly.

"I thought I'd go after lunch."

"Bad idea."

"I'm worried about him."

"You're worried about him. That maniac nut job."

"Yeah."

"You're not going alone."

"All right."

She went back to her careful work on the salad. Becca kept her face in the paper in order not to watch. Ten minutes later they heard the crunch of tires on the gravel—Chase in his father's red Camry.

By now the rain had lessened, but the water was high in places and Chase had to detour on the way to the motel. He went inside with Dana, only to learn that Sprague had checked out at seven that morning.

"Where now?" Chase said as they climbed back in the car. "Maybe he came to his senses and went home."

"I doubt that."

"Might as well try."

They set off, dodging through town to the riverfront. Chase switched off the ignition across from the Bow Street house.

"Is that a light in the front room?"

"You're right!"

He gave her a long look. "Sure you want to go in?"

"Yeah. But look, you don't have to do this."

"You think I'd let you go in there alone?"

She smiled down at her lap.

"Because I wouldn't."

"He's not a bad guy," she said. "I know that sounds strange."

"It does."

"But he's fighting this thing. You can see him struggling."

"I just want you safe."

"Me too." She gave him a nervous smile and popped open her door. Sharing the umbrella, they crossed to the house and thunked the heavy knocker. After half a minute they heard approaching steps. Chase gripped Dana's hand.

The man who opened the door looked very little like the haunted creature they'd shadowed last night. "Miss Landgrave!

Come in, come in. I see you've brought protection. You must be Chase."

"Yes, sir," said Chase. "Nice to meet you."

Nice! thought Dana distractedly. *What is this, a tea party?*

The doctor, large as ever, was dressed in a crisp sport shirt and pressed khakis. His loafers looked recently shined, his beard neatly trimmed.

She stared at him.

"Come," Sprague said. "Don't stand there in the rain."

She was baffled by his transformation. "I thought I'd see how you're doing," she said, stepping inside.

"As you see, bright and bushy." He led them to the living room. The shades were up and the books and papers, if not neat, were at least piled in stacks. No howling mastiffs from upstairs, Dana noted. The only sound she heard was the grumbling of a clothes dryer somewhere off the kitchen. "I was just making coffee," Sprague said. "You'll join me, I hope."

Chase and Dana looked at each other. "Sure," she said.

The teenagers sat on the couch with mugs of hazelnut decaf and a plate piled with cellophane-wrapped biscotti. Sprague took the chair. They were silent, taking one another in. Dana set her coffee down. "We saw you last night," she said.

A flicker of emotion crossed Sprague's face. He lifted his chin. "Then I can understand this visit," he said.

"We were concerned."

"As you should have been." He broke a biscotti and took a noisy bite. A tiny cloud of crumbs sifted down on his lap.

"So what happened?" she said.

"Direct as always." He glanced briefly at Chase. "Does your friend know anything about our situation?"

"I told him last night, after we saw you check in to the motel."

His eyes widened briefly. "You followed me that far."

She paused. Maybe she had admitted too much. "As I said, we were concerned."

"So you said."

The silence was uncomfortable. Sprague's chair creaked. "I was not at my best last night," he said. "I'd say I was very nearly at my worst. I'm sorry you saw that." He took another explosive bite and leaned back. "But all is well now."

Dana hesitated. It was awkward having Chase hear this. He was a third party in the room, like a court reporter. "How can you be sure?" she said finally.

"Because I faced him and I wrestled with him and I beat him. That's how I know. I suppose your friend here has very little idea what I'm talking about."

Chase stopped blowing the steam off his coffee. "Malveaux," he said.

Sprague perceptibly flinched. "You really did tell him everything."

"I had to," Dana said. "I'm sorry."

"Quite all right."

"Chase is okay," she said.

"I know that."

"He went to England with me. He was there when we discovered the body. We can trust him."

"As long as *you* can."

She threw Chase a glancing smile.

"Could I ask you something, doctor?" said Chase in his amenable voice. "Why the motel?"

Sprague leaned back. "The place where I was staying was no longer . . ." He made a dismissing gesture.

"You mean *he* was there?"

"Since you seem to know everything," said Sprague, frowning, "yes."

"When we saw you," said Dana, "you seemed in a hurry."

"Yes. His presence in the library had become oppressive. I thought it best to get out."

"You didn't have a coat on."

"No, I didn't have one with me. I heard the rain and just grabbed an old blanket."

"But he followed you?" Dana pressed.

"As you know, Miss Landgrave, he's as close as my heartbeat. I had to face that, finally, last night in the motel. We had it out." He gave a little laugh, as if it were a matter of small importance. "Fight of the century. Sprague versus Malveaux. Ten rounds."

"And?"

"Win by a knockout."

Dana glanced at Chase.

"You don't believe me," Sprague said.

"No, no, I do. But how . . . ?"

"I think I'll keep certain details to myself, if that's all right. The thing is, here I am, back in my house, the laundry in the dryer and coffee on the stove."

"You do seem so much better."

"Thank you, I am. I expect to be back at work next week." He leaned forward, smiling. "But you're not eating! More biscotti? I might be able to find some cookies."

Chase and Dana left a short time later, promising to come around in a day or two to see how things were going. Sprague gave a little wave from the doorway.

Dana looked at him quizzically. He never waved. He was

not a waver. Somehow that tiny gesture bothered her more than anything else.

They drove in silence to her house. The rain was picking up.

"Do you believe him?" Chase said as he pulled under the carport.

"I want to."

"He may have beaten this alter ego of his, but who knows when Malveaux will demand a rematch?"

"Not soon, I hope. Want to come in?"

He looked at the steering wheel. "I *would* . . ."

Dana felt the air pressure in the car suddenly drop. "Oh," she said.

"It's just a little confusing, that's all."

"I keep forgetting we're not . . ."

"Yeah."

"Are you still seeing her?"

"No," he said, giving her a serious look. "That's over."

"Sure?"

"She didn't make it easy, but yeah."

"Did she cry?"

"Yeah."

She gave him a long look. "So," she said, "you want to come in?"

He smiled and shook his head.

"Come on," she said. "My parents love you. Ben loves you." She paused, holding back. "And I love you."

"You do?"

"I've loved you for about two hundred and thirty years."

His smile slowly brightened. "Then how come you keep breaking up with me?"

"Who broke up with who?"

"That was a rebound breakup."

"Oh, I see. And that doesn't count."

"Shut up," he said, "and come over here."

He folded her in his arms and kissed her thoroughly and deeply, while the rain thrummed on the carport overhead.

Chapter Twenty-six

The Fall

"DANA! QUICK!" SAID TOM LANDGRAVE. "OH, HI, Chase," he said distractedly. "Hurry, Dana!"

She and Chase followed him up the staircase without a word. At the end of the corridor, framed against the lamplit room, stood Ben, wobbling slightly, holding on to the walker.

"Hey, Sis."

She stopped, stunned. "You—you're walking!" she managed finally.

"Not quite." His wobbling grew worse.

"Hokaydokay," said Renata, steadying the walker and supporting Ben around the waist. "Enough for one day." She helped him back into the wheelchair.

Dana ran up and hugged him, her tears, suddenly released, wetting his neck. "My God, my God," she murmured against him. "Oh, Ben."

"I told you we're going to beat this thing," he said.

"Oh, we are!"

Their father stood watching them, hands on his hips. "Ben," he said, shaking his head.

"Wait till Mom gets home," said Dana. "She's going to freak."

"Hold on a minute," said Ben. "It's not like I actually stood up."

"But you did! I saw you."

"Renata pulled me onto my feet and I stayed there a few seconds."

"Still, it's great."

"Soon," Renata said, squeezing Ben's shoulders, "he stands up on his own."

"Yeah," he said. "I will. Hey, I'm going to call Eric."

"Have him come over," said Tom. "Have him come for dinner. Chase, you're staying, aren't you? You too, Renata. We'll celebrate."

Ben didn't have a lot of energy for celebrating. He had managed to stay on his feet, briefly, and it had worn him out. But he looked triumphant as his father carried him down like royalty and set him in his downstairs wheelchair.

Pretty soon Eric arrived, out of breath and red-cheeked, water dripping off his slicker, and minutes later Becca came in bearing soggy groceries. Everyone was talking at once, and no one could hear anybody. Chase was ignored, which seemed to suit him fine. No one took note of the enormous fact that he was there, back from banishment. Smiling, he leaned against the kitchen counter, arms folded, sipping a ginger ale.

By the next morning the rain had finally gathered up its things and moved out. Sunlight blazed through the window, striking Dana's pillow with military brightness. She squinted awake.

It was earlier than she wanted to get up on a Sunday morning, but the sun gave her no choice. No nightmares, she realized with relief. There'd been no nightmares or insomnia for a while, ever since she'd found out who she'd been and what she'd really done all those centuries ago. She was innocent, at least of the main charges, after lifetimes of guilt. And yesterday her brother Ben had remained standing for almost a minute on his own two feet.

Dana sat on the edge of her bed, looking down at her fuzzy slippers. And then there was Chase, she thought. She couldn't believe how close she'd come to losing him. She'd never let that happen again. Was it too early to call?

Don't be a pest.

She reached for her cell.

They met for a coffee-shop breakfast and came back, laughing, around ten thirty, the screen door banging behind them. Ben was in his wheelchair at the table reading the comics, while Becca held her coffee cup at a careless angle and scanned the Week in Review. Dana's dad was down at the excavation site, Becca said, to check on the effects of yesterday's flooding. It didn't matter to him that it was Sunday and no one was working. He could be there for hours.

"You gotta get out, Ben," said Chase. "It's too beautiful."

"Yeah?"

"Come on. We'll take you."

"Can I finish *Hagar the Horrible*?"

"Hey, Mom," said Dana, "do we have anything in the fridge I can take to Dr. Sprague?"

"Can't he feed himself?"

"You don't know him."

"Well, take a look. Hands off the tuna nut loaf."

"I promise." She found several blueberry muffins on the sideboard and zipped them into a plastic bag.

"Do you think you'll be seeing your dad?" Becca said, holding up a brown bag. She wiggled it. "He forgot to take the lunch I made him."

"I guess we could swing around that way."

"He'd forget to eat if I didn't feed him. Oh," Becca called as Dana pushed open the screen door, "I want you to be careful with Dr. Sprague. Keep your distance if he's still sick."

"I will."

"School starts Thursday. I don't want any sniffles. That goes for you, too, Ben."

Sunlight in late summer is a wondrous thing in New England, warm and gold and laced with a breeze. Dana was glad they were looking in on Sprague. Maybe they could get him outside for a walk.

The trio jaunted through the sleepy, Sunday-morning town to Bow Street, where Dana strode to the door and clunked the knocker. Nothing happened. She knocked again, harder, then turned to Ben and Chase with a shrug. Finally, she heard a soft thumping, as of slippered feet coming down the stairs. There was a scrabbling of locks, and the door opened slightly. Sprague's large and unkempt head appeared in the narrow interval, his eyes confused.

"Hello?" he said, still not focusing.

His appearance put her off balance. "We brought you some muffins," she said lamely. "Did we wake you up or something?"

"No, no." Sprague looked past her at Ben in his wheelchair. "Who's that? Your brother?"

"That's Ben, yes. You won't believe what he did yesterday."

He looked at her, then at the Ziploc bag of muffins. As she watched, his face changed. His features seemed to relax, and a spooky smile slid along his lips. "Forgive me, dear," he said. "I'm forgetting my manners. Come in, for Heaven's sake."

"You're sure?"

His eyes crinkled. "Please," he said.

Soon everybody, and even the wheelchair, had crowded into

the living room. Ben, who'd never met Sprague before, was looking him over skeptically.

"Actually," said Dana, still standing, "we were hoping to take you out for a walk. It's a terrific day."

The doctor looked at Dana as though she'd proposed a trip to Angola.

"Really, sir," said Chase, "it might do you good."

Sprague held the bag of muffins, squeezing it slightly. "A walk. Well . . ." He seemed distracted by the sight of Ben sitting there in his wheelchair. "How about one of these nice muffins?" he said, bending toward him.

"Just ate."

"Ah."

"Oh, come on, Doc," said Dana.

"A walk, eh?"

"I won't take no."

He indulged a smile. "You seldom do." His look took in the three of them. "Can you wait while I get my shoes?"

"We can do that."

Sprague turned and stumped up the stairs. The kids glanced at each other.

It was almost ten minutes before Sprague appeared again, dressed more like late fall than late summer, his bulbous brown shoes poking out from under the cuffs of his corduroys. Instead of a shirt he wore a black turtleneck, which he probably thought sporty, and over it his tweed jacket. It was way too hot for today.

"Shall we?" he said. He waited for the others to go out and then set the burglar alarm.

Dana noticed. "The barking dog?"

"I call it my Cerberus system."

"I know who that is," piped Ben from his chair. They started along the deserted street. "He's the three-headed dog, right?"

"Very good!" said Sprague.

"Ben knows all about Greek myths," said Dana, scuffing the first fallen leaves of the season. "A whiz at heraldry, too."

"So I hear!" said Sprague.

He looked so bright and focused suddenly that Dana found herself glancing over at him. It was as if he were a different person.

"I understand," he went on, "you helped solve the mystery of Breen Hall."

Ben was watching the pavement rolling like a slow stream under his wheelchair. "Not really," he said.

"He was a huge help," said Dana.

"What did you think of the castle?"

Ben knew when he was being drawn out by an adult, but it really was an interesting subject. "At first it was neat," he said. "But later it got creepy."

They turned in at the entrance to Prescott Park and headed toward the water.

"Creepy how?"

"She probably told you."

"Ah, yes." Sprague nodded. "The dead boy."

They fell quiet and stared out at the glinting wavelets. Across the perfect sky a seagull chalked a quick straight line. A breeze blew Dana's curls across her face.

"That was me, you know," Ben said out of nowhere.

Sprague gave him a sharp glance. "What was you?"

Ben nodded significantly. *"Him."*

The doctor looked from Ben to Dana. "You mean the boy . . . ?"

"Yeah. I just saw his leg." Ben gave a little shiver. "I didn't know it, but I was, you know, looking at myself. Dana explained it to me later."

Sprague narrowed his eyes dreamily. "William Breen," he said.

"Yeah. Is that creepy?"

"Well," said Sprague with a smile, "welcome back."

They strolled by the water, talking of various things. Chase pushed the wheelchair while Sprague quizzed him amiably about his plans for college. Had he thought about Brown? Williams College had a wonderful liberal arts program, he thought. Dana walked a pace or two behind. She couldn't help thinking something was off. For one thing, the Sprague she'd known all these months wasn't a social talker. What did he care what colleges Chase was considering? He could be sharp, sarcastic, insistent, nasty, brilliant, any number of things, but . . . *chatty?*

At the same time he seemed to be avoiding her eyes.

Her unease grew when Sprague offered to take over pushing the wheelchair. Nothing wrong about that, of course. Chase could use the rest, and Dana's hand, although healed, still hurt when she put pressure on it.

But did he have to push the chair so fast?

"Say," she said, breaking into a trot to keep up, "why don't we see if Dad's over at the work site? I've got his lunch bag."

"Fine," said Sprague, striding smartly along. "Tell me where to turn."

"It's up there, by Mechanic Street."

Without slowing down, Sprague suddenly cut across the grass, soggy from the recent rain. Ben was practically bumped out of his chair. Finally they gained the street and lurched to a stop.

"Wow!" said Ben. "That was great!"

"You liked that?"

"Yeah! Dana's so careful all the time."

The work site was visible up ahead. Dana's heart fell to see that it was empty. She really wanted her father to be around.

"My dad's replacing the sewers," Ben announced as they approached the mesh fence.

"Something wrong with them?"

"They're, like, real old. The seventeen hundreds or something."

"Well! Let's take a look at this archeological dig," said Sprague.

"I don't know," Dana said doubtfully. "Dad's not here."

Chase squinted up the street. "I bet he's gone to grab lunch somewhere. He didn't know you were bringing it."

"May we look around?" Sprague said. "I'm always interested in the past."

"So's my dad," Ben said.

They made their way around the perimeter to the gate. "I'd think you'd be interested, too, knowing what you do," Sprague said.

"About what?"

Sprague gave the gate a shake. "About who you were." He scanned the top of the fence. The padlock clanked on its chain, but the chain hadn't been looped around the other post, so it really didn't lock anything. With a creak, the gate swung open.

"Well," said Chase, "there's a bit of luck."

"Providence, you mean," said Sprague. "Let's take a look, shall we?" Before Dana could object, he'd pushed the wheelchair through the entrance and started down the ramp. The others could only follow.

They passed a shovel standing in a mound of yellow dirt, and from it hung Tom Landgrave's green jacket.

Chase nodded to Dana. "Guess he'll be coming back."

"We should have waited."

A few yards farther on, a large orange machine was parked, like a dozing dinosaur. Two excavations lay nearby, each covered with a slab of plywood to prevent accidents. A roaring was audible from somewhere underneath.

"What's that?" said Ben.

"Let's see." Sprague pulled the plywood from one of the holes. The roar was suddenly louder. Straight down in darkness, water rushed madly past. He stared into it, his eyes glittering. "The *abyss*," he softly hissed.

"The water sounds real high," said Ben. "Must be all the flooding."

"I don't think we should be here," Dana said.

Chase was looking concerned himself. "Here. I'll take the wheelchair."

"I don't think that's wise," said Sprague, grabbing the handles.

"What are you doing?"

Sprague leveled his gaze at Chase. "You're not part of this," he said, his voice altered and low. "Stay out of it."

Chase and Dana exchanged a quick look. He turned to the doctor. "Let go of the wheelchair!"

"Can't do that."

"Are you crazy?"

Sprague's eyes narrowed. "Just finishing a job I didn't get to finish a long time ago." With that he shoved the wheelchair right to the lip of the hole.

"Hey!" Ben cried out, gripping the armrests and looking around wildly.

"Here you go, Master Breen," Sprague sneered. "Take a good look at Hell. You're about to enter it."

Chase ran and grabbed Sprague by the sleeve. The older man flung him back. When Chase came at him again, Sprague pulled something out of his jacket pocket. It was dark and metallic, but shiny at one end.

Chase reached for it, but Sprague lifted his arm away, and in that moment Dana recognized the sharpened crucifix she'd seen on Sprague's wall.

"No!" she cried out. She stared in horrified disbelief as the air glinted and his arm sliced down, driving the point into Chase's chest. The boy gasped, staggered backward, and fell.

"I told you to stay out of it!" Sprague growled. He grabbed the handles of Ben's wheelchair and started upending it into the sewer.

Ben screamed, and for a moment Dana stood frozen. A split second later she broke out of her daze and catapulted herself at the doctor, knocking him off his feet. Sprague fell with Dana on top of him, clawing at his face.

He's killed Chase! He's trying to kill Ben!

The two rolled in the wet dirt, while a few feet away the wheelchair tipped downward over the hole.

Ben cried out, gripping the wheels to keep from rolling. His muscles weren't strong enough to back the chair up over the lip. "Help!" he shouted, feeling his hands slipping. The chair edged forward. Loose dirt dribbled into the hole.

His sister, blood pounding in her ears, didn't hear him—and didn't hear Chase moaning as he struggled to raise himself to his knees. Half crushed under the doctor's weight, Dana kicked and punched desperately, till Sprague pulled back a moment, giving her the chance to squirm away. In a flash she was on him again, rage overpowering her completely. If she could have ripped his head off, she would have.

But Sprague, a large man, struggled to his feet, lifting Dana with him while she pummeled and bit him like a hive of bees, her face red with outrage.

Chase! He's killed Chase!

Unable to see, the doctor staggered several steps forward. At last, with a great roar, he grabbed Dana wherever he could and flung her down, knocking the wind out of her body.

For several seconds, all she saw were pins of light, great swarms of them, swooping toward her. Then the lights slowed and she saw through a blur Morton Sprague tipping Ben's wheelchair forward into the chasm while the boy screamed.

She tried to get up, but her body refused to respond. It lay helpless, gasping for air and consciousness.

Up now! Do it!

Later she would not remember the next several seconds, when the deepest part of her, her very soul, commanded her body to stand up, and showed her the rock in the loose dirt, and willed her to place one foot in front of the other, and ordered her to go up behind the doctor and slam the stone into the back of his head.

Sprague pitched forward over the wheelchair, over Ben's head, thumping against the sewer's rim before plunging into the howling hole. A brief splash, and he was swept away by the current.

Dana had no time to think about him. She was scrambling to grab the wheelchair, but it tipped to the side, one wheel slipping, and slid down into the sewer hole with Ben still in the seat.

"No!" she screamed as she saw her brother's face disappear into the blackness.

The chair, an unwieldy thing, had gone down at an angle and caught abruptly against the sides of the brick-lined hole. And suddenly there was Ben, scraped and bleeding, suspended over the deafening flood.

"Ben! Hold on!" Dana screamed.

There was nothing to hold on to. There was only the chair, wedged at an angle, supporting him for a last few seconds. With a groan, the chair slipped down several inches.

"Don't move, Ben!" she cried.

He stared up at her from the darkness, four feet below where she crouched, his eyes terrified. Blood trickled from a gash in his temple and threaded down his cheek.

"Don't move a muscle!" she called to him. Amid the howling of the water, she wasn't sure he could hear. "I'll get you up!"

Ben slowly nodded. Tears glinted in the corners of his eyes.

But how? He was farther down than she could reach.

She looked around desperately. That's when she saw him—Chase up on his knees, edging toward her, the metal crucifix protruding horribly from his chest just below his shoulder. His eyes were slits of determination.

"Take," he began, but faltered. He tried to pull at his belt buckle.

"Chase!" she cried. "Oh my God!" Her eyes filled with tears.

He shook his head. "Take my belt."

"Yes! Yes!" Dana carefully undid the buckle and pulled the belt through the loops. "You're *alive!*" she whispered, looking him in the face to make sure it was true.

He was too weak to do anything but nod. He sat back on his heels. "Hurry," he said.

She raised a shoulder to wipe the tears away, and then

reached down into the hole, gripping one end of the belt and letting the buckle end dangle down to her brother. Careful not to make a sudden move, Ben reached up. His fingertips just touched the edge of it.

"Good going!" Dana called. "You can do it."

It wasn't going to work; she could see that. Even if he got a good grip, he was much too weak to pull himself up.

The chair suddenly made a grinding sound and scraped its way two inches farther down along the sweating brick.

Ben's eyes widened.

"Don't worry!" Dana shouted. "I'm not going to lose you again!"

She stared at his face as if the mere power of sight could pull him to safety. "I love you, Benny!"

Just then, as she reached hopelessly into the darkness, an image flashed across her mind, and instead of her brother she found herself looking into the face of William Breen, the boy behind the altar, staring out at her, begging her to save him.

This time you're going to live!

"Don't move, Ben! I've just got to find something longer. Can you hold on?"

He nodded.

"I'll be right back. I promise."

She started to get up when she felt someone thump down beside her. "Try this."

It was her father, in a sweat from running the last block and a half. He held a rope in his hand.

"Dad!" Dana bit her lip. "Thank God! Can you get that down to him? Careful! Careful!"

A one-time fisherman, Tom Landgrave knew all about ropes. He quickly tied a loop at one end and lowered it to his son. "Ben!" he called over the noise of the water. "Can you get your arms through this?"

"Think so."

The rope was longer than the belt, but now that the chair had slipped farther down, it wasn't long enough. Tom pulled it back and tied the belt buckle to the end of it. That gave it a little more length, and Ben was able to reach it from where he sat.

"Good boy!" Tom shouted.

Ben could touch it, but couldn't reach far enough to get his arms through the loop.

"Ben, can you hear me?" his father called. "You're going to have to stand up!"

The boy shook his head.

"Listen. The rope isn't long enough. *You have to stand!*"

Dana had never seen such fear in her brother's eyes. "You almost did it before," she called to him. "At the house, with Renata. Remember?"

He barely nodded.

"You can do it now!"

"I can't!"

"Do it!" she yelled.

He started to say something, but just then there was a horrible grinding sound as the wheelchair began to scrape its way down the hole.

Ben raised himself halfway, his eyes fierce with effort, and grabbed the loop with both hands, just as the wheelchair shuddered and plunged into the current below.

"Hold on!" Tom shouted, pulling on the rope, hand over hand.

"You can do it!" cried his sister.

With his weak arms, there was no way Ben could support his body's weight. But he kept not letting go.

Grunting with effort, Tom hauled his son toward the light. Seconds later, Ben's head appeared at the top; and a second after that Dana had her arms around his shoulders and was dragging him out, gasping, onto the ground.

Chapter Twenty-seven

Ever After

DANA WAS AT THE HOSPITAL EVERY DAY, TALKING Chase through his pain, or playing game after game of Sorry during the hours of nothing to do. The first day of school came and went. She didn't even think about going.

She got to know the police pretty well during this time—also a couple of reporters who were keen to interview the Spunky Heroine Who Had Saved the Day. Chase's dad, as news producer at the station, had done what he could to shape the coverage, steering reporters away from any reference to the paranormal; but he couldn't shield Dana from their attention. The story was irresistible and led the newscast the first day. It dropped to the third item the next day, and to a thirty-second "tell story" the next. Newspaper coverage followed pretty much the same arc.

Dana was relieved to see the story die down. She'd taken no joy in her notoriety. After all, she had caused the death of a man she knew and cared about. It was something she'd have to deal with for the rest of this life—and maybe the next.

Meanwhile, the cards and visits from Chase's classmates continued. Once Mary Bing showed up. She gave Dana a flinching glance and stood uncertainly. Dana said hi and went out to wander the corridors. She felt an unexpected sympathy for the girl. For one thing, Mary had had the good taste and bad timing to love Chase Newcomer. Dana wondered what her past life must have been like to leave her so girly, frilly, and needy in this one.

After supper, Chase was shuffling cards for their Sorry game when he looked up at Dana. "Ever think about Malveaux?" he said.

"A lot."

"If you're right about all this," he said, "he's not really dead."

"I know. Just out of incarnation."

"Or else he's a newborn."

Dana gave a little laugh. "Pity the parents."

She picked up a card and took a man out of Start. "You know who I really miss?" she said. "I miss Sprague."

"Isn't he the same guy?"

"He's the other half. The better half."

"Well, he lost out."

"Maybe he'll win next time."

"Let's hope."

Arriving back at the house, Dana found an e-mail waiting for her from Graham Dunn. She read it with avid eyes. "My dear Miss Landgrave," it began.

> This probably doesn't surprise you at all, but we have examined the section of tapestry you indicated and are able to confirm your suspicions. I don't know where you get your information, but we did find signs of tampering, probably from the seventeenth or early eighteenth century, to judge by the materials used. Someone, no doubt offended by

the idea of a priest's being put to death, just blotted the evidence out.

What he did was paint over a small patch of the priest's black robe. On the reverse side of the tapestry, the original color can be clearly seen. And, yes, it is red. *Blood* red, you might say.

Thanks to you, we must now rethink our interpretation of *The Allegory of Time.* If you are ever moved to help us in this effort, please don't hesitate to contact me. Meanwhile, our deepest thanks.

Sincerely, Graham Dunn, Curator, Breen Hall, Bendelfin, Lancashire.

Dana stared at the screen.

She could understand why somebody would want to blur the disturbing elements. The *real* question was why the tapestry's *designer*, Paul Bertrand—herself as Bertrand—would want to inflict the wound in the first place. She rubbed her forehead, trying to think her way back into his mind.

She could imagine Bertrand's outrage, his need to settle the score—if only symbolically. His design was a coded accusation. A code that took centuries to break.

Dana hit the reply button. Her message was brief. "The man in black is not a priest. You've got to stop thinking that. He is a Calvinist spy. His name is John Malveaux. Yours truly, Dana Landgrave."

The next day Dana arrived at the hospital early, because Chase was being released. He was looking out the window when she entered, his small bag packed on the bed. She went right up and kissed him. "Ready to face the world?"

Chase did not look as happy as she thought he should. His wound was itching under the bandages and he couldn't scratch it. Also, he couldn't wear a regular shirt. "How can you dress decently when they've got you trussed up like something out of *The Mummy's Curse*?"

"Oh, I don't know." She cocked her head. "I think you look dashing."

"Right." He touched her cheek. They were silent. Honest eyes, gaze to gaze.

"Did we *really* know each other," he said, "back then?"

"Oh, yes."

"That's something."

"Yeah, it is."

"I love you, Dana—or Hannah, or whoever you are."

"Mm."

"How are you doing with those dreams?"

She gave a happy shrug. "Gone. You won't believe how stupid my dreams are now. Last night it was something about onions."

"Onions?"

"I think I was making a quiche and an onion dropped on the floor. I was crawling around and—"

"You know? I don't really need to know this."

Nick and Julie Newcomer came in then. They had hugs for Dana and more careful ones for their son. "Looks like you're ready to roll," Mr. Newcomer said.

"Doesn't he look dashing?" said Dana. "I was just telling him how dashing he looks."

Mrs. Newcomer patted her son's cheek. "He was born dashing."

"Thanks, Mom."

Chase's dad took the suitcase. "You'll come with us, won't you, Dana?"

"Sure!"

The Newcomers had a fat white Cadillac. It was several years old, but the cushy seats still had the new-leather smell. Chase was in the back with Dana. She lowered the window and let the warm wind bat her curls around.

"What a day, huh?"

Chase didn't reply. He was taking in the trees, buildings, people, like a kid in a new town. All that time indoors had made him hungry for the world.

"Hey," he said, as they approached the center of town. "Isn't that Gianna?"

Dana craned to see. It was Gianna all right, clumping along the sidewalk, her head jutting forward, determined about something. "She'll always land on her feet," Dana said.

"Or on someone else's."

Dana smiled.

They looked out their opposite windows awhile. It really was a perfect day.

Suddenly Dana gave a little gasp.

"What is it?" Chase looked over at her.

"I thought I saw . . ."

"What?"

"Nothing. A man."

"You saw a man? What kind of man?" Chase was looking worried.

"He ducked down that alley back there."

"*Where?*" Chase swung his head around.

"It's nothing. He was wearing a dark coat. He had it around his shoulders, that's all, and it looked sort of like a cape."

Chase frowned. "You're not thinking . . ."

"No." She shook her head. "No, no."

"Are you *sure*?"

"Oh, of course not. I'm sure it wasn't him."

"But . . . how do you *know*?"

Suddenly Dana burst out laughing. Chase stared at her as if she were deranged.

"I really got you that time, didn't I?" she hooted.

"You mean . . . ?"

"I was kidding!"

His mouth widened. "Oh my God!"

"I got you, boy."

He shook his head. "You really did."

They bubbled into laughter again, and then subsided. Their smiles faded slowly.

Dana stuck her head outside and let the wind buffet her. It was so rare that she could get the better of him like that. He must have been pretty concerned.

She glanced over. He was frowning down at his hands. The sight of him caught at her heart.

They rode the rest of the way in silence.